BROTHER TO BROTHER

SACRED HEARTS MC
BOOK 8

A.J. DOWNEY

Second Circle

COPYRIGHT

Book editing & design by Maggie Kern @ Ms.K Edits

Cover art by Dar Albert at Wicked Smart Designs

DEDICATION

To all the moms out there who have gotten down and dirty to take care of your kids. Especially those moms who have had to suck up their pride and accept help from the last place you've wanted to. The struggle is real, ladies, and you're making it. It might not be pretty, but you can do it. Just keep on keepin' on. Fitting this book's first draft was finished on Mother's Day weekend.

1

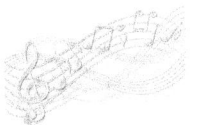

M elody…

I'd had my phone shut off and the little pre-paid go phone I'd purchased in case of an emergency didn't exactly have GPS, so I was doing this by way of the dinosaur; with a set of hastily scratched instructions on a napkin and an honest-to-god foldout map from the back room of a gas station. The attendant had even been surprised his dad had them back there and even though they were from something like the 1970s, they were still pretty functional. The gas station clerk's father had told me that I was looking for the juvenile correction center on the map, and that that was the place.

I put the map back down on my passenger seat and ignored it when it slipped to the floorboard. I was pulled over on the side of the road, and I looked into the back seat, twisting all the way around, to check on Noah, my son, in his car seat. He was fast asleep, and I sighed. The trip from Arizona all the way here by car had been a rough one on both of us.

"Okay, baby. We're almost there," I said under my breath, twisting back forward again. It was spring, early March according to the calendar but that didn't stop the sun. It was out bright and shining but I wasn't in Arizona anymore so it was considerably cooler than back home, that and it totally *showed*. Everything here was so *green* and I really loved it. It was easy on the eyes after so much flat, scorched brown desert tract.

I turned on my signal and pulled back out onto the three-lane rural highway. One lane in either direction, with a turn lane down the middle. I was close according to the map, and when I saw the wrought iron fence, the gate to it open wide but still less than inviting, I knew this was the place. The Sacred Hearts club in Arizona had been the same; less than inviting to look at, but the man I'd loved had been one of them, and now he was here, and so I had to try.

I pulled up into the driveway and turned off to park in the lot, the back of my car pointed at the front door of the building. I got out and shut the door quietly. I didn't want to wake Noah, and I would only be a few feet away. A clubhouse, even during the day when it was sedate, wasn't any place for a baby, which Noah still was, being barely past a year old.

I let out my breath slowly, my heart rate picking up speed. I was out of money, I was out of options, and I was desperate. It showed too; to have gone to the trouble to track Grinder down all the way here. I swallowed hard and wiped sweating palms off on my cut-off shorts. We'd parted on less than fabulous terms when I'd last seen him. In fact, he'd pretty solidly broken my heart, but I still somehow loved him, and I still somehow harbored the belief that there was a chance, and so I was here.

I put my sunglasses on the top of my head and went to the door, pulled it open and stepped into the gloom. The door swung shut behind me, and I jumped when it thumped closed. I stood still just inside it and waited for my eyes to adjust to the dim, daytime barroom gloom. There were two men at a table talking, and at least one behind the bar and I looked for the brother who looked like he was most likely in charge.

"Can I help you?" one of them at the table asked, standing, smoothing down his brown faux-hawk in front. I opened my mouth to ask for Grinder but was stopped cold before I could even vocalize anything.

"Oh no! Oh, hell no, you tramp. Get the fuck on out of here." A familiar voice, but not Grinder's, oh no, it was his brother, Archer, who spoke from the archway leading back further into the club. He approached me like an impending storm that was going to unleash all kinds of havoc on me and I shrank in on myself.

"Archer, I'm not here to cause any trouble, honest! I'm just looking for—"

"I don't give a *fuck!*" he barked and made long strides toward me. I felt myself shrink back even more, backing away into the closed door while he powered in my direction, rolling like a thunderhead across the sky. He grabbed me by the arm and pulled me forward, away from the door which swung inward as he jerked it open with his other hand.

"Archer, no! Please, I'm just looking for Grinder. I have to talk to him, *please* just tell him I'm here!" I babbled, trying to get him to listen to me as he dragged me out into the sun. He spied my car, eyes locking onto the Arizona plates. The two men from the table and the man from behind the bar piling out the door calling after him as he towed me toward my car.

"Archer! Man, let her go," one called; the other right over the top of him saying, "What the fuck are you *doing*, man?"

"Archer, please!" I hauled my body away from him, dug my sneakers into the gravel but he was hurting me, dragging me inexorably away from the building. I was sliding and I either let him tow me or I was going to go down and he'd drag me across the sharp unforgiving stones anyways. He was a man on a mission and that mission was to get rid of me at all costs and as soon as possible.

"I don't know what the fuck you were thinkin' comin' around here, Melody, but you damn sure ain't welcome. Now, get back in your car and take your ass back to Arizona! I mean it, too, *right* the fuck *now*," he was saying as I shouted and pleaded over his husky smoker's voice, which he'd always had. A lot of the girls finding it sexy until they actually slept with him. I don't ever remember any of the club girls doing it twice.

"Archer, I have to talk to Grinder, please let me go! Let me talk to him, you have to let me talk to him!"

He rounded on me and slammed me up against the side of my car and screamed, "Grinder's dead, you bitch! Whatever the fuck you told him to chase him out here, it was the last move he ever made! It fuckin' killed him, so *I don't have to do shit*!"

I cried out as my back made an impact with the back door and his words made an impact with my heart. I looked up at him, shocked, eyes wide and the tears gathering just as the high, thin wail of my son broke the clear day as he started to cry. The noise and the car rocking from mine and Archer's scuffle waking him.

Archer looked past me through the window glass at Noah's small face, and his eyes widened in shock. I stared up at Archer, and I stammered out, "I told him I was pregnant. That's why he left us." All I could think was, *oh my God, he must be lying, he must be lying, no Grinder can't be dead, he can't be dead… Oh my God, what was I going to do? It'd taken everything I had, all of my money, just to get us out here.*

"They didn't tell me, oh God, they *knew* and they didn't tell me… what am I going to do?" I heard myself say out loud. I looked up at Archer's familiar and angry face and asked the empty air, "What am I going to do?"

2

Archer…

She pushed me back and I was so fixed on the boy in the car seat I just sort of stepped back, poleaxed, while she opened the back door and brought him out where I could see him better. Jesus Christ, he looked just like Grind when he was a kid. I mean, this kid had Melody's bright blond hair, but the boy's eyes? They were the same hazel as my brother's and all I could do was stand there for a second and stare.

Fuck you, Grind. I thought at my dead brother, *fuck you, if what she says is true.* Which I knew it was. The proof was right in fuckin' front of me, staring at me with my dead brother's eyes.

"Archer, you fuckin' cool, man?" I turned and looked at Reaver, who was standing there with Data and Disney flanking him to either side, all three of them lookin' skeptical but Reaver's eyes especially cold.

"Mel, put the baby back in his seat," I ordered, staring Reaver down. He arched an eyebrow at me and I gave him a nod.

"What, why?"

"Just put him in the fuckin' cage, now!" I barked at her, and she jumped, the boy started up, screaming loud and she cuddled him close, making soothing noises and I cursed myself silently for scaring him.

I snatched her keys hanging out of her hip pocket and as soon as she shut the door, hauled her over to the passenger side of her own cage, dragging open the door and sitting her ass in the seat.

When I'd first seen her, the first thing I'd noticed was that she'd cut her hair, and that she'd filled out some in all the right ways, but now I knew why for the second. She'd had a fuckin' baby, *my brother's* baby. I shut her into the cage and went around to the driver's seat.

"Where you takin' her, Archer?" Reaver demanded, winter in his voice.

"My place," I uttered. "It'll have to fuckin' do for now." I got into the cage's driver's seat and turned it over, the guys walked back to the club and I pulled out in a spray of gravel. I could see 'em watching in the rearview mirror but I didn't care.

I glanced at Melody, who was staring at me wide eyed. I expected her to ask me where I was taking her and her boy, my brother's son, but she didn't, instead she asked me, voice hollow with shock and pain, "Is he really dead?"

Fuck.

"Yeah." I gritted my teeth a second to bite off the string of curses I had for every last one my brothers in my old chapter. "He's really dead," I said, and I didn't have a fuckin' thing else for her.

She turned her face out the window and stared blankly, and it was like I watched her shut down, like some kind of robot or something. Her eyes unfocused as she stared blankly as the scenery whipped by the window, and for her? Knowing where she'd come from? I knew it was nice scenery.

At least the boy was quiet now, too. I stared into the rearview mirror for a second and found him staring back at me, little cupid's bow of a mouth hanging open, my brother's eyes staring wide like I was the most interesting and awe-inspiring thing ever. I felt my jaw take on that familiar determined steel and shook my head, casting my eyes where they belonged on the road ahead. *I hated driving a fucking cage.*

3

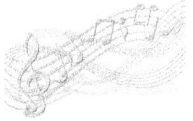

Melody...

He stopped the car in front of this old motel that appeared to have been renovated into apartments. I looked up at the place, it was as dilapidated as they got, and he shut off my car, pocketing the keys.

"Get the boy," he grunted.

"Noah," I said softly.

"What?"

"My son's name is Noah," I said and I got out of the car. He sat for a moment and I think seethed, but I didn't give a damn. I'd named my son after his father. Archer could and would just have to get over it.

I went around to the driver's side back door and opened it up, slinging Noah's diaper bag across my chest and ducking into the car to get him out of his car seat; my sweet boy looked distressed, and reached for me, calling "Mamma!" I pulled him out of the car and stood up with him in my arms, his chubby little arms wrapped tightly around my neck. He looked around, his father's hazel eyes scanning the cracked parking lot at the same time mine did. This place was a dump, but beggars couldn't be choosers.

"Get up here," Archer said, halfway up the cement steps with their rickety looking metal railing. I hugged Noah to me and followed him warily. He went to the door with a rusty, corroded metal number six nailed to it; rust stains running down the dirty beige-colored door like blood, and unlocked it ushering me quickly inside.

He shut the door behind us, and I stared. The living room was nothing more than a couch, television on an overturned milk crate, and a battered coffee table that looked like it'd come out of a pile marked 'free' on the side of the road. To the right was an old, seventies, equally battered four-seater table in front of every apartment kitchen you've ever seen. The table had four chairs around it, vinyl and equally as aged, yellow foam peeking from a slashed seat. The table at least looked like it *might* have come from a Goodwill or garage sale, the chairs though? They looked like they came out of the same 'free' pile the coffee table had come out of.

A doorway in the wall by the kitchen led back to the bedroom, which is where he took us next. I stared at the queen-sized bed with the wrought iron headboard – probably the nicest piece of furniture so far – and swallowed hard.

He gripped me by the upper arm and hauled me through the door when I hesitated too long, sitting me down on the end of the bed. I sat, and Noah looked around quietly; my heart broke just a little. Noah was usually a bubbly, talkative child, but kids *knew*, and my boy's silence as he slobbered all over his fist told me he was as apprehensive as his mamma. I looked up at Archer and he set his jaw.

"You can take the bedroom, I'll take the couch. I'm going to go pick up an extra shift. I'm taking your cage. I'll be back later tonight. Don't go anywhere." And just like that, he went out the bedroom door shutting it tightly behind him. I blinked and looked around the room.

Aside from the queen-sized bed, there was a battered garage sale dresser with a smaller television and DVD player on its top at the foot. One of those tall chest of drawers. There was a squat, longer dresser along the wall beside the bed where a doorway opened into a bathroom off to the side and by all appearances, the *only* bathroom in the place. The opposite wall had a window that was not only shuttered with venetian blinds but had a heavy military blanket tacked up over it.

That was it furniture wise; there was no more room for anything else in this bedroom with its stark walls and cracked ceiling. I looked at Noah, asking him, "Are you okay?"

"Yeah." His soft little breathy child's voice almost made me smile.

"You got a stinky butt?" I asked and he shook his head no, his fist resolutely back in his mouth and I closed my eyes for a second.

"I love you, my sweet boy," I murmured and kissed his soft hair. He chattered and murmured in his soft baby voice, his breath evening out and deepening and I sighed. He hadn't had much of a nap in the car. I slid the strap of his diaper bag off my shoulder and sat him down on the bed. He immediately started to fuss and whine until I picked him back up and he clung to me. I sighed... *I knew exactly how he felt.*

4

A rcher...

The bar was closed, and the shift had gone pretty well, and by well, I mean it'd been boring as shit. That's pretty much what you preferred when it came to this shit, and so I wasn't complaining, in fact, I was giving Cindy, one of the lead bartenders, a hand by mopping the floor while I waited for my two dumbass younger brothers to show up.

The place I worked some nights was a cowboy bar that was mostly on the right side of the tracks as compared to where I'd come from. It was popular, and usually pretty busy. A lot of the business was college kids, and ranch hands from some of the racehorse farms around here. Usually it blared country, but right now I had some Stone Temple Pilots on the system. I could only handle that country shit when patrons were around and it was your typical work night.

"Hey, Archer, wake up! Your brothers are at the door," Cindy called from behind the bar. I looked up, and sure enough, Rush and Nox stood outside and neither one of them looked very happy. I couldn't blame 'em, but this shit was important. I went to the door and unlocked it, letting them in, and locking right back up behind 'em.

"Dude, what is so fucking important that it couldn't wait? Some of us have to get our asses up and work for a living come tomorrow," Nox griped.

"Melody showed up today," I said and that shut him up. Rush eyed me, and I could see the gears turning.

"Spit it out, Arch. What's the rest?" he asked.

"She has her kid with her... Grind's kid," I said unhappily. Nox almost physically reeled, looking a lot like I'd felt when Grind's boy had first looked at me with our brother's eyes. He fell back against the bar lightly but leaned heavily on it.

"Holy fucking shit," Rush uttered, and swept the bandana off his head. He rubbed a hand back and forth over his close-cropped hair and shook his head in disbelief.

"You're sure it's Grind's?" Nox asked.

"Looks just like him," I said unhappily.

"Where they at?" Rush asked.

"My place, for now... there's more. She showed up here *looking* for Grind. Our old chapter, the brothers, didn't tell her. She didn't know he'd died."

"What the fuck? She been living under some kind of a rock?" Rush asked, the look on his face like he'd smelled something bad, which he had. *The distinct odor of bullshit,* I thought to myself and I wasn't happy. I wasn't happy at all.

"So, is that why Grind left?" Nox asked, and he looked as crushed with disappointment as I'd felt when Mel had told me.

"According to Mel, she told him she was pregnant and he upped and left her an' the boy both... came out here."

"Karma took that one too far," Nox muttered and sighed, swiping a hand over his face.

"I wanna see him," Rush said.

"It's late and she drove here by herself, all her shit's in garbage bags too, like she left in a big damn hurry. Nothing but pampers and clothes, I ain't seen anything like it."

"What's she running from?" Rush asked.

"Good question," Nox agreed.

"No idea. I dropped her and the boy off at my place and came here. What's a kid that's a year old even sleep in?"

"A crib, I think. How the fuck should I know?" Rush asked.

"Well I gotta get me one. Where the fuck you find one at three in the morning?"

"Twenty-four-hour Wally-World is my best guess," Nox said.

"Got a cage?" Rush wanted to know. "I ain't actually built any cribs yet."

"Yeah, hers. It's out back."

"Let's do this then," Rush said. "I ain't going home and crashing until I see this myself."

"Pitch in, I ain't leavin' 'til this place is closed up," I told them both. Closing was wrapped up double time and my brothers followed me first to Walmart then back to my apartment, a fuckin' crib tied to the roof of Mel's car.

The boys helped me bring it inside and I found everything exactly as I'd left it, bedroom door still shut and all. I worried for a sec that they'd be gone but when we opened the bedroom door it was to find them both racked out hard in my bed. Nox and Rush stood to either side of me and we watched them for a while.

Melody was drawn, and though she slept, the exhaustion was apparent in the tight lines of her face, even in sleep. The dark circles under her eyes made her seem a lot older than what I knew she was, too. Rush took a step forward like he was gonna go in and wake 'em up and I put a hand against his chest. He glared at me and I scowled right back, knowing he'd back down. I was scarier and we all knew it.

"Tomorrow," I grunted quietly.

"Yeah, let 'em sleep," Nox agreed, and I knew he'd back me. Out of all four of us brothers, he'd always been the softest.

I shut the door and sighed, looking at my two surviving brothers, first Rush then Nox, "After you both get off of work, come on back here."

"Need a hand bringing anything else in?" Nox asked.

"Nah, Bro, but thanks; I got it. Try and get some sleep and we'll see y'all tomorrow."

"What are you going to do?" Rush asked, brows knit together.

"Don't have a fuckin' clue, but for right now, until I figure it out, you're lookin' at it."

He and Nox nodded in unison and let themselves out while I set to putting the damn crib together for the living room. An hour and at least two beers later, it was done and I was dragging some ass, but I still brought up all of her and the baby's shit from the car, piling it on the dining room table.

I went over and flopped down on the couch after it was done, throwing an arm over my eyes. I had no fucking idea what I was doing, none whatsoever. All I knew? That boy in there was blood. Grinder's blood, sure, and even though we were foster brothers, coming up in the system together, it didn't matter. Grinder's blood, Rush or Nox's blood, it was as good as my own and you didn't abandon family.

Mel was the boy's mother, so like it or not that made her family too. I didn't have to like it, I just had to live with it. *Of course, living with it isn't exactly the worst hardship ever, now is it you fuckin' pussy?* I asked myself. I sighed and shifted on the couch uncomfortably. I'd always been a little jealous of Grind when it'd come to Mel. She'd been the prettiest of any of the girls to come around the club, but once Grind set his sights on a piece of ass…

Not so ancient history, but history nonetheless. I didn't make a habit of dwelling on what was in my rearview, and this was no exception. Besides, I needed to figure out the road ahead because this particular hairpin curve had been totally unexpected. It took me a while, but I managed to fall into an uneasy sleep. I could deal with this shit after the day job. It would just have to wait.

5

M elody...

Noah becoming fussy is what woke me. I pushed myself up and looked at him, asking automatically, "You got a stinky butt?" His best answer was to start fussing louder, beginning to cry.

"Okay, baby. Up we go!" I stood up and picked him up. Taking him and his diaper bag into the living room which seemingly had *exploded* with our belongings overnight.

"Wow," I uttered, Noah squirming in my arms.

I fetched a towel out of the pile of our clothes and stuff on the dining room table and laid it down on the carpet, along with Noah right on top of it. I played with my son, singing and rhyming and generally trying anything to keep him smiling and giggling while I worked him out of his choo choo train pajamas. Archer was asleep on the couch, and I was terrified of waking him. God knew what he'd do if we did.

I finished changing Noah and picked him up, hugging him and asking, "Are you hungry?"

"Yeah," he said in his soft baby voice and it was one of the things that made me smile. He was growing up so fast, and so many things he said were clear, but then he would come up with something silly and it was a never-ending source of joy… my only joy now.

"What does he eat?" My head snapped up and I quailed at Archer's voice. I started to immediately apologize and he gave me one of his withering looks, like he didn't give a fuck, so I quit while I was ahead and shut my mouth. "What does he eat?" he asked again.

"Anything, he isn't allergic to anything," I said.

"I meant formula, baby food, cereal? That kind of thing," he said and with a grunt he sat up.

"Oh, regular food like what you and I eat." Noah shifted in my arms and I readjusted him.

"Mamma, hungee!" he said, and Archer almost, *almost* cracked a smile. I couldn't help myself, *I* smiled.

"What do you want?" I asked.

"Chicken nuggets," he said clearly and I sighed.

"Okay, chicken nuggets is not breakfast food, how about cereal?" I asked.

"Pancakes good?" Archer asked.

"Pancakes!" Noah lit up and I laughed.

"I think you have a winner there," I said and Archer nodded, climbing to his feet.

"I'm gonna run out and get you guys breakfast, but I need your car to get to work," he said stretching.

"I thought you just got home from work," I said.

"Yeah, well, I've discovered you have to work twice as hard at a living when it's honest," he said with a frown.

"Oh," I murmured softly. Back in Arizona, I'd known the club to be in less than legitimate dealings. Drugs, money, weapons, you name it and they ran it for the cartels out of Mexico. Still, I wasn't so dumb that you would *ever* hear me talk about it.

"What am I supposed to do about lunch or dinner?" I asked.

"Don't worry about it for now, that's what. I'll bring back some rolls of quarters, since you'll be here all day you can sort out this mess," he said, gesturing to the piles of my and Noah's clothes.

"Okay." I was looking at the crib and asked, "Where did that come from?"

"Never mind," he grated. "I'll be back," and with that, he hauled himself onto his feet and left us. I sighed and hugged Noah, eyeing the TV.

"Cartoons, buddy?" I asked and Noah threw his arms around my neck with an enthusiastic, "Yah!"

I turned on the TV and looked for the remote, switching channels until I landed on *Billy & Mandy*, which would just have to do.

"Okay, bud?" I asked but he was already gone, fully absorbed in the happenings on the screen. I sighed. "Right, okay," I muttered to myself and began sorting through the rest of the mess on the table, sorting laundry by type—whites, coloreds, and darks.

I had no idea how I was supposed to do laundry with Noah, the laundry room being *downstairs? Somewhere? Maybe?* In any case, I wasn't *about* to leave my son alone not even for a minute. Too many things could happen, he could fall, he could choke, and I tried so hard, *I tried too hard*, to protect him.

Archer returning, opening up the front door, startled me. He froze and I did likewise, my hand pressed to my chest. He didn't say a word, just finished entering his small apartment, closing the door behind him. He had a couple of bags of fast food clutched in one hand.

"So, what happens now?" I asked softly.

"Now, you feed the boy and I go to work, I already said that," he said frowning.

"And after that?"

He sighed. "You both can stay here, for now, until you find something better. In exchange, I expect you to keep this place clean and to fix meals."

"Thank you," I murmured. "I'll find a job as soon as I can, start saving, get an apartment for me and Noah."

"Whatever," he grunted and dropped the bags on the coffee table. Noah got down off the couch and started to go through them and I sighed, going over to him and getting him out of the bags so I could take care of him.

"Anything you need, make a list. We'll get it taken care of tonight. This is the best I can do until I get off. Here's money for food, and the quarters. Order pizza for lunch or something." He paused and looked around. "I mean it, I expect this to be sorted out by the time I get back."

He dropped an envelope and two rolls of quarters onto the coffee table and turned to leave.

"And *I* mean it, Archer... thank you."

"The boy–"

"Noah," I said, and Archer scowled at the correction.

"Noah, is family. Grind ain't here to take on his responsibility; that leaves me," he said and it was less than a rousing endorsement, especially given his tone. He left the apartment, shutting the door tightly behind him, and I felt my shoulders drop. Archer *clearly* wasn't happy about our being here, but he was giving us a chance, and that was really all I could ask for. If he weren't awful to Noah, well, then that was really better than I expected. He could treat *me* poorly, but to be honest, given his track record thus far, I think both the best and worst I could expect was his cold indifference, which was fine.

Indifference beat getting slapped around, it also beat being derided and insulted on the regular. I didn't want Noah around either of those things. He needed to grow up understanding how to treat women. It was a big part of why I'd left Arizona in the first place. I hadn't known what to expect coming here, to be honest. So far, it was both better and worse than I imagined.

I fed myself with the breakfast sandwiches in the bag, and Noah with the pancakes and syrup cups. There were two things of orange juice in one of those cardboard drink carriers. I poured some into one of Noah's sippy cups for him and put the rest into the barren refrigerator. I drank the other and with a sigh, continued dealing with the piles of laundry.

Once they were all sorted, I had to figure out how to go about carting both them, and my one-year-old, back and forth to the laundry room with me. It was a daunting task to be sure. I gathered the first load into Archer's lone laundry basket and was about to open my mouth to tell Noah we were going to go when a knock fell on the front door.

"Melody!" a woman's voice called from the other side. "Melody, we're some of the ol' ladies from the club, can you open the door?"

I peeked out the blinds, through the window over the couch and sure enough, two petite women stood in front of Archer's front door. I went to it, and unlocked it at the knob, opening it up.

"Hi!" the one who'd called out said brightly.

"Um, hi," I said back nervously, stepping aside.

"I'm Ashton, this is Hayden. Trigger is my ol' man and Reaver is hers," she said and they both breezed into the living room, arms loaded with plastic bins; paper grocery bags in them.

"I'm sorry, I don't know any of the brothers' names here yet. Noah and I just got in yesterday." I shifted uncomfortably and closed the front door.

"I heard all about it," the one introduced as Hayden said, rolling her eyes.

"Was Reaver one of the men there, then?" I asked.

"Yeah, he's my husband," she said smiling.

"Look at you!" Ashton cooed, and she smiled, waving at Noah. "I'm Ashton, what's your name?" she asked and I went to Noah and picked him up.

"Can you say 'hi'?" I asked him.

"Hi," he said softly. For some reason I wanted to instantly like these women, but I was still reserving judgment. Back in Arizona, the ol' ladies of the club there wouldn't hesitate to throw you under the bus. Snakes in the grass, all of them.

"He's Archer's?" Hayden asked and looked tickled pink.

"Oh, no… he's Grinder's," I said softly.

"Oh, you poor thing!" Ashton said and touched my shoulder.

"I… I still don't know what happened," I said and my eyes welled. It was still so awful and new.

Hayden sighed. "Tell you what, let's get this place sorted, and laundry going and then we can all sit down and talk about it."

Ashton was nodding, tossing her long auburn braid over her shoulder. I bit my lower lip and asked, "Did Archer call you?"

Ashton and Hayden exchanged a look and rolled their eyes. "No, Reaver told me about you, and Ashton and I figured with Archer's bike still at the club he had you holed up here like some kind of prisoner, all by yourself, with an infant."

"We figured we'd come to the rescue with a welcome and some grown-up conversation, but don't you worry, we swung by the garage he works at to ask permission first. He told us you probably needed a few things like laundry soap, and some bins to stash your stuff, so here we are." Ashton smiled brightly and these two struck me as genuine. Still, I kept on my guard.

"Thank you," I murmured.

"Not a problem, and you're not you know," Hayden said.

"Not what?"

"A prisoner, silly!" Ashton laughed. "You get used to these guys acting like Neanderthals and doing what they want like you're some kind of afterthought." She made a face. "The good news is, they usually make it hard to be mad at them, because they're just doing it to protect you."

Hayden's look grew distant and she muttered something to the effect of, "Oh trust me, you can still be mad."

Ashton sighed. "He meant well," she said and I was bouncing between the two of them like a tennis match.

"Well you know what they say about hell and good intentions," she said dispassionately.

"I feel like I've missed something significant," I said, my curiosity getting the better of me.

"Trust us, it all ties in to what happened surrounding your man," Hayden said. I must have made a face, because she froze, both her and Ashton looking at me. "I'm sorry did I say something wrong?" she asked.

"Grinder was never technically 'my' anything," I uttered. "I was just a club..." I paused and looked at Noah who was playing with a lock of my hair against my shirt. "Well, you know..." I uttered.

"A club bunny?" Ashton supplied and I smiled.

"That's what we call them here," Hayden murmured. "It's a little more kid friendly and not quite as rude to the girls."

I laughed. "I've never met an ol' lady who cared about *that*."

"Well, we do things a bit different here," Ashton said and smiled.

"Right, so how do we want to do this?" Hayden asked, "All three of us to the laundry room?"

"Four," I said, boosting Noah higher on my hip. "And sure, I'm not quite comfortable letting my little man out of my sight just yet."

"Perfectly understandable." Ashton smiled.

"You have any?" I asked.

"I can't," she said and I could see it pained her.

"We've been trying, but no luck just yet," Hayden said, blushing.

"Revelator and Mandy have a seven-month-old girl named Eden, and they're already pregnant with their second. Ghost and Shelly are pregnant with their first, so there's that." Ashton beamed. She and Hayden had set down their bins and grocery items and were pulling the bags out and replacing them with laundry to carry down. Hayden popped an odd-looking container of laundry soap on top of one of the piles of clothes.

I asked Noah, "Go for a laundry basket ride?"

"Yah!"

"You going to hold still?" I asked.

"Yah!"

I nestled Noah in among the laundry in the basket I'd loaded and hefted it, groaning. "Oi! You're getting too big for this, monkey boy!"

"No!" he called laughing and giggling.

"Yes!"

My son and I bantered back and forth as I followed the two women out and downstairs in search of the laundry room. We found the door, down at the end, by way of following our noses and the smell of drier sheets on the crisp, but not terribly cold, spring air. It was warm in the laundry room where two of the seven driers were going. We took up three of the seven washers, the units stacked, washer on bottom, drier on top, along the little room's walls. Three on one end four along another wall, the remaining two walls containing a sink, a coin dispenser, and a powdered laundry soap dispenser. The free long wall had a Formica workbench where residents could fold their clothes.

"Shi-oot!" I cried, "I forgot the quarters on the coffee table."

"I'll get them," Hayden said brightly. "I'll be right back."

"Thank you," I called after her.

Ashton and I sorted laundry into the washers and Hayden returned with the quarters. Ashton opened the laundry soap container, extracting little pillow packs of detergent.

"I've never used those, are they any good?"

"Oh my God, *yes*," she said. "You have to use two for loads this size, but they are so convenient, you just have to make sure your hands are totally dry before you handle them or *big* mess."

"That and you should find someplace really high to keep them, they're shiny and pretty and awfully appealing to little ones to stick in their mouths." She made a face and I had to agree.

"Pretty sure he'd only do it once, but I'd rather not have to call poison control freaking out," I agreed.

I picked Noah up along with the laundry basket on the floor and we returned upstairs with our baskets and bins. Ashton set a timer on her phone to remind us to go back down and switch the laundry out to the driers and start the last two loads.

"Archer left me a little money for pizza for lunch. I um, I don't have anything to pay you for the laundry soap or—" the women started laughing, cutting me off.

"Trust me, Melody. Money is *no* object for me; consider this a 'welcome' present from the club." Ashton smiled and I shifted uncomfortably.

"She's serious, not to be rude, but she's a millionaire and while I come from old money; I do just fine for myself with interior decorating. This stuff," Hayden swept out a hand, "is really nothing, for either of us."

"It still doesn't feel right," I murmured.

"I've been where you are, starting from nothing…" Ashton said softly, and launched into the story about how she and Trigger first met, and how the club helped her.

"And your husband committed suicide?" I asked skeptically. Men like what she described him to be just didn't *do* that, at least not from what I knew and my own experiences. She and Hayden exchanged a telling look and said "Yes" in unison before dissolving into fits of laughter.

I filed that discreetly into the category of *I just didn't want to know* and moved on to what I *did* want to know. I looked over at Noah, who was reabsorbed in the cartoons on the screen, and turned back to the two women at the table.

"How did his father die?" I asked softly, and both of their expressions crushed down into sympathetic ones. Ashton reached out and took my hand.

"Grinder came out here in answer to a call from our club for help," she said softly and Hayden frowned.

"Ashton—"

"I know, it's club business, but she deserves to know the truth," she said.

"The truth?" I asked.

"They didn't tell you *anything?*" Hayden asked, horrified.

I shook my head, and it seemed to make up her mind. "Sorry I interrupted, Ashton, you're absolutely right," she said and sat back.

"I won't tell anyone you told me," I said, recognizing the position they were putting themselves in.

By all accounts, I was an outsider to them and this was clearly falling under the category of 'club business' and even if you did manage to find a bit of club business out, *you didn't share club business with outsiders.* It just wasn't done. *Period.*

"As I was saying, Grinder came out here to answer a call for help. There was another club, The Suicide Kings, and they did things to hurt The Sacred Hearts, things that required an answer—"

"I understand," I said softly. She really didn't need to say anymore. I knew how it worked. Disrespect couldn't go unanswered, any more than a physical attack of some kind could. It just wasn't the way things worked in the world of MC's. The rules were simpler than the rules of society, more basic, more primal, and certainly more barbaric but there was also a certain beauty to it. When these men loved, they loved harder and more deeply than any citizen could ever comprehend... or so I had thought.

I tried to banish the image of Grinder's face twisted up with anger and hate when I'd told him I was pregnant. The last image I would ever have of the man I loved was him turning his back on me, him riding away after telling me to abort my child... *our* child. After cursing me out for being so irresponsible as to get knocked up in the first place. As if I'd *planned* it, as if I had managed it all on my *own.* I refocused on what the women from this chapter were saying... I needed to know the truth.

"Some of them caught Grinder riding alone one night," Hayden said and she took up my other hand.

"They ran him off the road," Ashton said softly.

"Oh God," I moaned, tears slipping free of my closed lids and slicking hot down my face. I only had one question and I dreaded the answer, because as much as Grinder had hurt me, I had still loved him and not even *had*, he may be gone, but I loved him still. I swallowed hard and asked my question, voice cracking, "Was it quick?" Their silence was really all the answer I needed.

"The men, they all looked for him, it was cold; it was winter, but…" Hayden's shoulders dropped and she rushed it out, like ripping off a Band-Aid, as if that would make it better, "He was trapped under his bike and it took a day or two. I'm so sorry."

I cried, and they let me, the reality of the situation sinking in deep, until I was numb, all the way down deep into my bones. *Oh my God,* I thought and I wondered, *did he think about us? Did he wonder in all that time, trapped? Did he know he was going to die?* So many unanswered questions that would never *be* answered and the weight of them absolutely soul crushing.

"I don't understand why they didn't tell you," Ashton said, distressed. "They all came to the funeral."

Noah looked on from the couch and climbed down. He came to me and I lifted him into my lap. He put his tiny arms around my neck and hugged me tight; I hugged him back.

"Love you," he said. He was so *smart*. Far ahead where he should be with all of his talking. I was so proud of my boy. I loved him so, so much.

"I love you too, baby boy. I love you, too."

I sat there feeling guilty for taking comfort from my one-year-old, and at the same time, feeling so blessed that I had him; that I had a piece of Grinder still with me that I could love wholeheartedly with no regrets. It'd hurt so much when he'd turned away from me when I'd told him I was pregnant, and I'd been so sure he'd come back to us, but then he hadn't.

Pregnant club whores weren't exactly welcome around the club in Arizona, so I'd kept my distance. Besides that, I hadn't wanted any of the other brothers other than Grinder after he and I hooked up. He'd been the love of my life, for all that he wouldn't make me his ol' lady. I'd managed to hold on for a few months when it came to my apartment with my waitressing job, but without Grinder's help, and the mounting bills from the regular doctor's visits – even on a sliding scale – I hadn't been able to keep it up for very long and had been forced to move back in with my parents. Parents who weren't very happy with their twenty-six-year-old, knocked up, unwed, wayward daughter coming home.

I had tried so hard to get me and Noah out of there, had tried to save everything I'd made at my waitressing job, only to have to cut and run. The only place I had to run *to* was back to Grinder... or so I had thought. Now I was here, I really *was* alone, and I was scared. Scared out of my mind.

One day at a time, Melody, I thought to myself, and I had no other choice, truly. Ashton and Hayden were surprising, as far as a couple of ol' ladies went, but I still couldn't trust that there wasn't something awful about to come down the line. It was, unfortunately, a conditioned response.

They stayed, and seemingly, happily, helped me clean the apartment thoroughly. Switching out and bringing up laundry, joining Noah and I over pizza for lunch, and helping me make a shopping list of things I would still need; mostly of food and the like seeing as they'd brought just about every cleaning product I would need.

"He has *no* cooking utensils aside from a bunch of mismatched silver-ware, a bowl or two, and coffee mugs," I muttered from the kitchen floor. I was putting all the cleaning supplies away under the sink and thinking I would need child locks for the cabinet to keep little monkey boys out of it, but there really wasn't anyplace else for me to put any of it up high. The kitchen just wasn't built that way.

"At least he has a coffee maker." Hayden said brightly, and the three of us looked at each other and burst out laughing.

"Can you add child locks to that list?" I asked Ashton, and she put a finger to her nose and tapped twice.

"You're a good mom," she said and Noah piped up from behind her.

"Good mommy!"

We all laughed again and the front door opened, Nox came through and asked, "What's so funny?"

Out of the four brothers... well, three now, Nox was always the easiest to talk to. There was always something, I don't know, *softer* about him; gentler somehow.

I got up and went around the kitchen counter and quietly said, "Hi Nox." He smiled at me and opened up his arms and I felt my eyes get misty. I hugged him and he sighed when he felt me tremble with a silent sob.

"Where's my nephew?" he asked, giving me a slight squeeze.

"Noah, come here, baby," I called and he pushed off the couch, climbing down and toddling over. I picked him up and settled him on my hip and said, "I want you to meet your uncle Nox," I said gently and he looked at Nox blinking his wide eyes so like his father's.

"Hi, buddy!" Nox said and Noah just stared, chewing on his fingers. He smiled impishly and put his little head on my shoulder. Ashton and Hayden giggled quietly.

"Don't be shy, Noah! Say hi to your uncle Nox," I said, though my voice wasn't in the slightest bit chiding.

"Unca Nox, hi, Unca Nox," he said and I kissed his soft hair.

"Hi, Noah," Nox said and ruffled my boy's hair. He looked at me and I brazenly met his gaze, one brow raised in question.

"Picked Grind's name, huh?" he asked.

"I picked his father's name, yes."

"I thought Grinder's name was David," Hayden said softly.

"It *was* David Noah Chandler," I said. "He hated David."

Nox snorted. "He hated the whole damn thing. What's the last name you gave him?"

"What's your name, Noah?" I asked.

"Noah Jeramiah Beswick!" my baby proclaimed proudly.

"That's right!" I bounced him on my hip a little and said, "I'm proud of you. Can you tell your uncle Nox how old you are?" I asked. Noah looked at his little hand, and I urged him one more time. "Go on, hold it up," I said. Noah held up one finger with a cheesy grin and Nox smiled and praised him.

"Good job, buddy!"

Noah smiled and laughed and threw himself in Nox's direction, arms outstretched. I almost lost my grip, I hadn't expected him to do it. I said, "Woah, Noah hang on a second," but Nox was there, taking him from my arms.

"I got him, Mamma," he said gently and took Noah from me. Anxiety filled my chest and I folded my hands together to belay their trembling. Noah was busy, absorbed in playing with the buttons and colorful patches on Nox's cut.

I swallowed hard, "Be careful please?" I asked softly and Nox frowned at me.

"No worries, Mel. I got him," he said.

"I'm sorry," I immediately apologized. Ashton stepped up beside me and rubbed my back and I spooked, jumping lightly.

"You take good care of your mom, little man?" Nox asked Noah, but Noah was fully absorbed in a button on Nox's cut that said, 'fuck you,' which I was suddenly glad Noah and I were just beginning to work on his numbers one through ten and his ABC's. Reading was going to get interesting, along with all of the 'what's that' and 'what's that mean' questions that would likely follow.

"Well, I'm sure you'd like to catch up," Ashton murmured and I felt myself nod woodenly. She and Hayden gathered their purses and light jackets.

"Don't forget, you have one more load that needs to go in the dryer," Hayden reminded me and I nodded, taking a deep breath.

"Nox, can you bring Noah and come with me, so I can do it?" I asked.

"Yeah! Yeah, yeah, lead the way, Mamma."

"Thank you," I murmured, grateful that it was him and not Rush, or Archer.

We walked Ashton and Hayden out and I didn't want them to leave, but I got it, they had to. Damn the luck… I didn't know if I was ready for this.

6

A rcher...

It was getting on towards quittin' time when Dragon pulled up to the garage. I sighed, figuring he was here to talk about Mel and the goings on at his club the day before, and I wasn't exactly wrong. First thing he did was stride toward my bay and the Caprice I was working on.

"Archer," Dragon grunted, leaning a hip against the fender.

"What can I do for you, P.?" I asked him.

"Well, for starters, we have a little business to square up on," he said. I frowned and stood up, out from under the hood.

"Oh?" I asked.

"Now, I know you probably ain't been in a cage for a minute, but by-laws bein' what they are, do I really need to remind you that gettin' in one wearin' your colors goes against 'em?"

"Aw, fucking son of a bitch, that was totally my bad, Dragon, I'm sorry," I said.

"Be that as it may, yer fined fifty bucks and don't you ever disrespect the patch again, you get me?" he asked and I was already nodding and reaching for my wallet. Fuck, it was fifty bucks I really couldn't afford right now, but that served all the better to drive the message home, now didn't it?

"Don't pay me, you pay Ghost the next time you see 'im," he said and his tone brooked no argument. However, he did tone it down by quite a bit when he got to the question I could tell he really wanted to ask... "Who's the girl, and who's the kid? Better yet, where are they now?" he demanded, and I could tell I was probably looking forward to another talking to.

"She's just some club chippie from back in Arizona," I told him. "The boy is Grinder's."

"Shit," Dragon swore softly.

"Tell me about it, she showed up here lookin' for Grind, they didn't tell her, man. She came all the way out here expecting to see him."

"Way I hear it, you was none too gentle dropping the news." Dragon eyed me but showed no opinion one way or the other by his expression. I palmed the back of my neck and nodded.

"I didn't know that *she* didn't know. I feel like a right asshole about it now, that's no way for a boy to find out his father's dead."

"Boy? Hell, he ain't but a year or so old the way the boys that saw 'im tell it. That's damn sure no way to treat a *woman*, let alone the mother of your brother's child. Which brings me to my question that's gone unanswered... where are they?"

"I took 'em in, they're at my apartment. Nox and Rush are supposed to meet me there."

"Yeah? What you going to do about all this?" Dragon asked.

"Like you said, she's the mother of my brother's child. Noah's blood, he's family. They stay here and I'll get her on her feet. Noah will be taken care of and raised right, around family."

Dragon looked considerate for a minute and finally gave a nod. "She wasn't Grind's ol' lady, at all?"

"Never that he'd make it official," I said. "But they were pretty exclusive, at least as far as she knew."

Dragon gave another nod and said, "Well, anything they need, anything *you* need for 'em, as far as this chapter and this club is concerned, they're the property of a fallen brother and as such they'll be looked after."

I felt a tension in my shoulders ease and nodded. "I appreciate that, Dragon. I surely do," I said and he put a hand on my shoulder, giving it a squeeze. "Ashton and Hayden already came around first thing this morning, they should be with her for a minute today."

"Good, that's good," he said and went on with, "You can be a pain in the ass and hotheaded, Archer, but you're one of us. A brother, through and through. We may not always agree, but your problems are our problems just the same." He considered me for a long moment and asked, "May I give you some unsolicited advice? Not as your president, but as one brother to another?"

"Sure," I said and had a hard time looking at Dragon, staring fixedly at my hands which I was trying really hard to wipe off on a rag just as filthy as they were.

"She came runnin' out this way, I take it in that thing," he said indicating Mel's shitty, worn out hatchback. "Somethin' ain't right where she come from, she's runnin' from something and thought safety lay out this way with yer brother. What did she say on that anyways?"

"Said Grind bolted this direction as soon as she told him she was knocked up. Said she went back to the club with Noah, and they told her he was out here."

"They conveniently forget to mention they'd attended his funeral?" Dragon asked and looked downright stormy.

"Sounds about right," I said.

"Yeah, sounds like I need to make a trip to Arizona," he grumbled under his breath.

"You said you had some advice for me?" I asked, the curiosity burning me up from the inside out.

"I did." He took a deep breath and sighed out, "I know it ain't in your nature to go easy on nobody, but my advice to you? Take into consideration all of these things, her runnin', her findin' out the hardest way possible she's a single mom for real, her *bein'* a single mom. Think about all of that when you look at her and go easy on her, or at least try to."

I nodded, listening to his advice and takin' it in. "Do my best," I said and he gave a nod.

"You always do, brother, and trust me, I get it that sometimes you get ahead of yourself and in the way of yourself, but I'm here to tell you, you need *anything*, to talk, to drink, to duke things out, *all* your brothers got your back. Not just the ones you came up with."

"Thanks, man. I really mean that, too."

Dragon nodded, and we clasped hands. He pulled me in for a hug and we gave some hearty slaps on the back. The old man still had it, rattling my ribs like some fuckin' wind chimes. He wandered off to talk with Dray, his son and our V.P., and a minute later Dray looked up and in my direction.

"Hey, Archer!"

"Yeah, Boss?" I called back.

"Caprice ain't goin' nowhere tonight. Why don't you cut out of here a little early and see to your house?"

"Appreciate it, Boss, but I need the money," I called back.

"Did I say your paycheck would be negatively affected? It's a whole fuckin' hour, get you gone motherfucker!" He laughed and shook his head and I put down my tools.

"Thanks, Dray," I called over and he nodded.

"Don't mention it!"

I cleaned up my area, putting my tools away and hanging up my coveralls. I spent some time washing up my hands before pulling my jacket and cut down off the hook reserved for them. I didn't bother putting them on. It was why I was fined, it was in our by-laws; you didn't wear your cut in a cage, it was considered disrespect. I'd been so caught up with the goings on yesterday that I'd still had it on when I'd gotten into Melody's cage, right in front of no less than three brothers. I was lucky that all it was, was a fifty-dollar fine and that it wasn't an ass-whoopin' offense. Between Trig as the club's SAA and Reaver as the club's enforcer, I honestly didn't want it to come to that. I really didn't want to come up against either one of 'em.

I got into Mel's cage and sighed. Dragon was right, it wasn't bad as far as bein' a grocery getter on short, local trips, but it'd been a hell of a risk driving across the damn country in it. I knew Grind had kept it up for her, but there was only so much you could do with a bucket of bolts like this one. It was old, and old, in a lot of cases, meant fallible. I started it up and would be glad when I got my bike back tonight from the club where I'd left it parked.

I drove back to the apartment, my brothers' bikes parked in one of the stalls out front, and I parked next to 'em. When I went through my front door it was to the smell of clean, and everything in its place. Shit, I think she'd even *dusted* the place. She was sitting at the table, watching Rush and Nox with Noah on the floor. The few toys the boy had with 'em scattered between the three of them, but it wasn't nothing that couldn't be picked up in half a second.

"Unca Nox! Unca Rush! Again!" he cried laughing and my brothers laughed too.

"Hey," I said and Melody looked up at me.

"Hi," she said and chewed her bottom lip.

"Ready to go?" I asked and she rose from her seat.

"Just let me get Noah ready," she murmured and Rush piped up.

"Nah, he's good here with us, you guys go ahead. We'll be here when you get back and it'll let you get the things you need without half the struggle." He tickled the boy who laughed and writhed. Melody looked like some kind of cross between petrified and horrified.

"Oh no, that's okay. It's really no trouble at all. We just got here really and he doesn't know you guys yet, I'd have one foot out the door and you'd have a hell of a time," she kept on like that with every excuse in the book and I thought about what Dragon had said. Seems he was right, she *was* runnin' scared. It weren't none of my business, and I figured she'd tell me in her own time. I wasn't worried about whatever it was. She was here, and Noah was here, and I could handle it, if it chose to show up around these parts.

"Get him ready," I said. "I'm fuckin' tired and we can all go. Shit, it's just to pick up my bike and do some grocery shopping. I don't want to be out all night and I'm fuckin' hungry."

Melody was staring at me, the silence hanging thick between all of us. I broke first, "What're you fuckin' lookin' at?" I demanded gruffly and Melody's mouth worked a few times, opening and closing like a landed fish, like she were afraid of saying anything. She glanced at Grinder's boy and it seemed to make up her mind for her.

"*Language,*" she declared and stared at me evenly.

"What?" I asked, sort of mystified.

"I promise not to ask for anything, but when it comes to my son and raising him right, Archer, he can, and *will*, pick up *anything you say*, so *please*, watch what you say around my son." I blinked and stated the obvious.

"Doesn't much sound like you're asking, Mel. It sounds a lot like you're tellin' me."

She drew up a little straighter, and swallowed hard. "Fine, then I'm telling you. Watch your mouth around my son."

I shifted my weight to my other foot, simply because I'd been on my feet all day and Melody flinched. I froze for a second and felt my mouth press down into a thin line. She didn't move either but cowered just the same. I raised an eyebrow and said, "Alright, have it your way."

"Thank you," she murmured. "I'll get my purse." I held out her keys to her once she had everything gathered up, with one addition, I'd added a spare apartment key on there for her.

Nox picked up the boy. "I'll carry him down to the car, you've got your hands full," he said to Mel and that jittery unease was back in her.

"Sure," she said. "Just be careful."

"Christ, woman. The boy ain't made out of glass," I said sarcastically and she ducked her head down and went out past us. We all went down and she got Noah buckled into his car seat.

"You ready to go, baby boy?" she asked him.

"Not baby!"

"Yeah, sorry. That's my fault," Rush said.

She laughed a little and rolled her eyes at Rush. "He's growing up *so* fast, so try not to speed things along on me too much, okay?"

Nox laughed a little and Rush looked a little chagrinned. "Sorry, Mel," he muttered and she shut the door to the cage. I peeled off my cut.

"You want me to drive?" she asked.

"Gave you the keys, didn't I?"

She nodded carefully and asked, "Where to first?"

"I'd like to get my bike and get back here to put my feet up, you can handle the shopping, yeah?"

"Yeah, sure, absolutely."

"Don't worry about getting lost," Nox said. "I'll stick with you."

Mel looked relieved, "Thanks, Nox."

We piled into the cage, well Mel and I did, while Nox and Rush got on their bikes. They fired them up and it scared the shit out of Noah who started to cry.

"Easy, boy. Nothin' to be scared of," I said but it took Mel like five minutes to calm him down. Shit. This was gonna be different. I sighed and looked down at my cut across my knees. I'd be glad to be back in it, with my knees in the breeze.

"Can we get a move on?" I demanded and was about to say 'fuck' but stopped myself just in time. Mel backed out of the space and followed Rush and Nox. I shifted in my seat and thought back on what Dragon had said some more.

"Y'did real nice on my place," I grunted and she gave me a sideways glance like she was wondering who I was and if aliens had taken over my body.

"Thanks," she said softly and I gave a nod. I didn't really feel the need to talk much after that, content to let the rest of the ride go by in a tense silence. I glanced into the back seat about half way to the club and Noah was passed out.

"He didn't get a nap today. Truthfully, I'm surprised he lasted this long," she said.

"Tough guy, just like my brother," I stated and Mel's expression grew somber. She didn't say anything else after that, the intensity of the silence between us from before, doubling down even harder.

She followed Rush and Nox up into the driveway at the club and pulled to a stop. I got out and stretched, sliding my cut back on over my jacket.

"See you back at the house," I grunted and she nodded. Nox and Rush looked at each other, and Rush backed his bike into the line out front. I hated it when they did that creepy as fuck communicating without speaking. Some kind of freaky twin thing for all that they didn't look like each other. Shit, they didn't even share the same father. A one in a million genetic jackpot. Their mom dropped two eggs and fucked so many dudes close together on a kind of her being a hooker that one egg was fertilized by one John while the other got hit by another John's little swimmers. Wham, bam, half-brothers that were twins sharing the same womb for nine months.

Some seriously fucked up shit; that was for sure. Rush came over and clapped me on the shoulder.

"I need a fuckin' drink," I said.

"Limit one if you're riding," he said.

"Look at you, a regular fuckin' D.A.R.E. officer."

"Ha, ha. Man, like it or not, you've made yourself responsible for Grind's family. Fuck, I wouldn't know the first thing about takin' care of a woman and a kid full-time and I ain't ready for that kind of commitment. Better you than me, asshole."

Leave it to Rush to make it all about him. For being the older twin by virtue of eight and a half minutes, Nox ended up being the more mature and reliable of the two. Rush liked to live fast and was always in a big damn hurry, hence how he got his road name.

"Don't I know it?" I grumbled and followed him inside for that adult beverage. Not for the first time today, I wondered, *Just what in the fuck had I gotten myself into?* Just as quick, I answered myself, too, *You didn't. Grind did; and like always, you're left cleaning up his mess.*

Maybe I would make it *two* drinks. I had time.

7

M elody…

I walked through the door with Noah on my hip and groceries dangling from my other hand. Nox followed me in with the rest. I set them down and sighed with relief, Archer looking on from where he was slouched on the couch.

"Noah, stop!" I told my wriggling son, who I was going to drop if I didn't put him down. He toddled over to the couch and climbed up next to Archer.

"Me-mote!" he cried and Archer looked at him funny.

"What, kid?"

"Mimme the me-mote!"

Archer held up the remote control and Noah reached for it, Archer pulled it away. "No way, kid. I just got home a minute ago and the TV is mine." Noah stared at Archer aghast while basketball played out on the screen.

"Good luck with that," I uttered and hauled groceries into the kitchen to start putting them away while my one-year-old child and his forty-something child of an uncle argued over the remote control. Archer was going to win, it was just a question of if there would be screaming involved. *I sincerely hope not.*

I put away all the groceries and set to work making dinner which was hard to do with no real cookware. I would have to hit a Goodwill or second-hand store to stock the kitchen a little better. Right now, I had aluminum pans, paper plates and plastic cutlery to contend with on the short notice I had.

Dinner was a simple fare of shake and baked pork chops, mac and cheese, and canned green beans. Quick, easy, and by no means the extent of my culinary knowledge, it was just getting really close to being past Noah's bedtime. Nox was staying for dinner and I was grateful that he and Archer kept Noah busy while I cooked.

Eventually, the table was set and the food set out and Archer surprised me by turning off the television and ordering everyone to the table. Noah managed alright by kneeling up on one of the chairs, but I hovered nonetheless to make sure he didn't fall. He was hungry, inhaling his mac and cheese so fast I was afraid he'd choke, and equally demolishing his green beans. I was surprised. Usually he didn't want to have anything to do with his green beans but Nox ate his like they were the best thing ever and so Noah followed suit.

I washed Noah up, changed his diaper, got him into his jammies, and put him down in his crib. My little man was so tired he went down with a minimum of fuss. Nox left quietly, giving me a quick hug good-bye, while Archer had gone back to the couch, choosing this time to lay on it while he watched his game. By the time I was through cleaning up the aftermath of dinner, he was asleep too. I covered him up with the blanket from the back of the couch and turned off the TV with a sigh, dragging myself to bed to lay awake and listen to the bass and pounding rap music permeating the walls and through the floor.

I barely slept.

8

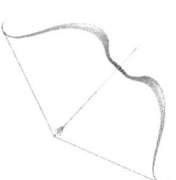

Archer...

I woke up first, surprised to find the boy still racked out in his crib. I got up and stretched and realized the only bathroom in the place was in my room, where Melody stayed. *Oh well.* I needed a shower and fresh clothes. I kicked off my boots and went to it, gathering up clean clothes and taking them into the bathroom with me. When I got out, it was to Mel's blue eyes looking at me.

"Wake you up?" I asked.

"Yes and no," she murmured.

"Gotta get ready for work."

"I know."

I sat down on the end of the bed to pull my socks on and got a good look at the rest of the room. She'd done good in here, too; their shit neatly folded and stored in some plastic bins between the bed and the wall.

"What time will you be home?" she asked, and I looked over my shoulder at her. She rubbed the sleep out of her eyes and looked at me expectantly.

"What, you gonna keep tabs on me now?" I demanded and her face fell.

"Actually, I just wanted to know what time to have dinner on the table," she said coolly.

Oh, well fuck me.

"Around six, maybe six-thirty," I grated.

"Okay then," she murmured.

"Got anywhere to be today?" I asked.

"I need to go to a Goodwill, you have nothing to cook with."

"What do you mean?" I frowned.

"No pots, no pans—"

"Got enough?" I asked.

"I should, there's still a little money left in the envelope you gave me."

"'Kay." I stood up and went back into the bathroom, pulling my long hair into a loose ponytail.

I heard her shifting around and glanced out the door, she was getting up, and pulling on a brightly colored flower pattern kimono type bathrobe over her white tank top and little white-and-blue striped boxer short things she'd been sleeping in. She pulled her bright blonde hair out of the collar and I felt myself twist my lips at how short it was now.

"How come you cut your hair?" It was out of my mouth before I even realized I was going to ask about it.

"You have a baby puke in hair that's nearly to your knees, and have to go wash it, only to have him do it again… you'd cut it too."

"Excuse the fuck out of me," I muttered under my breath and she went out into the living room, her light, feminine voice greeting Noah who must have been awake. I went out there and dropped onto the couch to pull on my boots.

"Breakfast?" she asked.

"Got anything quick?"

"Bacon and eggs?"

"Meh, not sure I have time."

She reached into a cabinet and opened a box, tossing me a package of on-the-go breakfast biscuits. I caught them and put them in my jacket pocket.

"We'll bring you by some lunch later," she said. I got up and swung into my jacket and cut.

"Don't bother," I grated and went out the door. Noah started up hollerin' as I closed it and Melody poked her head out.

"He wants you to say goodbye!" she called.

"I don't say goodbye, tell him I'll see him later," I called back. I was going to be late if I didn't move it, so I got on the bike and fired it up, backing out of the lot and leaving her to her own devices.

When I pulled up to the garage, it was opening up. Rush was in the bay next to mine, getting started on a Honda. I backed into my space and shut off the bike. Going about my business, getting into some coveralls to finish up the Caprice. Yesterday had been Rush's day off, and it didn't take long for him to wander over and start asking questions.

"So, how's the new home life?" he asked with a shit-eating grin and my mood, which wasn't stellar in the first place, soured even more.

"Fuck off, Rush," I grunted and ducked under the hood of the Caprice.

"Seriously? Your long-time crush moves in under your roof and you can't come up with a single bit of happy about that?"

I backed out from under the hood and fixed my younger brother with a hard glare. "I'm supposed to be happy?"

"Well, yeah. A little... aren't you?" he asked.

"You dumb shit, she was *Grind's* woman and shows up here with *Grind's* kid on her hip, doesn't know a fuckin' thing about the fact our brother's dead, I break it to her the worst fuckin' way possible, I'm sleeping on my *couch*, hemorrhaging cash I can't afford if I want to get out of that shithole apartment – I'm responsible for two other people who *really* don't need to be living in that shithole apartment with me... good Christ." I put my hands on my hips and let my eyes grab some garage floor so I didn't have to look at my shithead brother. The urge to punch him was a strong one. "What in the absolute fuck do I have to be happy about with this situation?" I demanded.

"You know, that's your problem Arch. You aren't *ever* happy with anything, Bro. Grind is gone and Mel is *here*, you should give it a go, man."

"Man, fuck you! Because you're sounding an awful lot like I should be grateful Grinder's *gone*."

"I didn't say that, asshole. You're just taking it that way. I'm just saying, let's hear it for second chances. Man, I loved Grinder just as much as you or Nox but he was a fucking *asshole* sometimes. Just like *you* are. Except Grinder's kind of asshole left that woman alone when she needed a *man*. I'm just sayin' you have a chance to *be* that man and it's good you're stepping up."

My brother's caramel brown eyes blazed at me, and he ran a hand over his short, light, tawny hair; back and forth, like he was trying to dust a bothersome insect off his head. Trouble was, that insect was me right this minute, and I hated that fuckin' feeling out of the little twerp.

Especially when Grind and I had changed his and Nox's shitty fuckin' diapers the first couple of years.

"Ain't no one else, *to* step up. I been cleaning up after all three of you fuckers a long time, this time is no exception."

Rush grunted. "Man sometimes you're a real fuckin' douche you know that?" he demanded.

"Go back to your fuckin' bay and quit bothering me," I demanded right back.

He didn't talk to me the rest of the day, which suited me just fine. Around noon-thirty, Melody pulled up with Noah in his car seat in the back. I gritted my teeth and glanced over at Rush who gave me a dirty look. I glared at him and walked out to the car as she cranked down the window.

"What're you doing here?" I demanded.

"Fulfilling my end of the bargain," she said handing me a sack out the window. Noah eyed me from the back seat, and when he caught me lookin' at him he grinned.

"Unca Atcha!" he said and held out his arms.

"Hey, boy," I said in return.

Melody gave me a cool look, as I looked in the bag, likely still pissy about this morning and me taking off with the kid squalling like he was. There was a sandwich and a thing of what looked like soup in the bottom of the bag.

"Better eat it while it's still hot," she said absently as she returned Rush's wave.

"Thought I told you not to bother," I said.

"You also told me it was my job to clean and keep you fed in exchange for staying, so which is it, Archer? Am I supposed to feed you or not bother?" she asked and sighed. I frowned. She looked fuckin' tired, her blonde hair in a lank ponytail, wisps escaping and hanging in her eyes. Her tee shirt had stains on it and her jeans were wrinkled. She was a far cry from the girl I knew in Arizona. Now she had the etched-in marks of a stressed out, frazzled mom.

"What's for dinner?" I asked her.

"I don't know yet, I hadn't gotten that far. Noah's been a challenge today."

"What have you done?" I asked and she sighed crossly but answered the question.

"Managed to get to a second-hand store, picked up some cooking utensils and dishes, made you lunch and brought it here. I plan on stopping into a diner or two looking for help, I have waitressing experience. I was going to head back, put Noah down for a nap, fill those applications out, and get dinner started."

"Busy day," I said dryly. She didn't say anything back. "I'll let you go," I said finally when the silence stretched too long between us.

She nodded, and said, "Can I impose upon you to watch Noah for a bit tonight, so I can get a shower?"

I blinked, *she hadn't showered since she got here?* I nodded finally when my brain caught up and got with the program. "Yeah, sure."

"Thank you, I'd better leave. I'd rather you not get in trouble with your boss," she uttered.

"Not likely, he's the club's V.P.," I said with a shrug.

"Good to know," she murmured. "See you later."

"Yeah, later," I said and knocked on her roof. I called out to Noah while she shifted it into reverse, "See you later, Little Man!"

"Bye!" he called out brightly.

"See, I told you, Noah. Uncle Archer told me to tell you…" I heard Melody say and I yelled, "That's right, I did!" I heard Noah laugh and they were gone. Mel's little hatchback buzzing up the road.

I sighed and pulled the sandwich out of the bag. Cold cuts and some hot chicken soup, probably out of a can, but it sure beat nothing, which is what I probably would have had if she hadn't defied me. I shrugged and let it slide. She made a good sandwich.

9

M elody...

I managed to get quite a bit at the Goodwill, not only cookware, but an almost complete, somewhat fancy set of it for a really reasonable price. I also managed an almost complete set of dishes. I had just enough cash left to get Noah a couple of toys, and that was what he was doing now—sitting on the living room floor, stacking and destroying blocks, laughing with little toddler maniacal glee at the destruction he wrought on the hapless colored wood. My child, super destructo-monkey.

I slid dinner into the oven and closed it up, blowing some of my bangs out of my eyes. I needed a trim badly, but it would have to wait until after Archer got home and Noah had someone to watch him. This place wasn't toddler-proofed enough, despite my best efforts. I had thick hair ties holding the cupboard under the sink closed. So tightly wrapped around the knobs on the cabinet, Noah's little fingers wouldn't have the strength to get them undone, nor would he have enough strength in him to get the doors open more than a couple of inches. I had all of the cleaning products and laundry soap shoved clear to the back of the cabinet and away from the doors. It was the best I could do. Still, I worried. If he tried, he could smash his fingers; I was exceptionally paranoid about the setup. I *needed* to get child safety locks for that cabinet, for *all* the kitchen cabinets.

I was standing there, hands flat on the kitchen counter, watching Noah play, when Archer came through the door. He stopped and looked at Noah, his face unreadable when he looked up and over at me. I raised an eyebrow with a slight smile over how he looked at my boy and he shut the door behind him, shrugging out of his jacket and cut.

"What smells good?" he asked.

I was secretly pleased by the light praise, and hoped it tasted as good as it smelled when I answered him, "Southwest casserole, it's got about ten minutes left."

"Go get your shower then, I can get it out of the oven and watch Little Man here."

"Thanks," I murmured and left to Archer getting down on the floor next to Noah and stacking blocks with him. Murmuring to my little boy and clapping with him when he knocked over the blocks in a spectacular display.

I felt a tension I hadn't realized rode me ease slightly. With a sigh that was a mix between exhaustion and relief I went in to shower, gathering some clean pajamas and a couple of clean towels out of the bins that sat on the floor between the bed and the wall, opposite the side with the dresser.

I spent a long time under the hot shower spray. Longer than ten minutes, for sure. I heard the timer I'd picked up at the Goodwill go off and Archer open the oven. I couldn't even bring myself to care too much that I'd forgotten to set the table, even though I still only had paper plates and plastic cutlery to do it with. I hadn't gotten around to washing the dishes I'd bought.

I startled when Archer called through the bathroom door a few minutes later, "That's enough, Mel. Food's on the table."

"I'll be right out!" I called and shut off the water.

I dried off and got dressed and took the two or three minutes to trim my bangs in the cracked mirror above the sink.

"Mel!" Archer called from the main room of the apartment.

"I'm coming!" I called back and set my scissors on the edge of the sink, the towel I let ride on my shoulders as I ran it over my hair, squeezing the water into the thick terrycloth.

"Thought you was drowning," Archer commented dryly and spooned some more food into Noah's mouth.

"Sorry, I had to trim my bangs and that shower felt *really* good. It's been a few days."

"Should have said something," he said, disapproval in his tone.

"I didn't want to be a bother."

"Too late for that."

Ouch. Motherfucker, he still has it, I thought. Archer always knew just how to hit below the belt in as few words as possible. I swallowed hard and sank into one of the seats. He had the casserole on a couple of pot holders on the end of the table far from Noah.

"You uh, know he can do that mostly by himself, right?" I asked watching him spoon more food into my child's mouth.

"Don't really know the first thing about kids; it's been a long fuckin' time since I had to wipe Rush and Nox's little asses."

"Language, please?" I said and let the pleading creep into my tone. I didn't want to get backhanded, but this was important to me. Of course, not getting backhanded in front of my son was equally as important. I wanted him to grow up learning what it was to properly treat a woman. Living this life, those lessons were going to likely be pretty tricky, but so far, my treatment in front of him had improved by leaps and bounds over where we'd just come from, so there was that.

Rome wasn't built in a day, Melody, I thought, but that still didn't stop my stepfather's voice from creeping in with some cold reality, asking me; *So why are you hanging around a bunch of dirty heathen bikers?* I took a deep breath and held it for a moment, answering that accusatory voice in my head; *Because, at the end of the day, those dirty heathen bikers are still treating me better than either you or Ma,* which was equal parts sad and pathetic.

"You should eat," Archer said eying me, and I felt myself blush. I hadn't thought to grab a robe or anything and I realized that the fitted white wife-beater and blue-and-white striped boxer shorts I wore rolled up at the top, didn't exactly do much to hide my figure – including my still pooched tummy. My hands drifted to it, to hide it and Archer raised a brow.

"You didn't come here pregnant, did you?" he demanded.

"What? No!" I cried.

"Good, I don't mind takin' care of Grind's kid, but I ain't springin' for any other man's child."

I felt tears begin to mist my eyes and stood, "I'm just self-conscious is all, I'll be right back; I'm going to grab my robe—"

"Sit *down*, Mel. Eat something. You ain't got nothin' to worry about; leastways not from me."

Perfect, just epically perfect, I thought and felt even worse when a tear snuck free. Noah's little gaze was on me, his small face solemn.

"Mamma sad," he said, and I wiped at the tear before Archer turned around to look.

"Mamma's fine, Baby," I told Noah. "Eat your dinner."

"Take your own advice, woman," Archer said.

"Just not very hungry I guess," I muttered but put some food on my plate anyways. I nibbled at it and spent more time pushing it around than actually eating it.

"That's too bad, it's good stuff," he said chewing a bite of his own. He'd relinquished the spoon to Noah and was watching him like a hawk as he ate. I realized he was afraid Noah might choke, which was something I feared too, and watched my son with the same careful eye as a result.

"Thanks," I murmured and that was pretty much it in the way of conversation.

I was clearing the table when Noah called, "Mamma! I stinky butt."

Archer heaved himself off the couch and went for Noah at the same time I tried to round the table to go to him.

"Go on, I got it. Changing diapers is a hard one to forget, it's like riding a bicycle," he said and I nodded carefully.

"Uncle Archer's gonna take care of your stinky butt, okay?" I asked Noah.

Noah looked at Archer with trepidation, but he was already laying Noah on the floor, pulling apart the snaps on the legs of his romper. I watched carefully while Noah fussed and cried a little while Archer wiped his bum.

"Does he have a rash again?" I asked.

"Looks like a little bit of one is starting," he called back over his shoulder.

"The cream for it is in the pocket of the diaper bag there." I pointed and Archer dug through a pocket. "Next one over," I directed.

"Prescription shit?" he asked.

"Doctors seem to think he has some kind of allergy to his own poop or pee, he gets it *really* bad sometimes, so they prescribed that. Am I almost out?"

"Naw, you got a ways to go."

"Okay." I closed my eyes and counted backwards from ten until the feeling of anxiety abated. I had no insurance, I had no way to refill the prescription without them finding out where we were… I didn't want to have to go to a doctor, not yet. *Damn it, why hadn't I thought to grab the extra tubes?* Because I'd been in a hurry, that's why.

"Hey, you okay?"

I opened my eyes to realize Archer was asking me, not Noah.

"I'm fine. Just not sleeping well, new place I think." I looked at my cheap watch, but Archer was already ahead of me.

"Okay, Little Man," he said, lifting Noah to his little feet, "all done, but if I'm not mistaken, it's bedtime for you."

He took Noah over to his crib and my little guy *was* tired. He went into it with a minimum of fuss and was out inside ten minutes while Archer channel surfed for a few and I finished wiping down the kitchen. After a little while he switched off the TV and stretched.

"I'm going to work, lock up after me and I'll see you in the morning."

"Okay, what do you want for breakfast?"

"The kid likes pancakes," he said and I nodded. "Then pancakes, if you've got the stuff for it."

I hazarded a smile and said, "I bought mix, but forgot the maple syrup, so is butter and jam okay?"

"I'll get some, we got some twenty-four-hour places around here that'll have it."

"Far cry from where we come from, where the sidewalks roll up at eight."

He grunted in agreement. "You ain't lyin', now get over here and do as I say, lock the door behind me."

"Of course," I said and he went out. I dutifully shot the deadbolt and twisted the little tab in the doorknob, too.

I went in to lie down, listening to the rap music thump and bump up through the floor. A car pulled up outside and was equally as loud. Laughter, shouting, a glass bottle breaking somewhere out in the parking lot... After an hour and a half of trying to sleep, I got up and peeked out the front blinds.

There was a glossy black, fancy new Dodge Charger with ridiculous looking rims on it down there, parked in the middle of the lot behind a bunch of other cars, all four doors open and the system pounding out into the night. I went back into the bedroom and hoped it would end soon, but I think I was just so tired that eventually it didn't matter. I fell asleep, albeit a fitful one. I must have been woken a half a dozen times during the night. Once by a man shouting down to the Charger from right outside the living room window – which woke Noah up causing him to fuss.

I got him back down and tried to go back to sleep, but I heard Archer come home when his second job was through.

"Hey, Little Man, what you doing up, huh?" I heard him say to my son, but I really wanted Noah to go back to sleep, so I stayed put. Maybe it was really because I was upset... I was *so tired*. I was so tired I couldn't sleep, so tired my eyes watered, the moisture slicking down my temples as I lay on my back in the dark. It was incredibly frustrating, but what could I do about it?

I think I fell into a light slumber, but it was shattered by my phone going off. The alarm I'd set so I could fix Archer breakfast before work, shattering the exhausted moments of calm I'd found. I got up, slipping into my flowered kimono-type robe, a deep blue with bright bursts of pink peonies on it. It'd been a gift from Grinder once upon a time… I felt a deep stab of loss borne of a longing to see or have something you would never have again, but I stuffed it ruthlessly down.

I had a child to take care of. A son who was everything to me, and who I wouldn't trade for the moon *and* the stars, let alone the world. I couldn't dwell on what could and would never be. I just couldn't.

I stopped in the doorway to the bedroom and let myself fall into the doorjamb, my shoulder propped against the poorly painted wood as my eyes fell on my boy. He was sprawled over Archer's chest, his little cheek pressed against Archer's worn, light blue tee, his little thumb in his mouth. Archer's lashes formed crescents against his much lighter skin, the last year or so out of the Arizona heat greatly diminishing his once golden-bronze tan. He had one hand on Noah's butt so my child wouldn't slip but both of them were fast asleep. I couldn't help but indulge myself in the moment for a little while.

This is what I had wanted, so badly, for my son. For him to have a father, a man to look up to and who would look out for him. I thought that Grinder would have come around. I thought that his father would be that man eventually, but Grinder hadn't come home and when things got so bad, and I'd gone to find him… I felt my eyes mist, but not from loss this time.

I could put up with Archer's cold hatred of me, his caustic dislike. I could put up with being single and alone for the rest of my days, as long as he treated my son like he was now. I could do this. I could do this for as long as it took, for the rest of my life, as long as Noah had men to look up to. As long as my son had every idea of what brother-hood and family was *supposed to be.*

For the first time since arriving here, in this strange town, so very far away from anything and anyone I'd ever known, I knew no fear and had no regrets. I stood in the doorway of Archer's bedroom and drank every detail of this morning in. The light growing, and casting lines across the man and my boy through the slats of the blinds.

You can do this Melody. You have to… for him, I thought, and as I ever did, took strength from it. I took a picture, and I did what every mother before me had likely done—I went into the kitchen, forgot my tired, made coffee, and started breakfast like it was just any other day and I hadn't just seen something that profoundly changed me, or mattered to me.

10

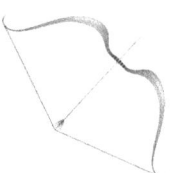

A **rcher...**

I woke up with the boy on my chest and to the quiet sounds of Mel moving through the kitchen. My stomach growled and I looked down, but the boy was still out cold. Kids. They could sleep through a nuclear holocaust and this particular kid was no different.

I sat up slowly, carefully, and got up, taking Noah to his crib and laying him down. He didn't so much as stir. Might as well have been comatose. When I turned to look, Mel was watching me over the stove, spatula in hand. I raised an eyebrow at her somber, almost sad, expression and realized – she looked like shit. Like she hadn't slept in a fucking age. I didn't comment on that, I just waited her out because it looked like she had something to say.

"You can treat me however you'd like," she said softly, flipping the pancake she had going in the skillet. "As long as you don't do it in front of him and as long as you treat him the way you just did, always. Am I clear?"

I frowned. "Where the fuck did that come from?" I asked.

She shook her head. "Never mind that, I just need to know, am I perfectly clear on this?"

Truth be told, her intensity was kind of freaking me out, so I nodded and when she raised her eyebrows I realized she wanted to hear it, or maybe *needed* to hear me say it out loud, "Yeah, Mel. You're clear, I get you—"

"Thank you," she uttered and flipped the pancakes she had going in the skillet onto a plate after a few heartbeats more.

I just wanted to get off this super fucking weird bent she was on, it was seriously creepy as fuck, so I asked, "Is there coffee?"

"Absolutely, still take it with cream and no sugar?" she asked and again I blinked. I hadn't realized that she'd ever paid that much attention to anything that wasn't my brother, Grinder's, dick.

"Yeah."

She made me coffee, she served my food and I was glad I'd remembered the syrup. Of course, when I said I would do something I did it. I was a man of my word. Maybe that was why she'd been so adamant about whatever the fuck it was that put a wild hair up her ass the minute before.

"Wanna tell me what that was all about?" I asked, shoveling some pancake drowned in syrup in my mouth – my curiosity winning out more than my desire to let it lie.

"No," she murmured.

"Suit yourself," I said with a shrug. I let it go, I didn't want to pursue it that fuckin' bad. Females, who the fuck knew why they did half the shit they did?

I ate, and she watched me, sitting at the opposite end of the table from me, her hands wrapped around a fresh, steaming mug of coffee, huddled in on herself like she was cold or something. She had on this thin cotton bathrobe with the wide sleeves, like something outta China or something. It looked good on her. Suited her color, or whatever, but I'd be fucked if I'd tell her so. I didn't need her going back to primping and fucking with makeup in a mirror forever like she had when she'd been nailing my brother. I needed her to take care of her boy, and maybe get a job if that's what she wanted.

"Get any of them applications in?" I asked.

"Yes," she said with a worried frown.

"What's that look for?"

"With as much as you work, I don't know how I'm going to—"

"What do you mean?" She gave me an exasperated look and it pissed me off some so I told her, "Quit lookin' at me like I'm stupid or some shit and spit it out."

"Who's going to watch Noah?" I asked.

"Mm, I'll figure it out." She stared at me wide eyed, her mouth very nearly hanging open. "What?" I demanded.

"Nothing, I… I just…" I pinned her with a look, what, didn't she fuckin' trust me? Jesus Christ, I took her and the kid's ass in, didn't that earn me a little bit of trust? She was saved from answering me, and I was stopped from saying anything else because right then was when the boy chose to stir, pushing himself into a sit and rubbing his eyes.

"Good morning!" Melody said, and her worried expression was just gone – poof, just like that; like it hadn't been carved into every line of her face just a second before.

"I gotta get to work," I grumbled, and took my ass into the bedroom. I grabbed like a five-minute shower, a cold one to wake up that really had absolutely nothing to do with Mel and that little robe of hers. I redressed quick in a fresh shirt, fresh pair of boxers and the same pair of jeans from the day before. I grabbed a fresh pair of socks and sat on the end of the bed to put them on.

Mel was talking to Noah and I watched her for a minute as she interacted with her boy. She was different than the girl we'd all left behind in Arizona. More mature, more grown up. *I think the word you're looking for is* responsible, *you dick,* I thought to myself and it sounded suspiciously like Grinder's voice in my head.

I knew it was all me, though. I didn't believe in ghosts or any kind of afterlife. You died and that was it. It was like turning off a television set. The picture went out, the screen went dark and that was that. I also believed that you only got this one life. That there weren't any do overs. There was no such thing as heaven and if there was a hell? Well we very surely were livin' in it.

"You okay?" Mel asked, and I snapped out of it, shaking my head a bit, to clear it.

Blinking a few times, I answered her, "Yeah, just deep thinkin' I guess."

"You're going to be late," she murmured.

"Don't nag me, woman," I said, and I meant it in jest but all it did was make her blanch.

"I'm sorry, I didn't mean it that way... I'll keep my mouth shut," she uttered and I frowned.

"Yeah, okay." I got up and went over to the couch pulling my boots on. "See you, same bat time, same bat channel, you be good for your mom, kiddo," I told Noah.

"Unca Atcha, bye-bye," Noah said and opened and closed his little hand in a wave. I felt myself smile in spite of myself and waved back at him.

"See you later, squirt," and with that, I opened the front door. "Lock up after me," I ordered Mel and she nodded, rising gracefully from her seat in that way that only women could.

"See you tonight," she said, and I gave a nod, shutting the door tight so I wouldn't have to look at her and the worry that was carving ruts into her face and the dark circles that were taking up residence under her blue eyes.

~

"You rang?" Dragon asked, making lazy strides in my direction a few hours later at the garage.

"Yeah, I need your help with somethin', P."

Dragon arched a salt and pepper eyebrow and said, "Oh yeah? You got my interest, what might that be?"

I couldn't get my back and forth with Mel that morning out of my head and it was taking over just about every thought I had like some kind of cancer.

"You got a way with scared females, like you're the fuckin' pussy whisperer or somethin'," I said with a sniff. Dragon laughed, a deep belly laugh that started off a chuckle and grew into a dull roar.

"Somethin' goin' on with Grind's baby mamma I should know about?" he asked, wiping a tear from his eye.

"I don't know," I said honestly, "but I got my suspicions that there's more than meets the eye, her comin' here like she did."

"Ah, I see." He was quiet a minute, real thoughtful. "Bring her by the club on Friday, I'll have a talk with her."

I gave a nod. "Thanks, Dragon," I said relieved. I still didn't give a shit about whatever might follow her out this way, but damn – something had to give, she looked like she was gonna worry herself sick.

"Anything for a brother, that's how we operate. How many times I gotta tell you that?"

"Well, he's got an awful thick skull," Rush said, striding up. He'd missed most of the conversation, but he'd at least caught Dragon's last line.

"Yeah? Fuck you, asshole," I told my brother and threw my rag at him which he deftly dodged with a shit-eating grin.

"See you and this mystery girl on Friday," Dragon said and Rush's expression fell.

"Something wrong with Mel and Noah?" he asked.

"Nope, now mind your own fuckin' business and get your ass back to work," I said.

"Hey, here you're not the boss of me," Rush said with a wink, but he missed that Dray was coming up on his ass.

"No, but I am, now get your ass back to work," Dray said. Rush gave me a one-fingered salute and Dray a proper one and ducked under the hood of his latest project. Dray bent and picked up my rag off the garage floor, handing it to me.

"What's up?" I asked him, half expecting him to ask what I'd brought his pops over here for, but he didn't. He asked me about a car I'd worked on a couple of weeks before and it was business as usual after that – for real this time. I was finally able to put Mel and her weird requests and busted-ass expressions to the back of my mind for the time being.

I finished out the day pretty strong and rode back home. I walked into a noisy disaster. It looked like the honeymoon of having a toddler added to the equation was over. Noah was running around shouting a bunch of nonsense while Mel stood in the kitchen rubbing her forehead yelling for him to stop. She meant business, too; busting out every little kid's worst nightmare... the dreaded parental countdown.

"One!" she called out but it was too late, Noah crashed into the front of my legs hard enough to knock him flat on his ass. He looked up at me and I looked down at him and I demanded.

"Just what do you think yer doin'?" He burst into noisy alligator tears. I looked at Mel with a clear look that asked, *Why the fuck is your kid crying?* But all she could do was look back at me, her shoulders dropping in sheer, worn out, exhaustion and I had a feeling it'd pretty much been like this all day.

Fuckin' great.

I left Noah where he was and shut the door behind me, and by the time I turned back around Mel had scooped him up.

"Why are you crying?" she demanded tersely and sounded just like every other mother I'd ever heard who was damn near at the end of her rope. I called in the cavalry, I shot a text off to Rush and Nox both.

"Unca Atcha scawy!" Noah said and broke into a fresh peal of screeching toddler whining cry. I couldn't stand that shit.

"I'm gonna get a shower, and when I get back out here, you're gonna be stopped. You hear me?" I asked him, which only made him wail harder despite my attempt at a tickle.

"I'm so sorry, Archer, he's just been like this all day, and I've been trying to keep up and I was trying to get dinner done and you're home already and I don't know where the time went and—" I raised a hand to stem the tide of Mel's babbling.

"I don't care, Mel. I'm going to grab a shower and by the time I get out, he'll be settled down. Shit, I just want some dinner and a night in." I went past her and Noah and into my room shutting the door. Sure enough, when I got out of the shower, the boy was quiet, and I could hear Nox out there playing with him.

I threw on fresh jeans and a clean shirt and went out, tying my hair up and back into a damp ponytail. I went into the kitchen and took the spoon out of Mel's hand.

"What have you got going on in here?" I asked.

"Tomato soup and grilled cheese?" I raised an eyebrow and shook my head. She'd had a hell of a day.

"I think I can manage, go lie down, take a nap or something," I grated and she very nearly slunk out of the kitchen. Nox and I exchanged a look and when the door shut quietly behind her, he mouthed at me 'what the fuck?'

It was a good question, I didn't have an answer. I finished up the food and Nox fed the kid and we put him down after a talking to that I think *maybe* only like twenty-five percent of it got through his little toddler brain.

I looked in on Mel and she was passed *out.* I let her sleep.

"I gotta run, man," Nox said quietly and I nodded.

"Thanks for comin'," I said.

"No problem, he's my nephew, too. What's going on with Mel?" I gave a one shouldered shrug.

"Not sleepin' so hot, I guess. I'm not really sure. She hasn't said shit to me."

Nox gave me a look like I was a dumbass. "Not like you're the easiest guy to fuckin' talk to," he said and I gave another shrug. "Right," he said dubiously, "I'll see you around."

"See you around, little brother," I affirmed and shut the door behind him.

I checked my phone, and Rush had texted back some dumbass excuse as to why he couldn't come around tonight. I didn't care, Nox had been enough. I went over to the couch and dropped onto it with an overblown sigh, Noah watching me through the bars of his crib.

"Go to sleep, kid."

He grinned his adorable baby grin at me and I felt my mouth quirk up on one side into a smile I couldn't resist. Even on a bad night, it wasn't so bad havin' 'em here. I was kind of surprised by that, and by how easy they'd fit into things. I didn't have much time to dwell on it though, I think I passed out before the kid even had a chance.

11

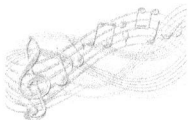

M elody...
I'd done as Archer had ordered and had gone to lie down. I hadn't meant to sleep for so long, but exhaustion had sucked me under and held me in some kind of comatose death grip, because the next thing I knew, I was dragged back up out of sleep by the alarm on my phone.

I hadn't even changed for bed, and still in my clothes from the day before, I sat up, pushed my hair off my forehead and clambered to my feet, waiting for my sleep fogged brain to orient itself.

Breakfast, I need to cook breakfast...

I went out into the living room and spied the empty couch, Noah's attention rapt on the TV screen as cartoons played. I turned to look and Archer stood in the kitchen, eyeing me.

"Sit down before you fall down, Mel."

I walked over to the little four-person dining table and sank into one of the chairs. Archer brought over a glass of orange juice and set it down in front of me. I picked it up with a shaky grip and sucked some of it down.

"Better?" he asked, and I nodded. "When was the last time you ate something?" he asked me, and I thought about it. He sighed and said, "If you have to think about it, it's been too fuckin' long. Jesus, Mel. How do you expect to take care of him if you can't even take care of yourself?"

Ouch again. He was right, of course he was, but his comment more than stung. The knife went deep and twisted in my heart and I focused my gaze on my sweet little boy, transfixed by ninja turtles on the small screen. I felt tears slip free and wiped them away quickly. I didn't answer Archer, figuring the question was rhetorical, but I couldn't help but wonder what it was exactly that I'd done to make him hate me so much.

"Here, eat this," he said dropping a plate in front of me. He called to my son, "Come on, Noah. Come help your mommy eat her breakfast." I closed my eyes and drew a deep, steadying breath. I reminded myself, that as long as he treated Noah well, and Noah didn't know anything was amiss, I could take whatever he dished out. I'd done it with my mother and stepfather in Arizona, but anything Archer did was a pale imitation of their cruelty.

You can do this, Melody. You have to… for Noah, I told myself.

"Mommy, up!" I opened my eyes and plastered on a brave smile for my brave little boy and lifted him up onto my lap.

"Good morning," I said and he hugged me. I loved that he loved me, despite how much of an utter failure I was.

Eggs and bacon, alongside toast loaded with butter and jam sat on the plate in front of Noah and me, and as always, I made sure my child was full before I bothered to feed myself. Archer sat with his own plate in front of him, drinking coffee and watching us. When Noah had enough and started to squirm, I put him down and he went back to the couch, climbing back up onto it and resuming his cartoons. I finished the food on the plate, my cheeks burning under Archer's cold, green-gold gaze.

"I didn't mean to sleep for so long," I murmured.

"You obviously needed it. I don't mind so long as you don't make a habit of pawning breakfast off on me." I winced at that and couldn't meet his gaze.

"Jesus, Mel. What the fuck happened to you?" he asked and I looked up sharply.

"Language in front of Noah, please."

"Sorry," he grimaced. "My question stands though, what's going on? You're not the same woman we left behind."

"Of course, I'm not," I said gently. "The girl you all left in Arizona was scared and pregnant with her first child; the woman you see now is a mother to a one-and-a-half-year-old boy. They're worlds apart, Archer."

He looked like he tasted something bad, took a drink of his coffee to wash it down and said, "Well regardless, the pres out here wants to see you and the boy on Friday, so fix you and the kid some dinner and meet me at the club after I get off work," he said. I felt myself pale and he eyed me, before asking, "Now what's wrong?"

"Nothing, he isn't... I mean I won't be expected to..."

"Naw, he just wants to meet you. May not have been official, you bein' Grinder's ol' lady, but the chapter out here agreed it's best that you be treated that way."

"What way?" I asked needing to hear precisely what he meant.

"As the property of a fallen brother, with all the protections and aide that comes with it. You know how it goes, Mel. We take care of our own," he said softly.

I nodded. I knew how it was *supposed* to work, yes, but the Arizona chapter sometimes had its own ideas, and back there, Noah and I were nothing but a laughing stock and little better than trash. I may have earned it, I may have gotten in way over my head as little better than a slut to be passed around between brothers, but it'd been better than the alternative of staying under my parents' roof. Plus, title aside, I didn't *feel* like a slut. Grinder was the only brother I'd really been with. He'd protected me from the others despite his refusal to be faithful to me, or to make me any kind of an official girlfriend or ol' lady.

When I'd come up pregnant, I might as well have turned into a leper as far as the rest of the guys had been concerned and when Grinder had left? Well, I found myself alone and I didn't want to be passed around, so I simply had stopped going around the club and its brothers. At least until I started to really show, and by then, it was like they'd all decided I was contagious or something. None of them wanted anything to do with the pregnant me. I'd thought it was because I was the reason Grinder had left... now I knew different. Now I knew it was likely because he had died, and the Arizona chapter's president had told the lot of them not to tell me.

"Mel?" I snapped out of it before I could dwell on it too much, my refusal had spurned the Arizona chapter's pres but good. I'd had to think about Noah, and Dom's reputation for turning out girls, getting them hooked and strung out and eventually turning tricks for him – well I'd wanted no part in that. Not with a baby on the way.

"What the fuck you thinkin' about so hard in there?" Archer demanded and I rubbed my face with my hands.

"A lot of things," I said and drew in a shaky breath.

"Well lay it on me. I'm not too keen on the zombie staring off into space routine when I'm tryin' to talk to you," he said and I flinched inwardly. Shit, last thing I wanted was to trip Archer's famous temper.

"After you left, to follow Grind out here, Dom started making hints about taking me for his own for a while. 'Trying me on for size,' he called it. I turned him down, told him I was pregnant, and it was Grinder's. It seemed to piss him off. They all left me alone for the most part after that. I think that's why no one told me. Dom told them not to, because I wouldn't go there, you know?"

Archer chewed the corner of his bottom lip and gave a single nod, once down, once up. "Yeah, I could see Dom pullin' some shit like that. If word got out he got a pregnant bitch hooked on his shit and was turnin' her out for profit, especially with Dragon and the mother chapter sniffing around, things would've gone really, really bad for him. These boys out here don't play that kind of shit at all. It's supposed to be one of the club's tenants – 'No women, no children –' but Dom always had a slightly different idea of what that means." Archer heaved a sigh. "It get much worse once Grind wasn't there to keep him in check anymore?"

"I honestly don't know, I stayed away once Grind left. I wanted to protect Noah, I thought he'd come around, you know? Come back, or send for me... I never in a million years thought he would just up and leave us like that."

Archer grunted. "He never got the chance to come around, at least not really. I'd like to think he would have too, but honestly I don't know that he would. We had a real fucked up upbringing comin' up in the system like we did. Grind was always pretty fuckin' adamant that he never wanted kids. I think it really freaked him the fuck out when you turned up knocked up. He probably thought you did it on purpose to trap him or some shit."

I felt my face crumble, that was pretty much exactly what Grinder had accused me of, and it'd crushed me. I closed my eyes and whispered, "Please, please, *please,* watch your language around Noah?"

"Shi-ffffu-da- I am so not good at this, am I?" he asked and I couldn't help the smile.

"Not really, but if it helps, neither am I. I feel like I'm a terrible mother."

"From what I've seen so far, you do alright. You haven't killed him yet, and kids are pretty resilient."

Thanks for the rousing endorsement, I thought to myself and tried not to feel sick.

"Anything else I should know about back home?"

"Like what?" I asked, keeping my tone light despite how dry my mouth had just gone.

"Nothing, I guess. Just miss it from time to time."

"I don't see how; it's beautiful here, so lush and green."

Archer nodded and I perked up. "Aren't you going to be late for work?"

"Yeah, I'll just stay a little late to make up. It's not a big deal, we don't have set hours as long as we work eight hours, five days a week or ten hours, four days a week. Dray doesn't give a fu—" I raised my eyebrows and stopped him with a look. "Yeah, that's the look I remember," he said with a bit of a grin.

"We'll bring you lunch later since I failed to make one for you."

"Good deal, thanks."

"Just living up to my end of the bargain," I said under my breath.

"Good thing, too. No deadbeats allowed."

I nodded, and again failed to look at him. I would feel like a monumental deadbeat until I got a job, but I still didn't know what to do about childcare… if I put Noah in daycare, it would probably take my entire salary and then some… such was the way of the world for the working class, American, single mother.

Welfare office, here I come. It was going to be an ugly eventuality. One I would have to undertake sooner, rather than later.

"I'll see you tonight," Archer said shrugging into his jacket and cut, trapping his ponytail in the collar. That always drove me nuts that he did that. At least Grinder would let me braid his hair when he'd kept it long so he didn't have to deal with the wind tangling it, although he never had kept it as long as Archer did.

I missed him with a sudden and fierce ache in the center of my chest. I looked at Noah and that ache eased.

"Mel?"

I shook myself. "Sorry, having a bit of a tougher time today for some reason." I cleared my throat. "Did I miss something?"

"Yeah, I said don't bother to wait up, and if you can, have my dinner packed up to go. I'm working the bar tonight and won't have time to eat here."

"Sure, I'll bring both lunch and dinner by the shop then, save you the extra trip of having to come here, does that sound alright?"

"Yeah, sure, thanks."

He ducked out into the brightly lit morning and I dutifully went to the door and locked up behind him. I sagged against the inside of its scarred wooden surface and sighed. My wits were scrambled this morning and I was all over the map emotionally. I frowned and looked at my watch and the date in the corner, rolling my eyes.

"PMS'll do that to you, Mel." I forced out a rushed sigh and set to work cleaning the kitchen which was not as big of a disaster area as I'd expected it to be. As soon as it was clean and orderly, I set to work making both an acceptable lunch and dinner for Archer as well as the needed snacks for the day for Noah.

It was busy work, but right now, with as much as my mind was wandering, I needed busy work, so that was okay.

12

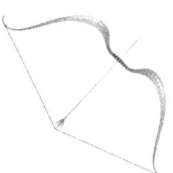

A rcher...

When I walked into the club on Friday, it was to a bunch of curious lookie-loos craning their necks and trying to get a look around me at Mel and Noah. Dragon sat at his usual table, cigarette dangling between his lips, glasses perched on the end of his nose and a newspaper open in front of him. Mel drew up even with me, her and Noah scanning the room.

"Unca Nox! Unca Rush!" Noah pointed at my two foster brothers and Rush called out to him, "Hey, buddy!"

"Hi Noah!" Ashton cried and Noah smiled.

"Ashden!"

"Did he just say Ashden?" Reaver asked, grinning. "Is that anything like Tom-Kat or Brangelina?"

"Shut up!" Hayden said giving him a light slap in the chest and rolling her eyes. "Hey, Melody," she greeted Mel and Mel smiled nervously.

"Hi," she said back hefting Noah, hauling him up higher on her hip.

Dragon folded his newspaper shut and set it down on his table, stubbing out his cigarette in the glass ashtray perched next to it. He took off his glasses and folded in the arms, tucking them into an inside pocket of his cut.

"So, this is her, eh?" he asked.

I gave a nod. "Mel, Dragon, Dragon this is Melody."

"Pleased to meet you," Mel said, voice strained.

Dragon looked her and Noah up and down. "Who's the little guy?" he asked, smiling at the kid. Noah smiled back shyly his fingers in his mouth. Dragon curled his fingers up and down in a child's wave for Noah and Noah imitated it with his free hand.

"Can you say hi to Uncle Dragon?" Nox asked.

"Unca Dragon?" Noah asked, and Dray chuckled.

"More like 'Grandpa Dragon,'" he said and there was some laughter.

"Boompa?" Noah asked, and his face twisted, Mel immediately soothed Noah.

"No, no, no, Grandpa Phillip isn't here, baby. This is Dragon."

"Boompa Dragon?" he asked.

"Sure, if yah like," Dragon chuckled, and Noah twisted in his mother's arms. I frowned, some suspicions coming up to the surface. I knew Phil was her stepdad and I also knew he was some kind of a dick, at least according to Grind. Noah's odd discomfiture sent up some red flags.

"Well, c'mere you two," Dragon said, and Mel edged further into the room. The guys moved out of her way and the girls edged back further too and the word must have gotten out because literally *everyone* was here, except for Rev and Red, they were probably held up by their kid.

"Have a seat," Dragon said. "All of y'all give the woman some breathing room, would you?" he called out and everyone turned and started milling about for a second before moving off to do whatever they were either up to when we arrived, or off to do something else. I watched Dani and R.T. drift off out back towards Dani's shop, Shelly and Ghost moving off with them.

The dynamic ol' lady duo of Sunshine and Doll took off toward the media room with Ev, the three of them laughing. No surprise, Trig, Reaver, and Dray followed along right after, like their dicks were some kind of leash. I chuckled and turned back to Dragon and Mel who were staring at me and my two foster brothers.

"Do I need to put it more plainly?" Dragon asked.

Rush laughed. "What?"

"Apparently I do," Dragon said. "Fuck off, and take your nephew with you. Go watch some cartoons or some shit down in the media room."

I eyed Melody who looked like she was sweating it out big time. "You gonna let him swear like that in front of the boy, but you gripe my shit?"

"He's the president, he can do whatever he wants," she said, breathily.

Dragon laughed, a big booming belly laugh at that. "Well, sweetheart, that ain't quite how it works, and I apologize. It's been a minute since I've been around a little one that could pick up bad words."

Nox went and took Noah from Mel, he made a noise of protest but then he got a look at one of the buttons on Nox's cut and he started to play with it and disaster averted.

"Come on, Little Man, let's go watch some cartoons in my room," Nox said.

"You alright?" I asked Mel and she nodded stiffly. I nodded back and followed my brother's out who were fully absorbed in our nephew, but me, for some reason, I couldn't resist one last look back at Mel who sat small and afraid in the chair opposite my P. The nagging feeling that shit just wasn't right getting stronger by the minute. I was hoping Dragon would get to the bottom of it, he was just plain better at this shit than I was.

13

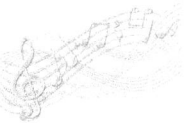

Melody...

Silence hung between us, an almost physical veil. I waited while he looked at me, coal dark eyes raking me over, bouncing across every detail of my face. Finally, he pulled back the curtain, breaking the silence first.

"So, what made you come out here?" he asked, leaning back in his chair.

"I wanted Noah to know who his father was. I wanted to see if I could change Grinder's mind," I said truthfully, and it was true... mostly. I swallowed hard, my eyes tearing, and Dragon's expression drew down into something considering. I could see the gears turning as he twisted his mouth back and forth. Finally, he pulled a pack of cigarettes from his cut and held them up.

"You mind?" I shook my head. "You want one?" he asked and I found my voice.

"I don't smoke."

"Hmm, you look like you could use one, can I get you a drink instead?" he asked. I shook my head, and he sighed. "Archer told me you got all the way out here just to find out Grind was gone."

I nodded and felt my face crumble, the pain welling fresh. I couldn't stop myself. Between that and the stress, I started to cry. I hid my face behind my hands and looked up sharply when his chair creaked. He held out a black bandana to me and I took it with shaking fingers.

"You wanna see him?" he asked and I looked up sharply.

"He's here?" I asked confused.

"Buried here, yeah. In a plot at the local cemetery, for any brother that didn't have any place else to *be* buried. For brothers that don't have any other family than the club. I got some questions about that, but they can wait. This is important."

I nodded numbly, and asked, "Can we go by Archer's apartment first?" I asked. "I'd like to bring something, you know?"

"I do," he said, and sighed. "Tell you what, if you have us stop there, can I stop someplace too? I'd like to pick up some flowers for my wife if we're going out there."

"Of course," I said, surprised he would ask.

"Okay then, you good to ride? I don't do cages."

"Sure," I agreed.

We went back to check on Noah, and to tell Archer, Rush, and Nox where we were going. They wanted to go too, but Dragon vetoed that.

"You know where he's at, you can go anytime. Let the lady mourn the father of her child in peace. She don't need an audience for this," he'd told them. I don't think he cared that I was standing right there, and I wasn't about to try and correct the president of the mother chapter.

"I need to go by the apartment," I murmured, and Archer fixed me with his cold, gold-green gaze.

"You have a key," he drawled.

Dragon turned to leave the room and looked over his shoulder. "One of you knuckleheads should have brought her out to see 'im by now." He shook his head and muttered "Jesus Christmas," and with that parting shot, he left the room. I felt my cheeks burn hotly and quickly gave Noah a kiss. I ducked my head, following Dragon out and back across the grass to the club's main building, trotting to catch up to him.

"I wish you hadn't said that," I murmured, and he arched an eyebrow and looked sideways at me.

"Any of 'em ever lay a hand on you?" he asked.

"No, why?" I asked.

"I don't just mean here, but back in Arizona either," he said.

"No, I mean, Grind once or twice but they were mistakes and we kept them just between us. I mean, it was my fault really. I got him too worked up and…"

I fell silent when he stopped and eyed me. "If he weren't dead I'd have Reave cut his balls off. That's not what this club is about, honey. Never has been, never will be. I got some questions for sure about the happenings back in Arizona, but they can wait. Come on."

I felt my heart sink and was afraid of what questions he'd ask me. Not that I'd lie, just… what if they found out? *Dom would probably kill you,* I thought to myself and sighed softly in resignation. *How did I always end up in these damn situations?*

We rode back to Archer's and it felt good to be on the back of a bike again. Dragon waited, looking around the parking lot while he sat on the front of his bike smoking a cigarette while I ran upstairs to get what I came for.

I found them quickly and went back downstairs, the neighbors out there with their Charger, music pounding like always. I got onto the back of the bike behind Dragon and he fired it up, drowning out the thumping bass from the cage with the angry growl from his engine. He turned us out of the parking lot and turned us toward the cemetery, making a quick stop at a flower shop on the way.

It was a slow, respectful ride through the old, wrought iron gates and along the sweeping paved pathways only wide enough for a car. We stopped and he tapped me. I got off the bike and he heeled down the kickstand, shutting her off.

"He's up that way," he said with a solemn sigh and I held out the deep red rose he'd bought out to him. He took it with a nod of thanks and got off his Harley himself.

"Thank you," I murmured, and I went up to the little fenced in area he'd indicated. There was no gate, and it was actually a pretty big expanse in the new spring grass. There weren't too many headstones inside the spindly, decorative fence, and it was easy to spot Grinder's grave as it was the newest. I went over to it and felt my eyes well.

David 'Grinder' Chandler
Riding Free

THAT WAS IT. No birth and death dates, just 'riding free' and a little oval set into the stone with a picture of him leaning against his bike, proud in his cut. I remembered that day. I'd taken the photo outside the club in Arizona. I knelt down carefully and took the photographs of Noah I'd brought out of my jacket pocket.

"I never expected to find you like this," I whispered and had to clear my throat; it was closing up, I was choking up from the rising tide of hot tears. "We had a boy, I named him Noah. I know you hated your middle name and I think part of why I named him that was because I wanted him to have a part of you and to piss you off... because let's face it, your leaving us pissed *me* off, but not as much as it *hurt.*"

I sniffed and wiped at the moisture under my eyes and leaned the two pictures up against the main part of the black stone, along the little ledge where it attached to the carved, thicker base.

"He's so beautiful, and such a sweet boy. It was hard, being all alone when I had him. I didn't know what to do and things didn't go… well. Not to say he didn't come out perfect! He did, I just… I just wish you'd been there. I wish *anyone* had been there. I wish you were here now to see your beautiful son and I wish I had a chance to fix things. I wish a lot of things, but I guess… I guess I don't want you to worry about us. I'm trying really hard and Noah is healthy and happy and Archer is letting us stay with him. Who'd have thought, right?" I laughed but it came out forced and broken.

"Why did this have to happen to us?" I whispered brokenly, and it was the sixty-four-thousand-dollar question. One with no answer except a cold slab of silent marble set in new spring grass under an endless blue sky full of fluffy, fat white clouds.

I let my gaze stray from that endless sky to a stone set about forty paces outside the fence, further along on the hilltop where Dragon's lumbering frame knelt, head bowed, hand on a white marble stone. The lone, deep crimson rose he'd purchased sitting in a bronze fluted vase with a lovely green patina that was attached to the headstone. His shoulders shook as he wept openly, and I didn't feel nearly so alone in my grief. It'd been so long since I hadn't felt alone, like it was simply me against the world, standing between it and my son.

I looked back down at Grinder's name carved into the black marble, my gaze riveting to the picture I'd taken so long ago with his phone. I missed him with a fierce burning ache, deep in the center of my chest where my heart still beat, battered and bruised. I lay down on the grass and stared into the sky like we used to do a thousand times back home, picking shapes out of the clouds.

I tried to think of every question he would possibly ask me about Noah, and I answered every single one. Telling him everything about his son, and how we came to be here and I have to say… I felt better. Much lighter than I had before. When I finished, Dragon was waiting back at his Harley, wraparound sunglasses in place. I said my goodbyes and left the pictures of Noah with his father, heading back down the hill to go back to my son and make good on everything I promised in the time I'd been there.

Dragon's expression was inscrutable from behind his wraparounds, but I could tell, now would come the questions he spoke of before. The first thing he asked was what exactly the hell was going on with the Arizona chapter that they would send me all the way out here on a wild-goose chase?

I told him everything and of course, the next question on the heels of the first, was about Dom, specifically what it was about him that made me say no.

"I'll tell you on one condition," I said softly and braced myself.

"What's that?" he asked me.

"That Archer, Rush, and Nox won't be in trouble for not selling out their brothers," I said.

Dragon huffed a bit of a laugh. "They ever involved in what I'm worried might come out your mouth?" he asked.

"Only insofar as looking the other way. They never had a direct hand in it that I know of. Of course, I'm just a dumb club whore and this probably falls under club business… At least it did according to Dom."

"You worried he might come out here holding a grudge?" Dragon asked.

"Insightful," I said. "And yes, yes I am."

Dragon sighed. "Just what're you runnin' from, sweetheart? We can't protect you if we don't know what the big bad is all about."

"It's nothing club related. I went to the club in Arizona to find out where Grinder had gone, remember? They told me, they just conveniently left out some of the important details."

"Right now, I'm just askin'," he said gently. "Don't make me have to order you, honey. I don't want to be like the guys you just left."

He pulled off his glasses and even red-rimmed from weeping, his gaze was so sincere... I told him. I told him about Dom and turning out the girls. I told him about all of it and then I begged him to keep it between us unless it became absolutely necessary to tell Noah's uncles.

He nodded. "Your secrets are yours to keep. I'm satisfied with what you've told me and I gotta say, you understand you're safe out here right? That the club is gonna protect you and your boy. Archer explained to you that you're being treated as Grinder's property with all that entails, yeah?"

I nodded. "I guess it's just been so long, you know? Feels like if I didn't have bad luck, I wouldn't have any luck at all." I huddled in my jacket. "Usually, if it's too good to be true, it undoubtedly is, you know?"

He nodded and sighed. "Maybe you're just due for a little good luck, eh?"

"I don't disagree, but it's still so hard to believe."

"Well, believe it, sugar, you're gonna be okay. We aren't perfect, but as far as this club is concerned, you and your boy are family. Speaking of which, you ready to get back to him?" he asked; I nodded. "Okay, let's go."

Dragon was as good as his word – he took me back to my son, who was sitting and playing in the midst of the media room floor with another, younger baby, while everyone stood around cooing and awing. I was passed to Ashton and Hayden who took it upon themselves to introduce me to the rest of the ol' ladies while Dragon quietly called a church meeting.

There was Everett, who belonged to Dray and Mandy, her best friend, who was the mother of the little girl my son played with; she belonged to a brother named Revelator. Shelly was next, and she positively glowed, her belly just beginning to show. She belonged to a brother called Ghost. Dani introduced herself; she said the love of her life was a man who went by Thirteen. I felt adopted right into their circle and it was the first time in a long time I felt like I belonged anywhere. It was nice, even when the men came out looking equal parts pissed off and grim. Archer, Rush, and Nox stared at me and I cringed inwardly, afraid they would take my candor as a betrayal.

"You good, Mel?" Archer asked and I felt some of the tension in my chest ease. I nodded and he gave a quick nod before turning and putting his head together with Rush's and Nox's. The women provided a fantastic distraction from the goings on around me and Noah, and for that, I was grateful. My son remained happy and safe, and above all, oblivious to the very adult goings on around him.

The rest of the early evening passed into night and when I took Noah home, Archer riding before us like some kind of vanguard, the anxiety returned and I worried what awaited me when I got us there. I put my sweet little sleeping boy down and turned, expecting Archer to have something to say, but all he did was drop heavily onto the couch with a sigh.

"Nothing?" I asked softly.

"Yeah, g'night Mel," he said gently and I went back into the bedroom a little shocked. I closed the door and changed for bed but laid awake. This time for a completely different reason than the thumping and bumping of bass through the walls.

14

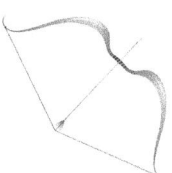

A rcher...

It'd been weeks, more than a month, I couldn't say for sure if it'd been more than two, but Mel, Noah, and I had settled into a kind of routine. In that time, Mel had even gotten a job; working a day shift over at some diner taking care of the lunch rush. She was bringing in good tips, and I'd told her to keep 'em to get her and Noah set up.

I say all this, because it was weird as hell that she'd be calling me in the middle of the day at the garage. She should be at work, slinging plates to a bunch of blue-collar working stiffs like myself.

I picked it up on the third buzz and asked, "Everything okay?"

"Yeah, I was just calling to let you know that Rev called me, said Noah wasn't feeling well. Jake is letting me off to go get him, so I'll be home when you get there."

"You usually are," I said tucking the phone between my shoulder and ear, so I could turn a socket wrench and get a bolt off my latest project.

"Yeah, I usually am, but not with a sick kid... I just figured you'd want to know in case things get ugly."

"Ugly how?"

"Could be anything," she said. "A snotty nose, rapid diaper changes, throwing up…"

"The joys of mommy hood," I said sarcastically and I think I heard her smile, which she still hadn't really done since getting here; leastways not around me. "Thanks for the warning," I said.

"No problem."

"See you later then."

"Yeah, bye."

I put in the rest of my hours and headed home, giving Mel a call before I headed out. It took her a while to answer and she got the phone right before it went to voicemail.

"Yeah, hello?"

I could hear Noah squealing in the background and Mel sounded frazzled. "Not sick I take it?"

"One awful diaper later he was right as rain. I think he just had an upset tummy because he's acting fine now. Noah, stop running!"

"Was calling to check and see if you needed anything from the store for him but it sounds like you're all good."

"All except for him making up for lost time," she said and I could hear her blow her bangs off her forehead. Yep. Definitely worn out chasing after the kid. Of course, it wasn't like Mel ever seemed fully rested. "Noah, I said stop!"

"I'll let you go so you can rein him in," I said and she said something but even *I* heard Noah hit, a loud thump coming over the line followed by him crying in the background.

"I've got to go!" Mel cried and the line went dead. I sighed and tucked my phone away, starting up my bike. I knew something was wrong when about three minutes into my eight-minute ride home, my phone started buzzing off the hook. It stopped, probably when it went to voicemail, but then immediately started up again.

"Aw shit," I muttered under my breath and poured on the speed. I parked the bike and took the stairs two at a time, my keys already at the ready to get into the apartment. Mel sat at the dining table, Noah in her lap, a wad of bloody paper towels pressed against his forehead while the kid just *screamed* in those hiccuping sobs. Mel was white as a fuckin' sheet and sobbing just as hard as her son.

"What happened?" I demanded and she was tripping over herself to get it out, talking so fast I couldn't understand her, Noah screaming even louder over her and it was so fucking noisy and he was obviously bleeding and it looked bad... *fuck!*

I finally had to grip the back of my head with both hands, fingers laced and take a few deep breaths so I didn't scream at them both to just shut the fuck up and tell me what the fuck had just happened. Finally, I put it together from Mel's babbling that Noah had been running around the apartment, unsteady as fuck being a fairly new walker, hell, toddlers his age were always unsteady, it was what it was. He'd tripped over his own damn feet and had crashed headfirst into the doorjamb to the bedroom, except he'd gone down just right and had hit his head on the corner of the strike plate, where the thing from the doorknob went into.

"Alright, legit, let me see," I ordered and she pulled the paper towels away. That was going to need a stich or two. No doubt about it. "Right, we're going to the hospital, gimme your keys, I'll drive. You try to keep him calm; can you work on that? Can you do that?" I asked over the noise of Noah's rhythmic howling. God, it was enough to drive anybody nuts.

"I don't have insurance for him!" she cried and I looked at her.

"Doesn't matter, I'll figure it out, but let's get that looked at, come on." I grabbed her keys off the counter where I spotted them and we rushed down to her cage. I didn't bother dealing with my cut on account of the emergency and had already decided we were lucky to be nearest Doc's hospital. I opened the back door for Mel and she got in the cage, I got in the front.

"What if they think I hurt my son?" she asked and I shook my head.

"If anything, they're gonna take one look at me and think *I* hurt him," I told her. "We'll cross that bridge when we come to it. Right now, the important thing is to get him looked at. That's what we're doing. One problem at a fucking time," I grated and I knew I sounded pissed. I wasn't pissed at her, or anyone for that matter. I guess I was more pissed that there wasn't anything I could do other than what I was doing and that didn't seem like very damn much at all. I couldn't fix this one, and that chapped my fucking ass.

We pulled into the parking lot at Doc's ER and I let Mel out the back door. "Go in, get everything going, I'll be right there."

She nodded and carried Noah in. She hadn't let him go since I'd gotten to them, and I didn't see that changing. I parked the car and took a couple extra deep breaths, hitting the steering wheel a couple of times to vent before I went in there and tore into any hospital personnel, making this any worse than it already was.

I got out the car and went in, to find no sign of Mel and Noah, they were in the back already. Good. I went that way and ignored the nurse behind the admin desk who yelled out, "Sir, you can't go back there!" The fuck I couldn't, Noah was blood. I'd be damned if anybody would keep me from him.

I found Mel and Noah in an alcove and sat down. A hospital security guy pulled back the curtain a second after me.

"It's okay," Mel said, "he's my baby's uncle."

"You can't be back here without one of these," the admin desk nurse said holding up a 'visitor' sticker. I plucked it from her fingers and stuck it on the front of my cut.

"Happy?"

"No!"

"Too damn bad," I said and put my hand on Mel's shoulder giving it a squeeze. "Doc look at him yet?"

"No, I ain't looked at him yet, he only just got here. Should've guessed it was you when one of the nurses said it was a biker causing trouble in my ER. What seems to be the problem?"

Mel looked up at Doc; a disarming mix of wide-eyed and dumb-founded while he pulled some latex gloves out of a box on the wall, slipping his hands into them. "He was running," she said. "I told him to stop but he tripped and hit his head on that metal door thingy before I could get to him to make him stop," she said and Doc looked at her funny.

"Metal door thingy?" he asked.

"Strike plate," I said.

"You saw it?" he asked.

"Yeah," I lied. I'd heard everything; that was close enough. Mel looked startled but kept her mouth shut. The admin nurse and the security guard wandered away when Doc waved them off.

"Let's have a look," he said rolling over a stool and pulling the paper towels away. "Oh yeah, see that's not so bad. If he were a little bit older, I wouldn't even stitch it, I'd just put a couple butterfly bandages on it, but given he'd likely just pull 'em off... Let me have a nurse set up a suture kit. You hold this here, like you been doing and I'll be right back." He pressed a thick square of fresh gauze over the cut and threw the paper towels away before stripping off the medical gloves he'd put on and throwing them in the trash right behind the bloody mess.

Noah was quieting down and sat huddled against Mel who held him like somebody was going to snatch him any second. She mouthed 'thank you' over his light blond curls and I nodded. A nurse came by a few seconds later with a tray full of the goods Doc was going to need.

Noah screamed bloody hell when Doc gave him the shot of the numbing agent. Melody looked green and I asked her if she wanted me to take him. She remained mute, but adamantly shook her head. Stitches went in, one and two and the boy was all done. Doc slapped a Scooby-Doo Band-Aid over the cut and he was done. It really wasn't nothin'.

"Might want to get him some pediatric drink, he might be a little dehydrated from the diarrhea you said he had and all this cryin'."

"I'll do that," Mel said quickly.

"And for you, I'm prescribing a glass or two of wine or a margarita or something." He looked up at me. "Think you can handle that?"

I gave a sharp nod. "I believe I can," I told him and held out my hand. We shook, and he gave me a lopsided grin.

"Y'all need to stick to seeing me at the club," he said and I nodded again. I could do without this shit and Mel looked like she was shattered into a million fuckin' pieces.

"We'll do that, too," I said.

"Go on, then. Get on out of here."

"Thank you, Doc," Mel said and she sounded bottom of her heart grateful.

"I got no problem takin' care of family," he said and with that, he left us.

I took Mel and Noah home, and left 'em just long enough to go get some of that drink shit at the drugstore, like Doc recommended. By the time I got back, Noah was napping in his crib and Mel was sitting on the edge of the couch staring at him.

"You need to go get a shower and come on back out here and have a drink," I uttered.

"Do you think the hospital is going to call child services?" she asked.

I snorted. "No."

"Am I a horrible mother?" she asked and tears leaked out of her eyes, she still hadn't looked at me. Her gaze locked on her sleeping son.

"Naw, I'd say you're a damn good mom," I said.

"You really think so?"

"What I really think is you need a hot shower and to take the medicine the doctor prescribed you. I picked up your favorite tequila along with his juice stuff." She finally looked at me and I said, "It's pretty bad when the clerk rings you up and says 'I know exactly how you feel.'"

Nothing. Not even a smile. Just that vacant, traumatized stare. I sighed and gave her an order, "Mel, I'll watch him, go take a shower."

She got up as if pulled by strings and floated over to the doorway leading into my room, she stopped and looked down at the strike plate, her shoulders bouncing once, twice, a third time before she rushed into the bathroom and closed the door. I could hear her crying but sometimes, with bitches, that's all they needed was to cry it out, so I left her to it while I went and grabbed a couple of shot glasses. I took one shot while she cried and downed another when the shower started up.

"Well, that escalated quickly," I muttered to myself, my own eyes locked on the sleeping boy. I didn't know what to think, the fact that the whole thing had jump started my heart as hard as it had.

Maybe it was more like I didn't want to admit how much I was beginning to feel. Not just for Noah, but for his mother too.

Shit.

15

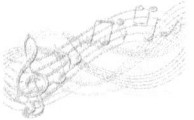

Melody...

A month or more had passed since the incident with Noah and his stitches, and my little boy's cut had healed admirably. His first permanent mark was forever etched in a straight notch through his eyebrow, however. When he was older, it would probably make him look more edgy, perhaps even devilish, the way his father had looked. Grinder very nearly had the same scar, only on the opposite side, though his story had been much more sinister at how he had arrived at it.

I wish I could say that I was fully recovered from the incident, but after my hot shower and a shot of tequila which Archer had insisted I take on the doctor's orders, I had slept and I had slept hard and well. However, all good things must come to an end and I think that was the *last* good night's sleep I'd had since.

Archer was barely at the apartment at night, and even so, I swear he could sleep through just about anything short of a nuclear bomb blast. It was as if he and Noah were father and son in that regard. My little boy could sleep through just about anything too. I envied them their particular superpower.

If it wasn't the Charger out front, it was one of the neighboring apartments. If it wasn't music, it was the couple in apartment number two downstairs and to the right of ours. They fought near constantly and their screaming should have been heard for miles. I was exhausted, I wanted sleep, I wanted sleep so bad I cried nearly every night until it found me... because let's face it, I very rarely, if ever, found *it*.

I blame my total lack of sleep on the monumental mistake I made coming back to the apartment that day. It was sunny, and warm. Unseasonably warm according to the radio. I was loving it. Except for the fact the air was so humid as compared to the dry desert heat of Arizona, it was very nearly just like being home.

I had gone to the grocery store to pick up just a few items and I had them tucked in the crook of one arm against my hip, while I had Noah in the other, equally balanced on the other hip as I kicked the back door of my sad little hatchback closed. I didn't even bother to lock it. There wasn't anything worth stealing in it. It didn't even have a CD player, but rather the factory radio and a broken tape deck. I figured if anyone wanted to go through it *that* badly, they could have at it; I might as well save myself the broken window which I wouldn't be able to afford to get fixed anyways.

I was saving my ass off for first, last, and deposit on a place for me and Noah that was anywhere but here, and like I said, I blame the lack of sleep when it came to my frayed rope and what happened next. I was headed toward the stairs up to the second floor when the owner of the Charger started blaring his bass-heavy rap music and without even thinking, my last thread of sanity snapped.

"Oh, will you give it a fucking *rest* already! You know there are people who actually live here who would like to *sleep* every once in a while," I said over my shoulder.

The owner of the car stood up straight out of the car and turned. "What did you say to me you fat white bitch?" he demanded and I carried on up the stairs.

"You obviously heard me just fine," I called back crossly and the young man, probably younger than even I was at a mere twenty-eight, started up the stairs in my direction. I dropped the groceries and fumbled the keys into the lock, my hand shaking while Noah stared at the man with wide innocent eyes.

"Oh, I *know,* you ain't talkin' to me that way, I'm about to teach yo ass some respect! What you think you doin' talkin' to a nigga like that?" I shoved open the door and went to slam it in his face but I was too late. He kicked in the door and cradling Noah in my arms I protected him with my body as we both went down.

My son shrieked in terror and I heard my voice echo his as the man towered over us both, and I went sprawling into the living room of Archer's apartment. Noah struggled out of my grip and crawled away, sitting up. His voice rising in a panicked cry I could do little to comfort him because the gangbanger standing in the doorway had all of my attention.

I put my hands up and beseeched him, "Please, not in front of my son, don't shoot me in front of my son."

"Oh, I might shoot you bitch, but I got a different lesson in mind," he said, licking his bottom lip and grabbing his crotch with his other hand. I felt myself blanch.

"I'll do anything you ask, just please, not in front of my son."

I started to cry, the tears of pure terror slipping down my cheeks, and I did nothing to wipe them away. I was frozen, adrenaline pounding through my veins with every heartbeat. I wanted to pick up my son, but I didn't dare move. The man smiled, his deep ebony skin making his teeth seem so very white, the metal in his mouth from several gold teeth gleaming. I would say his smile was like the Cheshire cat's in a way, however, it was far too malevolent for that. I was staring pure evil in the face and I found myself silently praying to Grinder, to God, and to anyone else who would listen, to give me the strength and cunning to get my son and I both out of this intact.

"Take off them panties," he ordered and I broke into a sob.

"Please don't, not in front of my son!" I begged and he cocked the gun shoving it forcefully in the air in my direction.

"I suggest you do what I tell you and maybe I won't!" he shouted.

I shook and moved mechanically to comply. I was still in my work uniform, which was a little light turquoise 1950s dress with white apron and white accents at the collar and short sleeves. They were paired with white ankle socks and white Chuck Taylor sneakers and fit the diner I worked at. I had loved the uniform when I started, but right now, sprawled on my butt in the living room with the short, mid-thigh-length skirt riding up after my tumble, I loathed it for giving this creature the perverse idea to rape me in front of my *child*.

I shimmied my white cotton underwear midway down my thighs while the pervert pointed a gun in my face and I was about to resign myself to my fate when he froze and looked like he was about to shit himself. I stopped and it was Noah's screaming cry of, "Unca Atcha!" that let me know who was behind the thug.

Archer took a slight step to the right and I could see him framed in the open door, a gun of his own pressed into the close-shaven scalp of our assailant, a calm, but angry look on his face. He nudged the man's scalp and said, "Hand over your piece before I redecorate the inside of this place with your face." The man put up his hands and Archer took the gun, shoving it into the back of his waistband.

"What the fuck you think you doin' in here? Huh?" Archer demanded.

"Man, I was teaching yo bitch a lesson!"

"Yeah, well, you don't teach my bitch *anything*, that's my job."

"Well you need to teach her some respect, you dig?"

"Well you need to get the fuck out of my place and let me handle these things, *you* dig?" Archer demanded back, pressing the gun barrel harder into the man's skull, moving to the side to let him switch places and to put him closer to the door.

"Man, you is makin' a mistake comin' at me like this—" the Charger's driver said, and Archer cut him off.

"Shut the fuck up! Don't think I don't know who your fuckin' boss is. The only mistake *you* made was coming into a Sacred Heart's place. Somehow, I don't think that's a can of whoopass you're going to want to open. Now you might want to get the fuck out, before I change my mind about redecorating," Archer said coldly.

I swallowed hard, and the man changed his tune but only slightly, upon hearing the club's name.

"Alright, alright, we cool, we cool. I'm leavin'. What about my gun?"

"Consider it the cost of doing business," Archer said, and he already had the man almost halfway out the door. "Newsflash for you, slick. You tell your homies and the rest of your crew that this apartment, everything and every*one* in it, is *mine*. You get me? There won't be a next time for any of this shit either."

He then shut the door in the gangbanger's face and turned to me, asking softly, "You alright?"

I pushed to my feet, bile rising in my throat and gasped out, "Take care of Noah," before I stepped out of my panties and practically ran for the bathroom, slamming the bedroom door behind me. When I did, I saw Archer picking up my son and cradling him against his chest the way any protective father would.

I threw up, and I don't remember much, but the next thing I *did* remember was sitting on the end of Archer's bed hugging myself, knees tightly together, one hand pressed over my mouth as I sobbed while trying valiantly to make no noise, so my child wouldn't hear. Archer came in the room and I saw past him that Nox and Rush had Noah. I only caught a glimpse before Archer closed the door but it was enough to send me into more sobs as the adrenaline wore off and I crashed and burned.

Archer sat down next to me and did something unprecedented. He put his arms around me and tucked me tightly into his chest. He breathed out a heavy sigh and pressed his lips to the top of my hair.

"You should have killed him," I said, voice cracking.

"Oh, I'm going to, but I need to go about it the right way," he said and I knew he was completely, one hundred percent serious, however, I couldn't bring myself to feel anything but relieved.

"When you calm down, you can tell me what happened but right now, just shhhh," he soothed and it was just so *nice* of him and completely out of the ordinary. I was grateful for the reprieve though, so I just soaked it up while I could and let myself calm down.

I swallowed hard, and told him everything and when I was finished, he sighed asking, "Why didn't you tell me you weren't sleeping because of that asshole?"

"I didn't want to be a bother, I guess I figured you wouldn't really care. I mean, it wasn't affecting Noah, so why bother, right?"

He went deathly silent for a minute and I could almost hear him thinking. Finally he said, "Right," but it came out so incredibly bitter. I wondered for a glimmer of a moment if I had hurt his feelings with that little revelation.

"What are we going to do?" I asked weakly, fear for mine and Noah's safety creeping in.

"'We' aren't going to do anything. *You* are going to stay here with Rush and Nox, *I* am going to go have a talk with Dragon. I need you to sit tight. Clean yourself up and go comfort your boy. I'll be back when I can."

I nodded and he let me go; I suddenly felt bereft and incredibly selfish. Of course my son needed me, and here I was, in Archer's room, hiding from him. I felt deep shame over that, even deeper than I had a moment before. I didn't have the time or ability to fall apart for myself when Noah needed me, now did I? I swallowed hard and looked up at Archer.

"Be careful?" I asked and he searched my face, his green-gold eyes almost troubled.

"Always am," he said and got up, going back out into the living room.

16

A rcher...

"She okay?" Rush asked and I shook my head handing him the piece I took off the banger.

"No, I need you two to stay here and keep her and Noah safe. I've gotta go see Dragon and get in front of this before it gets worse."

"Yeah, we can do that, fly low fly fast, Brother," Nox said and with that, I was out of there. I went out, the Charger was gone, and I put my headphones in and plugged them into my phone, dialing up Dragon as I fired up the bike.

"Yeah?" he answered by way of greeting.

"We got a situation, P. One of the Fiddy Street Crew's boys just busted into my place and tried to rape Mel."

"Jesus Fucking Christ! What would he go and do a damn fool thing like that for?"

"Perceived disrespect, she told him to turn his music down in a less than polite way. What's worse, he was gonna do it in front of Noah."

"Shit, they okay?"

"Shook up, scared as fuck, I got Rush and Nox there watching 'em but we need to get ahead of this before all hell breaks loose."

"You on your way here?" he asked.

"Yeah," I shouted above the road noise. "Be there in like ten more."

"Noted, I'll get us a sit-down with their shot caller," he said.

"Be there soon," I said to the empty air, Dragon had already hung up on me.

SOMETHING LIKE AN HOUR LATER; Dragon, me, Reaver, Duracell, and Blue were riding up on neutral territory. The man of the hour, the shot caller for the Fiddy Street Crew, waited with some of his street soldiers outside a couple of tricked out black Escalades.

"To what do I owe this pleasure?" he called out when we'd shut off the bikes.

"Seems to me you might want to tug on a leash or two before me an' mine get a mite upset," Dragon said dispassionately.

I stood in my appointed place and tuned out the conversation. The last thing I wanted was for the club to get into another war, and the last thing I needed was to get pissed off and shove us headlong in that direction. I'd called Dragon for a reason, because if anyone could get us out of this using diplomacy it was him. Additionally, if there was anyone who could get me the other thing I wanted, it was him... and what I really, *really* wanted was that motherfucker's head on a pike.

"So, you're telling me that if you don't get this cat's head that it's gonna be war?" I heard the shot caller say.

"That's about the size of it, yeah."

Go Dragon, I thought. Color me impressed, I didn't expect him to be that direct. The shot caller looked skeptically at us for a full minute, taking our measure as to how serious he thought we were being.

"Man, you must be some kind of crazy," he said, the skepticism in his eyes coloring his voice. It was Reaver who beat me to saying it…

"Tell that to the Suicide Kings," he said and I tried not to smirk and failed. So, did the rest of the guys on our side of the proverbial line in the sand.

The shot caller called back over his shoulder to one of his men something that sounded like 'groan main' which was the weirdest fuckin' name I'd ever heard, and with our road names, I'd heard some fuckin' doozies. I didn't comment, I wanted to see what was what.

"Yeah, Boss?"

"Who runs out of the apartments on Twenty-Sixth and Vine?" he asked.

"That'd be Shorty Mac, Boss."

"Uh huh," he said and licked his bottom lip, head back, lookin' down his nose at all of us. I gritted my teeth and I could see Duracell doin' the same.

"Alright, y'all do you. You disappear this one man with no interference from me an' mine we cool?"

"Oh yeah, we'd be cool," Dragon said.

The shot caller nodded slowly, considering, "Y'all some badass motherfuckers, we want no beef wit' you. You want him, you can have him. Rapin' girls in front of their kids is bad for business as is evidenced by this little party we're havin' right here."

"I don't disagree," Dragon said.

"Cool, we cool then?"

"No interference from you and yours, we'll be cool as soon as the job is done."

"So be it."

"Pleasure doing business with you," Dragon said with a wicked smile, before he turned to me. "You want you should do this, they're bein' your declared property an' all?"

"Absolutely," I said.

"Awww!" Reaver stuck his bottom lip out and pouted.

"You're welcome to join me," I told him and he gave a feral grin.

"Yay!"

The men from the Fiddy Street Crew gave Reaver a weird look, the shot caller saying, "Man, you're one weird cat."

Reaver bobbed his head happily in the dude's direction. "Uh huh!"

"Right then, meeting adjourned," Dragon muttered and we started up the bikes, leaving out the way we came. About half way to the clubhouse, Reaver and I broke off and went our own way.

17

M elody…

The bedroom door opened, and I looked up sharply from where Noah lay sleeping. It was late, and for once the apartments were silent, but of course I couldn't sleep. Archer stood in the doorway and I sat up. He came into the room and shut the door behind him, his gaze roaming over me and Noah, his lips thinning down into a straight line.

"Marry me," he said and I blinked.

"I'm sorry, but did you just ask me to—"

"I'll say it again, *marry me*, Mel. I've been thinking about it. I can do so much more for you, and for Noah. I can put you both on my insurance at the shop, I can adopt Noah and be a father to him, I can give you both the protection you need and with the tax breaks and shit, I can get us into a house faster, and start saving for the boy's education… all of it." He scanned my face and I sat, shocked into silence. Everything he said was true but…

"Why? Why would you do this? I mean, what's in it for you?"

"A family. A real one," he said. "You agree to bear me at least one child, you be a mother to them, that's all I want, Mel."

"How do I know you won't treat Noah like something… less, once you have a child of your own?" I asked, voice quavering.

"You have my word, and have I ever gone back on my word in all the time you've known me?"

I closed my eyes and breathed slow and even. This was big. This was a lot and so very quickly. I opened them and stared at Archer which was when I noticed a few errant stains on his tee. Stains that hadn't been there when he'd come home the first time. Stains that looked suspiciously like blood. I looked Archer in the eye and swallowed hard.

He sank to the end of the bed, never breaking eye contact and said, "Just think about it, you don't have to answer me now—"

"Yes," I said, voice hollow. It was impulsive, but it was far from irrational. In fact, it made perfect sense. It was just daunting, but I would do anything, and I mean *anything* for my child and this? This was no exception.

He adjusted himself, lying down on the other side of Noah, I laid down too, facing him, my child between us.

"Yes?" he asked and I eased onto my side, so I could face him across the pillows.

"Yes."

He closed his eyes and nodded faintly, opening them again and voice rough with an undefined emotion he murmured, "Sleep. I'm here to stand watch, you're safe, Noah's safe and no one is going to hurt either of you; not anymore."

I closed my eyes and nodded faintly, and when I opened them again, Archer was gone and Noah was nose-to-nose with me.

"Moooooommy! Wake up!" he said and I smiled in spite of myself.

"Good morning," I said softly and he grinned.

"I'm hungee," he whispered and I sat up.

"Cereal?" I asked.

"Tix!"

"Trix it is," I said and stood, picking him up when he reached for me. We went out into the living room where we found Archer, standing with a concerned looking Rush and Nox.

"Did you seriously agree to marry this asshole?" Rush asked and I immediately scowled at him.

"Language!" I admonished.

"That doesn't answer the question," he said.

"Yes, and it's my business and Archer's," I told him.

"Oh my God, *why?* Why would you do that?" he asked and looked completely baffled.

"Do you really have to ask?" Nox leveled his twin with a downright tempestuous look.

"Shit, man. I just never thought I'd see the day, let alone that it'd be—" he stopped mid-sentence and looked like he was struggling.

"What? That'd it'd be Grinder's leftovers?" I asked softly.

Silence met my question and I set Noah down in a chair at the table. I brought down a bowl and filled it with his favorite cereal and added milk, bringing it and a spoon over to him. I sat down with my son and helped him eat, we were doing really well with him feeding himself and making less mess in the process. I smoothed down his bed head and watched him for a moment while the guys all stood around looking guilty or just plain at a loss for anything to say.

"I've said it before and I'll say it again, you can say whatever you'd like about me, treat me how ever you'd like, as long as Noah is treated well, and you don't treat me poorly in front of him, okay?"

"Rush, Nox, I think you guys had better go for now," Archer said pinching the bridge of his nose, squeezing his eyes shut. Nox punched Rush in the arm.

"Ow!"

"Shut up, you big baby, let's go," Nox said and he didn't sound at all happy with his twin. I didn't blame him. Rush had a bad habit of opening his mouth and inserting his foot. This was no exception.

The boys piled out of the apartment's front door and shut it behind them leaving Archer and I staring at one another over my baby's head as he happily munched his cereal, apparently none the worse for wear over what'd happened the day before.

"Change your mind?" he asked. I shook my head silently.

Archer nodded and rolled his lips. "I'll uh, get us an appointment at the courthouse."

I nodded and swallowed hard. "You should let your brothers know, not just Rush and Nox, but the rest of the club, you know? So that they can be there; they might get upset if they feel left out. It's kind of an important milestone."

"Yeah, that's a good idea. You know it's Saturday. You don't have work, why don't we go over to the club and let folks know what's up. I don't think it's a good idea you hanging around here today, you know, after what happened."

I nodded again and smoothed my lips together. "That's a good idea," I murmured.

Archer sank into the seat next to mine and asked, "What's bothering you?"

"A lot of things," I said quietly.

"Talk to me," he said and I closed my eyes.

"It's okay," I told him. "You don't have to pretend all of a sudden to care because I've agreed to marry you—"

He sat up straight and shifted in his seat, leaning back. "If I didn't care, I wouldn't have asked you to in the first place; don't you think?"

I sighed and fixed my gaze to the tabletop, "I know the reason you're doing this is for Noah, and that's okay. I'm used to being an afterthought."

"Right, can I ask you something?"

"Of course."

"Why do you put words in my mouth?"

I looked up sharply. "Excuse me?"

"Have I ever said you're an afterthought?"

"No—"

"Okay then," he stood up, "finish feeding our little man, I'm going to grab a shower then I want you to get dressed so we can get going."

"Okay," I murmured, once again feeling thoroughly dismissed. He went into the bedroom and I sighed, putting my face in my hands.

"Mamma sad?"

"No, baby. Mamma's just frustrated."

"Okay," he said and I had to smile. I don't recall if I'd ever gone over 'frustrated,' but we had a long way to go yet so it didn't much matter.

When Archer came out of the bedroom, freshly dressed and running a towel over his hair, I had Noah wrapped up with coloring on some plain sheets of butcher paper with crayons. I rose quietly and went to slip past Archer and he stopped me with a light grip on my arm. I startled and looked up into his green-gold eyes which had always been so intense and slightly ethereal with how beautiful they were. Not that I'd ever admit it to him, that just seemed like such an awkward thing to do.

"You don't have anything to ever be afraid of out of me," he said. "You have my word."

I stood there open mouthed for a moment, the proclamation from him being totally unexpected. I didn't know what to say and what came out of my mouth was the best I could think of with how simply overloaded my mind was. "Thank you," I said and it was apparently the right thing to say. He let me go and inclined his head in a gentle nod and I let my feet carry me the rest of the way to the bedroom.

I dug out clothes to wear, some jeans and an old club ladies cut tee from the Arizona chapter. I showered and pulled my hair into a pony-tail while it was still wet. I dressed slowly and deliberately and when I finished, I sat for several long moments asking myself just what it was I had done by agreeing to marry Archer... I mean, I barely knew anything about him!

I think it was just finally hitting me, and even though I knew in my heart of hearts that it was the right decision for Noah, I was afraid. For all that we'd been living together for the last few months, Archer and I might as well have been ships passing in the night with our working schedules. We didn't speak much beyond what was for dinner, or anything not regarding Noah. We didn't talk about old times, he didn't bother to ask anything about me, and I had treated him with the same regard.

It wasn't like open curiosity was welcomed by the man. At best, he was coldly indifferent about my presence, at worst, he regarded it with open disdain. I had been both lucky and grateful that Archer at his worst didn't show up but once or twice since I had arrived, the worst of it being upon my arrival and he had kept true to his word. Any negative remarks in the time since, he had kept either to himself, or had leveled them at me well outside of Noah's presence.

Yet here I was, three or so months into mine and Noah's stay and I had readily agreed to marry the man who might as well have been a stranger to me. Not only had I agreed to marry him, I had agreed to bear him at least one child, right along with everything that entailed. I swallowed hard and gave myself one last passing glance in the cracked mirror above the bathroom sink before rejoining my son and his uncle... my soon to be *husband*, out in the living area of the sad, one-bedroom apartment.

Oh my God, I thought to myself, *what had I agreed to do?*

One look at my son and it all came rushing back. I smiled bravely at my little boy and reminded myself, likely not for the last time, *I secured him a better future. That's what I did...* and it was true.

"Ready to go?" Archer asked and I gathered my purse and my keys. Noah's diaper bag remained in the car.

"Ready," I affirmed and hoped I looked braver than I felt. Archer looked me over with what appeared to be new eyes in that moment.

He nodded and said, "I'll lead."

I nodded again and found myself thinking, *isn't that what you've always done?*

18

Archer...

"How's she doing?" Trigger asked as we all stood around watching her disappear back into the media room.

"She's okay, she's tougher than she thinks she is," I said. "Probably why she agreed to marry me so fast."

Silence met my proclamation. "You're getting *married?*" Dray demanded.

"Yeah, I need to set an appointment down at the courthouse for some time this week—"

"Oh the fuck you are! Archer if I knew your first, middle, and last name I would *so* be using it right now. You are *not,* I repeat, you are *so not* taking that away from her!"

"Woman, what the fuck are you on about?" Ghost demanded and all of us turned to where his pregnant ol' lady, Shelly, was coming out of one of the bathrooms.

"Bad enough she drives across the country out of that hellhole she was living in, bad enough she's had it almost as rough since she got here, now you want to take her special day away from her too? No, just *no*. I need you, I need *all* of you to think for just a damn minute about this. Did you even get down on one knee? Did you even bother to get her a ring? I bet you didn't."

The look on my face must have said it all, because she scoffed. "Gah! You're such a *jackass!*" Shelly cried and Ghost went to her, gripping her by the arm and giving her a flat and unfriendly look.

"Shells, I'm not going to have you disrespect a brother, not now not ever. You need to cool it right the fuck now," he said, consternation in his tone.

"Me? Oh that's rich, Ghost. That's real rich! What about *him?* You're all freaking unbelievable!"

"Shut it, woman! Does she even want a wedding?"

"You didn't even ask, so how would you know she *doesn't?*"

By now, women were filtering out into the hall, apparently Shelly's harpy call had brought the rest of them out of the media room. Melody was among them, Noah on Hayden's hip looked on curiously, but my eyes were on Mel whose eyes glinted with tears.

"Archer, I think the reason Shelly is so upset, is because when we're little girls, it's all about the day when we grow up and we get married. It's supposed to be our one special day. Every little girl dreams about the day that her perfect knight in shining armor gets down on one knee and asks her to be his forever. It's so much a part of the very fiber of our being. While she gets the *why* of it, the how is really hard to understand," Red said gently, and I looked back to Mel where Everett hugged her gently into her side, her one hand stroking up and down Mel's shoulder in a comforting gesture.

I didn't physically roll my eyes, but it was a very near thing. I sighed out and used the best argument I had in my defense, "Weddings are expensive as shit, and I ain't got that kind of money. Nor do I want to waste a whole bunch of fuckin' time on this either." Mel very nearly flinched and I kicked myself again. I was batting a thousand with my mouth with these bitches. All I wanted to do was get shit taken care of where she and Noah were concerned. Take on the burden that dulled her sparkle so damn much. She used to laugh and smile back when she was with Grind and it made her beautiful. In the months she'd been here, I could count on one hand the number of times she'd smiled and have fingers left over. None of those smiles had been what they once were, either.

Dragon hadn't had much luck getting the full meal deal out of her about what had fucked her shit up back in Arizona, just that it hadn't all been the club to do it. I remember Grind had said that her mamma and stepdaddy were a piece of work, so I'd surmised that whatever it was had more to do with them. She didn't trust me or anyone here enough to open up about it, and I had a feeling that had a lot more to do with them and the Arizona chapter both than it did with any of us.

I sighed, and looked at the shine in Mel's eyes, the fear radiating out of her and as ever, Ashton to the fuckin' rescue.

"Give me a week, a week and a half," the diminutive woman piped up. All eyes drifted in her direction. "I love a good wedding, and I'd be happy to pay for it, that's your only stumbling block isn't it? Affordability?"

Trigger was positively beaming at his woman and he was a good brother so I gave a sharp nod. "If I want to get us out of that shithole apartment and into something more suitable for a family, yeah, it is."

"Good! Then it's settled, you work on that, we'll work on the wedding, and everyone can be happy," Shelly said and I couldn't disagree without looking like even more of an asshole than I already did. I caught Dani giving me a meaningful look from the back and I scowled. She cocked her head and raised an eyebrow, and when she was sure no one was looking, gave me the finger… her ring finger that is. I did roll my eyes at that point. I hadn't exactly *planned* to ask Mel like I did. I'd thought about it, sure, but it'd sort of slipped out in the heat of the moment –looking at her and the kid laying there all busted up and exhausted. I'd just wanted to make things better and here I was, so it seemed, just making everything worse… again. *Fuck I sucked ass at these things.*

"Fine, sure, yeah, do whatever the fuck you want. You have two weeks. Make you happy? I just want this shit done and over with by Friday week after next. Think you can handle that?"

"Does the Pope shit in the woods?" Reaver asked, "These women can handle anything."

"Love you, baby," Hayden called and Reaver grinned.

"Right, let's all stop hanging out in the hallway with our dicks in our hands and get this church outta the way. Leave these girls to it," Dragon grunted.

"Best fuckin' idea I've heard all morning," I grated and followed my pres back out into the main room. Rush slipped behind the bar and poured a line of shots for everyone.

"The fuck, boy? It ain't even noon," Dragon laughed.

"The fuck, man. Archer's *getting married,*" my jackass little brother said and Nox started laughing silently, his shoulders shaking. "Might as well be the fucking apocalypse, surprised there ain't blood raining out of the sky and shit—"

"Alright, knock it the fuck off!" I griped.

"Rush is right, I need a fuckin' drink. Can't believe you're getting married before me," Trig said, and Reaver grinned.

"I beat all of y'all motherfuckers to that finish line," Reave said, beaming proudly and Ghost looked a bit stormy.

"After that little display, I'm not sure if that's worthy of any kind of bragging rights," he said picking up a shot. We all downed one in agreement.

"Could have been worse," Rev said, and Ghost coughed a bit, looking dubious.

"Don't I know it?"

I closed my eyes, the tequila going down smooth and tried not to let the ribbing get to me. I hadn't exactly pictured this going down for me either... like at all. I'd actually been caught off guard when she'd agreed. Fuck me swingin'.

"Right, congratulations Brother Archer, now let's get this shit started and out of the way," Dragon said. Anything to get the attention off of me, I was all for it.

"Let's," I agreed under my breath and Reaver started laughing his ass off at me.

Duracell and Blue came through the front door and Cell asked, "What's so funny?"

"Archer's getting married in two weeks," Reaver said, tears leaking out of his eyes. Blue grinned and gave me a silent nod of approval while Cell made things worse by bursting out laughing harder than Reave.

Fuck. My. Life.

"Awright, knock this shit off! I'm callin' this shit to order," Dragon said and I could have blessed him. Didn't take long for business as fuckin' usual after that. Thank fuck. I wasn't good when the focus was on me.

Meeting went fast, the rest of the club brought up to speed on the happenings of the night before. A lot of these motherfuckers weren't laughing so hard about my impending marital status after that. If anything, their humor turned to looks of respect in some cases, a little pity in a couple of more. I kept my mouth shut. I didn't feel like talkin' about it. Talkin' didn't settle a lot of shit for me. In fact, it was pretty fuckin' useless all said and done.

Nox caught up to me after the meeting was adjourned, and asked me, "You sure about this, man?"

"Yeah."

He looked grim and nodded carefully, thoughtfully. "Okay."

"Thanks," I said and he nodded.

"Anything I can do?"

"Just do what you been doin', help out with Noah and the like. Be a good uncle."

"Always," he said gravely.

I nodded, he slapped me on the back and moved off in a different direction. Dragon came over to me and asked, "You want to handle the ride to Arizona before or after this wedding?" he asked.

We'd been meaning to put a ride together to head out that way but the weather in parts of the country heading over wasn't exactly favorable. With a lot of the brothers having kids or weddings of their own coming up, we didn't want to risk injury or death on this run, so we decided to wait the few weeks for the conditions to become more favorable across the board. Now we were a chunk of the way into summer, it being June, and we could finally go – except in two weeks I was getting married, now. Fuck.

"After and we'd be coming from a stronger position, don't you think?"

"That we would," he agreed.

"After it is, then."

He nodded. "Any designs on your honeymoon?" he asked and I hung my head and sighed out harshly.

"Not you too, man."

"No, not me too. I'm bein' serious. Shelly had a point back there for all she's like you and goes about deliverin' it wrong nine times outta ten. If you hadn't thought about it, let me be the first one to offer you a weekend down at the honeymoon cabin at the lodge. You might want to see to startin' this marriage thing off right – well, at least better than you have so far," he said and I nodded, listening to him. He'd been married to Tilly a long time. Hell, as far as he was considered, her death hadn't changed that. He still wore the ring.

"Yeah, speaking of, I better talk to Dani, she was making hints about rings and shit."

"Sounds like a good idea, Arch. This woman is about to be your wife, and if there's one thing I've learned about you, you're like me. A forever kind of guy. In that vein, you might wanna not fuck this up."

"Man, I am just not good at shit like this," I confessed and he slapped me on the back.

"We know, which is why, in case you haven't noticed, the club has your back in this too. Your honeymoon is where yer trainin' wheels come off though. Just gonna be you and her."

"It's been me and her for a few months," I said and Dragon shook his head and led me over to the bar.

"Sit your happy ass down, boy. I can tell we need to talk."

I scowled but did as I was told. "What the fuck now?" I demanded.

"Lemme ask you somethin' and fuck all if it's gonna get personal, but I'm just tryin' to get you some perspective here."

"Right, go ahead."

"You been fuckin' her these last three months?"

"Hell no, I've been sleepin' on my fuckin' couch."

"Exactly." He gave me a pointed look, inclining his head and raising his eyebrows.

"You ain't sayin' I should get on that are you?"

"Not your style, Arch. I'm sayin' you should do you, but I'm also sayin' she's a person too. I'm sayin' that if you want this marriage thing to work there's work involved. You get me?"

"Yes and no, speak your fuckin' mind man. We're both adults."

"That's exactly my point. You ain't a mind reader and neither is she. You need to speak your fuckin' mind to her and y'all need to *communicate*. Only way any of this shit works."

Fuckin' Dragon. Always had a way of illustrating his point while he made it. I nodded and harrumphed.

"Message received, loud and clear, Boss."

"Good. I'ma let you stew on that."

"Thanks," I uttered and Disney slid a drink across the bar to me.

I eyed him, and he shrugged. "All of us have your back," he said cryptically and I gave him a nod as he wandered down to the other end to commiserate with Ghost who was still bitchin' about his woman and her mouth. Something about it gettin' ten times worse since he knocked her up. I sipped the whiskey in the glass and figured I probably had looked as nervous as I felt right now.

I tried to be rational about it. I'd been lookin' after Mel and Noah since they'd hit my doorstep, so why was this any different. Short answer? I was getting' fuckin' married and Dragon was exactly right; I was a forever kind of guy. I figured if it ever happened I was only ever gonna do it once and here it was… happening. Fuck it all, it still seemed like the right thing to do, but now all of a sudden, the nerves were setting in. Why?

Because now this shit is outside your control, that's why. That voice in my head that sounded an awful lot like Grind's was back again.

Ain't nothin' outside my control, I thought back at it.

Keep tellin' yourself that, it shot back. I tossed back the rest of the whiskey in the glass. *I will, godammit, I will.*

19

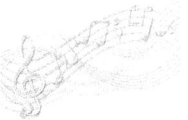

Melody...

I feared that if Archer were anything like Phil, I would be hearing all about Shelly's well-intentioned meltdown on my behalf. The thing was, I hadn't complained, I hadn't even said *anything* about the whole getting married thing at all; I wasn't going to, I mean I hadn't planned to. I knew at least one thing about Archer in the time we'd lived with one another and that one thing was that he was an *intensely* private man.

"You okay, Melody?" Ashton asked softly and I nodded mutely.

Shelly sighed, grumbling under her breath, "Men are so *stupid.*"

Soft laughter tittered among the rest of the women present but Ashton just smiled and it looked as brittle as mine felt. She mouthed at me, '*we'll talk later*' and I nodded. I could see it plainly that somehow, Ashton *knew* and I drew a certain strength and comfort both in that shared solidarity.

"Okay, first things first, we need the basics from you to make two weeks work," Hayden was saying. Mandy handed her a spiral bound notebook and a pen and pencil both. Hayden thanked Mandy and rolled up the sleeves on her blouse. Everyone was looking at me expectantly, Noah wriggling in my lap to make me let go where I sat on the floor in front of the big couch and equally big television.

"I don't even know where to start," I murmured.

"Well, where did you picture yourself getting married?" Everett asked. "You must have thought about it."

I felt myself blush a deep red with embarrassment. I mean, I had thought about it, but the man I'd always pictured waiting for me at the end of the aisle was Grinder, certainly not his brother Archer. I felt the earlier threatening tears rise in a hot rush and my face crumble under their weight.

"Oh, Honey!" Ashton's voice was sympathetic and her hug warm and supportive. It only made me crumble harder.

The women around me were wonderful, and genuinely supportive. I cried it out rather quickly and when I looked a little stronger, Hayden gently suggested, "Maybe not location first, how about we start with colors, how does that sound?"

I nodded, a bit stupidly and said, "I like purple, like amethyst, does that help?"

"That's a great start," Everett said and smiled, Shelly was nodding and Mandy was too.

"Okay, what's a good color to go with dark purple? Wedding colors are typically two sometimes three."

"Purple and white?" I asked.

"Sure! I can do a lot with that," Hayden said cheerfully.

Dani had a little book of her own open in her lap with some drawing pencils. She looked up from the sketch pad and asked, "What's Noah's birthday?"

"February eleventh, why?"

Dani smiled. "Is that why you like amethyst?" she asked.

"I always liked the color, but yeah, it being Noah's birthstone makes me like it even more."

"When's your birthday?" she asked.

"April, I just turned twenty-eight," I murmured, and everyone stared at me.

"You mean your birthday was like a month and a half ago and you didn't say anything? You got here in March! What kind of shit is that? We totally would have done something if we'd known," Shelly ranted.

"It just didn't seem that important, I guess." Which was true. Grinder had always remembered my birthday. Had always gotten me something small, but precious – at least to me. We'd shared three of them together and all three things he'd gotten me, as well as the Christmas gifts, I'd managed to keep even during mine and Noah's quick escape. They were tucked at the bottom of one of the plastic bins buried beneath my clothes.

"Oh, I swear to Christ, if Archer knew and didn't do anything I'm going to bury my foot up his ass," Shelly went on and I shook my head.

"I don't think he either ever knew or paid attention enough to remember and please, it's really not that big of a deal… at least not enough to say anything or make a big stink. It's enough that he's taken Noah and I in. I don't want to rock the boat."

I got a lot of blank stares and exchanged looks from the women in the room and it was Everett who sat back in her seat on the couch and asked, "Is Archer mistreating you at all?"

I shook my head quickly. "No, we barely see each other and for Archer, he's been incredibly patient with me."

Dani was the one to laugh and nod at that. "I know precisely what you mean," she said and smiled at me.

"Honestly, I might as well not even be there," I said.

"That ain't right either," Shelly griped.

"No, it really isn't," Everett agreed.

"It's fine," I said. "Can we please leave it alone?"

"I'm sure things will change now, given these new set of circumstances," Ashton said lightly.

"They'd better, that's no way to treat a person let alone your wife." Shelly's tone was dispassionate and I sighed inwardly. I was afraid I was making this worse instead of better. Archer didn't treat me *badly* per se, it was more of an indifference to my being there one way or the other. Our conversations tended to be limited to Noah and his needs, or 'what do you want to eat?' that sort of thing. We simply didn't talk, not that I wouldn't, it just felt like trying to engage him in simple small talk would be... bothersome to him. I didn't want to be a bother, I mean, I was already bother enough just being here, a constant reminder; at least it felt that way to me.

"Okay, so an amethyst purple and white for the colors. Would you want it indoors or outdoors?" Hayden asked, changing the subject.

"Outside sounds nice," I said perking up a bit. It was definitely cool enough and so pretty out here.

"We could do it here at the club," Everett suggested and I think the look on my face said it all.

"Actually, if it's okay, I would like to have it anywhere *but* the club. I mean, I don't mind the club members being at my wedding, but I just can't... I don't..." I shook my head and Hayden smiled.

"I got married here, but mine was kind of a guerilla wedding. I totally get that it's not for everyone. So outside, to be determined," she said as she jotted it down.

"I don't want to be any trouble, if it's easiest to have it here—"

"Melody, sugar, baby, honey child, this is *your* special day. It may not be the one you had imagined, but it's still *yours*, it's not supposed to be about what's *easy*, it's supposed to be about what makes you feel special and it's supposed to be a day you remember forever," Shelly said. "So let's get with the program, and make it a day you can look back on and *smile* and be *happy* with."

Every head in the room was nodding in agreement, and I felt a tension in my shoulders and chest ease. I nodded and Mandy asked, "You like chocolate or white for the cake?"

"I always pictured having cupcakes at my wedding, rather than a traditional three-tiered cake, would that be too hard?"

Mandy grinned. "Actually, no! I have the perfect thing I saw on Pinterest that I've been dying to try—"

"Oh Lord." Everett rolled her eyes. "The Pinterest Queen is in the house."

Laughter ensued, and I felt like the atmosphere became a bit lighter. The questions came rapid and fierce after that and before the day was through, we had colors and cake, table covers and a guest list, which sadly involved no one but Noah on my side of things.

Ashton and Hayden volunteered to be my bridesmaids and I graciously accepted; they took it upon themselves to appoint Rush and Nox as groomsmen. They also volunteered Dragon to officiate which left me a bit flabbergasted.

"He did my wedding," Hayden said.

"And mine!" Mandy piped up.

"Ours too," Shelly said with a grin.

"Trigger and I got engaged around last Christmas, we're planning on a winter wedding *next* Christmas, and he'll likely do ours too," Ashton said.

"You really don't think he'll mind?" I asked.

"This is a case of too bad, so sad, if he does," Everett said with a wink and the rest of the women laughed.

"Things are far different out here than they were in Arizona, apparently," Shelly said dryly.

"We're all treated very well, and we're all so, very loved here," Dani said. "They make sure of it. The last club I was with..." she shook her head. "Trust me, we all know how very lucky we are."

Solemn nods of agreement from every last one of them made me feel vaguely jealous and so very happy for them all at the same time. It was an odd mix of feelings to be sure. I thought I'd had what they did with Grinder, until I'd become accidentally pregnant with Noah. I'd been through so many emotions in that time, I'd even wanted to hate my baby for chasing Grinder away, but then he'd been born. Even with how awful that had been, the moment I'd gotten to see him, to hold him in my arms, it'd been instant love and devotion.

That love, that devotion, it'd only grown stronger and hadn't waivered not one bit which is why, even now, I was readily agreeing to enter into a loveless marriage. Not only that, but to sacrifice my body and even another piece of my heart, so that I could bear this man another child, one that, undoubtedly, I would love, too. All so I could secure a solid and better future for the sweet boy whose attention was rapt on the large television screen while I talked with the rest of the women of this chapter.

"Okay, everyone, I think we might be overwhelming her a little bit, let's take it down a notch," I heard Everett say and it was as if her word was the final say among them, everyone falling quiescent.

"I'm sorry," I said shaking my head. "I didn't mean to get so wrapped up inside my own head."

"It's okay," Dani said with a slight smile. "You're marrying *Archer*, and I, for one, totally get how that would be enough to drive *anyone* to distraction."

I looked at her, almost with new eyes in that moment as she brought her long, dark hair over her shoulder, running it through her hands, sketchpad and pencils balanced on her knees.

"Archer runs hot then cold, then hot again. It can be tough keeping track sometimes," I admitted and that was putting it mildly. I remember listening to the girls talk, back in Arizona. About how, when he did happen to indulge in a club girl, he could be less than gentle. If they were being generous, they would say how he simply liked it rough sometimes, other times they said he didn't care one way or the other. That he was demanding in the sack. Words like, rough, punishing, and painful, were commonly used as was the phrase 'too much to take.'

It made me nervous, knowing exactly how babies were made, that I was volunteering for that kind of sex, although Grinder could be all of those things too, I'd been in love with him. I'd at the very least liked him enough to *want* him. Archer was an unknown quantity. Attractive? Sure, but it took a lot more than rugged good looks for me to want a man and Archer was nothing like Grinder had been. He had none of the qualities that had made me love his brother.

Grind had been charming, and sweet. He'd talked to me and taken an interest in me. He'd shared things with me, not just likes and dislikes, but hopes and dreams as well. We'd gone on rides together, had shared meals and experiences beyond just sex... I had none of that with Archer. No foundation at all with which to build off of. Nothing but fear and mostly that of the unknown.

I'd seen Archer hurt men for something as little as a dirty look cast in his direction. I'd even watched him and Grind fist fight on occasion. Archer was formidable and terrifying in those memories and there was only one thing I had taken away from the experience of watching him throw down… *don't piss him off. Don't make him angry or give him a reason to turn any of that intensity on* you.

"Mamma?" I blinked and smiled down at my son.

"Yes, baby?"

"Outside?" he asked.

"You wanna go outside?" I asked and he gave me his stunning little baby grin.

"Yah!" he cried and reached up, opening and closing his little fists in a bid for me to pick him up.

"Okay, up you go!" I stood and picked up my son and Dani stood fluidly out of her perch on the edge of the recliner she'd claimed.

"I'll walk with you, I need to go out to my shop anyways," she said. I smiled and nodded.

"Thanks," I murmured before asking, "Is there anything else you guys need from me right now?"

Ashton looked up from where she, Everett, Hayden, and Mandy had their heads bowed together. She smiled at me and shook her head. Shelly came back from, presumably the bathroom again and asked, "Where you going?"

"Out back to let Noah run wild for a minute," Dani told her, smiling.

"Good luck keeping up, Mamma," she said to me with a smile.

I smiled back. "It'll be your turn soon enough," I said, and Shelly smiled.

"Two months and counting, I just hope it's a boy so Ghost can be a happy camper."

"You don't know?"

"Keeping it a surprise," she said with a smile, "but Ghost really wants to start with a boy."

"Plan on having many?" I asked.

"As many as my body will give me before it's had enough," she said smiling.

"Careful what you wish for," Everett called out. "You could end up like that broad on TV with like nineteen kids."

Shelly rolled her eyes. "I'll stop at six, I promise."

"Any luck and there will be twins or a set of triplets in there to speed things along," I told her.

"Rough birth with this guy?" she asked tickling Noah and my look must have said it all. She sobered and cocked her head to the side.

"Oh, I'm sorry," she said.

"It's okay, just really scary is all. He's perfect, that's really all I can ask for. Everything turned out okay."

She nodded, smiling and I smiled bravely back. Noah's birth had been a nightmare from the moment I'd shown up at the hospital in labor. I didn't have the heart to scare her or Mandy, although, by all appearances, Mandy seemed to have had a good birthing experience with Eden. She showed no traces of fear about being pregnant and about to do it again.

I was scared to death about becoming pregnant again but I kept resolutely silent about it, shoving that fear down and to the background. I had so much to do, so much to get through before it became an eventuality, that I wouldn't let that fear rule me; not just yet.

A little more small talk and I followed Dani out to the bright grassy backyard of the club house. To the left, was a big sheet metal shop building with three bays. The first bay was Dani's shop, the second appeared to be random storage, and the third? Well that appeared to be Rush's wood-shop. He had the huge bay door rolled up and was running a sander over whatever his latest project was, Nox sitting on a stool nearby, arms crossed over his chest as he talked with his twin. He spied me and Noah first and smiled, though he kept speaking to Rush, giving me a nod.

Rush looked up and turned off his sander, calling out, "Hey Mel! Hey Noah! Whatcha guys up to?"

It struck me in that moment that I knew more about the twins than I did about Archer and the misgivings about readily agreeing to marry their brother began to set in. I marched across the grass with my son in my arms, parting with Dani at the oval tract of road as she headed for her shop.

"Noah wanted to come outside and play," I said and Rush grinned.

"Pretty soon he'll have all sorts of fun times out here," he said patting the plank of wood he was working on. Noah was looking at the rich, red grain, fascinated.

"Oh? What are you building?" I asked.

"With Noah and Eden and so many kids on the way, I figured it was time this club had a swing set for the kids to play on. Figured we could all chip in and go buy one, but what's the fun in that?"

"You're building a swing set?" I asked incredulously.

"Eh," he gave a shrug, "among other things." He gave me a smile that I couldn't help but match with one of my own.

"I see your handiwork isn't limited to the kids." I gave a nod in the direction of some wooden lounge chairs around a brick constructed firepit out in the grass.

"Aw, yeah, I been keepin' myself busy."

"Seriously, Rush, I told you in Arizona and I'm telling you now, you should make a website and sell some of this stuff. It's incredible."

Rush smiled and Nox smiled with him. "Maybe someday," he agreed which was more than I'd ever gotten from him before.

An awkward and uncomfortable silence ensued, no one wanting to really address the elephant in the room. Finally, it was Nox who drew a breath to ask but I stopped him, exhaling sharply and hitching Noah up higher on my hip.

"Don't ask me, please?" I said and he and Rush exchanged a nervous glance.

"Why?" Nox asked and I knew his meaning and answered him honestly.

"Because it really is the best thing I could do for Noah, and if you start asking I'm going to start questioning and pick it apart. I've made up my mind and I don't want to do that. Let's just... let's just not make it any harder than it already is, okay?" Both of them shut their mouths and nodded almost in unison. "Thanks."

"Man, I can't wait for him to be old enough to play Jenga, I've been wanting to make a set forever."

"So, what's stopping you?" I asked.

He thought about it a second. "You know what? Good point. I can always make it a wedding gift, am I right?" I smiled and nodded and Rush smiled back.

"Well, I for one, welcome the opportunity to call you family, Mel. Always thought Grind was a dumbass for not making it official," Nox said. "Here's to second chances."

I knew he meant well, but sometimes Nox just lived up to his name-sake inadvertently. He didn't mean to come off obnoxious, he just did sometimes. Rush was looking at him horrified but I just smiled and took what he said for the compliment he meant it to be, rather than for the painful truths he'd dragged out of the darkness and unleashed into the bright light of day.

"Thank you, Nox. That means a lot," I said.

He smiled and asked, "You mind if Little Man and I go play?" he asked and Noah smiled and reached for Nox. I relinquished my son into his uncle's care and Rush said, "As long as you can keep him busy to give Mel a break and let me keep working, it's all good, Brother."

"Wanna go play?" he asked Noah.

"Yah!"

I watched them go out into the grass and took up Nox's spot on his stool to watch after him and my boy as they played horsy. I had a feeling with all of the brothers, he would be a rather adept rider in no time.

"I can't not ask," Rush said quietly, "you're sure? You're really sure?"

I nodded, pressing my lips together. "I'd be lying if I said I weren't scared, but I'm sure, Rush. It's the best thing for my son. He needs healthcare, he needs a father, and Archer treats him really well."

"And what about you, Mel? How do you factor into all of this?"

I smiled a little sadly, eyes fixed on my laughing and squealing child, and answered Rush truthfully, as much as it ached to do it, "I don't, Rush. I don't matter at all."

He snorted harshly. "Bullshit," he said and sighed. "I think once you crack that thick as fuck shell around my brother, you might be surprised at what Archer has to offer you," he said. I turned to look at him, his rich, warm brown eyes fixing on mine.

"I hope you're right," I said with a faint echo of a smile which I know held a lot of sadness.

He nodded and said, "Just give him time and a little more credit than you feel he deserves. He's a good guy deep down. I mean, he's stuck with me and Nox this long, hasn't he?"

He switched his sander on, effectively drowning out whatever reply I could have made so I didn't bother. Instead I smiled and waved at Noah, bringing out my phone to take pictures of him and Nox and his epic uncle pony ride. His laughter making my heart lighter and reminding me, solidly, that I had everything to laugh, live, love, and be happy for in one neat little package. Nothing else mattered.

20

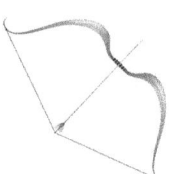

A**rcher...**

"You've been movin' around this place like some kind of ghost since we got back from the club. It's driving me nuts, so how about you tell me what's up? You having second thoughts or some shit?"

Melody looked up from where she sat, Indian style in the middle of the bed. It'd been something like two or three days since we'd been at the club and she'd been quieter than usual, which she'd practically been a fuckin' church mouse to begin with. Her phone forgotten in her hands she opened her mouth to speak, thought better of it, closed it, opened it again only to turn around and shut it again.

To make my point that I wasn't going anywhere until I got some kind of an answer, I crossed my arms over my chest and leaned a shoulder against the edge of the open doorway. She leaned way over to get a look around me into the living room.

"He's out cold already," I assured her, and she leaned back slowly, resuming her seated position in the middle of my bed. I'd kept sleeping on the couch, figuring I'd be back in it soon enough once she and I were married, a couple of weeks more didn't make much difference.

She pinned me with those beautiful blue eyes of her and nervously pushed some of that gorgeous blonde hair of hers behind her ear. Melody damn sure was a beautiful woman. I was lucky on that score. Even luckier that she was a fine mother and homemaker. Still, I was getting tired of her looking so rundown and fuckin' scared all the time, but I couldn't fix it if I didn't know *what* was freaking her out so hard.

"I'm scared," she admitted finally, and it was a start.

"Of what?" I asked, needing to know which dragon to slay would be an even better starting point, but I could tell by the expression on her face I was gonna have to drag it out of her. I hated that. Why couldn't women ever be straightforward like most dudes? I ask a question, I expect an answer but if what I suspected were true...

"Of... of you," she said finally and my suspicions were dead on confirmed. Well, shit. *Now how did I go about fixing that?*

"Okay," I said judiciously. "Why? What am I doing to scare you? Give me some specifics."

She smoothed her lips together and I realized I was looking forward to seeing if they were as soft as they looked. She swallowed hard, and voice trembling, said, "I don't know if it's anything specific—" I snorted and she looked like a deer caught in the fuckin' headlights.

"Don't bullshit me, Mel. I promise not to get pissed off, but you gotta tell me, else I can't work on it, or fix it, now can I?"

"No, I suppose not," she said softly and I had to wait her out. I could see her trying to gather up her thoughts. The slight line that developed between her eyes as she thought furiously how best to say it, was cute on her.

Still, I didn't have endless patience so I finally sighed and said, "Just gimme the short version, and spill it. I gotta try and get some sleep tonight."

"I don't know how I'm supposed to... I don't know if I can..."

"Fuck me?" I asked, the heat lending a sweet blush of color across her cheeks cluing me in.

"I've never done sex without love... You're attractive, Archer, don't get me wrong but I'm a woman and feelings... we have to have feelings as a part of it, it's just how it works, I guess..." She covered her face with her hands. "Oh, God!" She groaned. "I'm saying this all wrong and I don't want to hurt your feelings but it's important and I'm so sorry, but I'm really struggling and the girls back in Arizona always said you were rough and that scares me too, and I just am trying to get my head around it and I'm struggling... I'm sorry." I let her babble and repeat herself and waited her out until she was finished and somewhat beyond that.

I could feel the slight smirk on my lips, a defense mechanism if I were being totally honest, because what she said *did* sting, but I had to be honest with myself, it wasn't totally unexpected. Finally, she gave me what I wanted, lowering her hands and looking at me.

"First of all, those girls back in Arizona? I don't and didn't give a fuck about them, so why would I give a shit? They weren't mine, and I was just in it to get my rocks off, meet a physical need, you get me?"

Again, with that adorable little thoughtful frown. Mel nodded slowly, and I was pretty sure she didn't get what I was saying but I wasn't too terribly worried about it, because soon enough she would. I was a 'doer' by nature. I didn't really dig sitting around talking about shit, the only reason I was indulging her in it now, was because I thought she was gonna worry herself sick and back out of getting married unless I did something about it.

"Second of all, I hear what you're saying and the only solution I can see is I need to make you fall in love with me. That's gonna take some time unfortunately, and I'm probably not going to be able to pull it off by our wedding night, but it's not like I ain't gonna have the rest of our lives so I ain't really worried about it too much." I gave a one shouldered shrug and watched her mouth drop open, incredulous.

She scoffed, "Archer, you can't just *make* someone fall in love with you!"

I smiled and I knew it wasn't exactly friendly, but I had no problem accepting this particular challenge she'd set in front of me. "Oh yeah?" I said, and I nodded thoughtfully. "You just watch me."

Her mouth dropped open again with a little 'ah!' of disbelief and I dropped my hands to my hips asking her, "Is there anything else I should work on while I'm at it?"

"I... I don't know..." she uttered and I could see I'd caught her completely flatfooted.

I nodded and told her, "You tell me if you think of anything, you hear?"

She nodded dumbly and I could tell her mind was more on what I'd just said. I silently gave myself a strong reminder to thank Rush for cluing me in that there could be trouble down the line. He'd been asking a little too much about Mel the last day or two at the shop and I'd finally told him to spit it the fuck out, which is when he'd come clean about their discussion in his woodshop the day I'd broke the news about us getting hitched to the rest of the club.

I turned to leave the room, her voice stopping me, "Why are you asking me these things?"

I looked back over my shoulder and said, "Because despite what you got in that head of yours, you're a person, Mel, and the people in my life, especially the ones sharing my roof, matter a great deal. I don't want to hear about you sayin' you don't count again, okay?"

Her eyes turned glassy and I didn't want to see her fuckin' cry or get all emotional, so I slipped back out of the room and shut the door tight on her, to give her some privacy and let her get her shit together. I stopped and looked down at Noah who was out cold in his crib, bending to tug his blanket up over him, tucking him in real gentle like. Only about a week and a half or so and he'd be *my* son. Well, not really, it would take several more steps and a metric fuck-ton of paperwork to call him my son legally, but for all intents and purposes he would be mine. I had a few mixed feelings about that.

I sighed and bowed my head. "Not trying to erase you, Grind. Just trying to make sure your legacy stays whole," I murmured, then had to laugh at myself a little. Grind was dead and didn't give one shit over the other about what happened on this rock anymore. Really it was just me trying to assuage my guilty feelings about lettin' Grind go. If I hadn't been a stubborn ass about relocating, if I'd just done it sooner… maybe Grind would still be here.

I sighed out; if it was one thing about the past it was that it was set in stone. The future though? It'd yet to be carved, and I meant for Mel and Noah's future to be a lot brighter than a single working mom living off government assistance barely able to make ends meet. I wanted to make sure Noah never had a night going hungry for lack of food, and to make sure he had clothes with no holes in them. I wanted to make sure Mel was warm at night, though it would take a lot of work for a woman as clearly damaged as she was to feel what pitiful excuse for love I had to give her.

Still, I would do my damnedest to provide, because that's what a man did. Not just food, clothes and a roof over their heads either; but love and support and sure, guidance where it was needed.

Truthfully, I'd about given up on ever having a family of my own but it could never be said that I wouldn't seize the opportunity for anything when life presented it. This was no exception, either.

The door to the bedroom opened and I looked over. Mel stilled when she saw me standing over Noah and his crib, but then the tension in her posture eased and she sort of softened.

"Think of something else?" I asked softly.

She shook her head and licked her lips. "I was looking at some pictures

I took, and I thought I would share them; see if maybe you'd like to see them."

I straightened and looked her over, at the sincerity on her face and realized that she didn't really know how to relate, or whatever, which was a failing we both apparently shared. I nodded carefully and said, "Sure, show me what you got."

She slipped out of the bedroom in that white tank top and those blue-and-white striped short boxer things she slept in and not for the first time, I felt my cock stir in my own shorts. I sat down with her on the couch and let her drive, as she carefully flipped through pictures of Noah on her phone, mostly ones she'd taken since she'd gotten here.

"I have more on a couple of flash drives, pictures of us in the hospital that one of the nurses took, but I don't have anything to plug it in to, so I can show you."

I blinked and took the phone gently from her fingers, staring down at the picture she'd just swiped to of me, passed out on the couch, Noah sleeping soundly on my chest.

"I'd like to have a copy of this one. Can you do that for me?"

She looked up at me with those true-blue eyes of hers beneath the veil of her long lashes and nodded gently. "What size?"

"I want one for the wall of our new house, but I want you to get me one of those wallet-sized ones too if you can."

She smiled, the first genuine, warm, smile that was purely Mel, light and free. The kind I hadn't seen since Arizona, the kind she used to waste on my brother, Grind, all the time who clearly hadn't deserved a single damn one of 'em, abandoning his family like he did.

"Sure," she murmured and with that smile? I felt like we'd finally cracked the ice some.

"Thanks," I muttered back and let her resume scrolling through, all the way to the beginning of the photos on this piece of shit go-phone. It was another thing I needed to replace for her, even if it was only to get a better camera for her. I learned something new about Mel that night that I probably should have learned a month or more ago – she liked to take pictures. A lot of pictures. It was actually kind of nice; I liked it.

21

Melody...

I sat in front of a mirror on a little dressing table and stared at my wide-eyed reflection in the glass and felt more than a little shell-shocked at the woman looking back at me. She was beautiful, in an elegant, classy sort of style that I'd never before possessed. Her hair was perfectly coifed into a French twist, the ends hidden and tucked neatly, the seam where her hair was pinned was lined with these tiny, deep purple, and superbly fragrant little blossoms that smelled like vanilla, or some kind of pie.

Her makeup was subtle and she had this natural glow about her, and I couldn't help but turn this way and that, surprised every time that the woman in the mirror matched my movements because I was her.

The dress was a vintage 1920s satin affair, floor length with a slight train and a sweetheart neckline. It had a lace and light gauzy overlay with short sleeves and was entirely appropriate for the warm, early summer weather outside. The overlay lay in what I would describe as petals, falling to my knees and a little past, the hemline asymmetrical and giving me a long, luxurious silhouette. The material a light cream with age as the dress was the real deal, found by Hayden in an antique store in the older part of town.

Ashton had paid not only a small fortune for the dress itself, but also a small fortune to have it taken in on time by a professional tailor that hadn't been afraid to touch it. They'd found the dress something like five days ago but had only found the tailor something like the day before yesterday.

I wish I could say I felt guilty, but the girls had slowly, but surely, been eking me out of my shell and they had been absolutely right about one thing – I was only getting married once. When Archer said forever, he meant it, and so if this were my one shot at what was supposed to be the happiest day of my life, I had better take it, and so I had. Now it was here, staring me in the face and all I could think was how much I wanted it over.

I was terrified, but there was certainly no going back now, and there was certainly no pretending that this was a happy occasion. At least not in that moment, not for me.

While I had certainly accepted that this was going to happen, I still felt like I was about to marry a perfect stranger. Archer and I were talking a little bit more, I'd even shared some photos with him a little over a week and a half ago. Still, despite our impending marital status, he had resolutely and in quite the old-fashioned manor, remained on the couch. A fact I still didn't know if I was grateful for or not.

Hell, we hadn't even kissed! I realized, horrified. Our first kiss was going to be in front of all of those *people* waiting downstairs, which was, admittedly, just the club, all of the ol' ladies and a few of the waitresses and my boss from the diner. Shelly had invited them, while I just as soon as never told them I was getting married at all. Still, somehow, it'd helped me. For now I felt as if I must keep up appearances, which was something I was accustomed to doing thanks to Phil and my mother.

"Honey, breathe," Everett said gently and I looked past my reflection to hers in the mirror. "It's going to be okay."

I nodded and she smiled gently, asking me, "Are you ready?"

"I think so," I said and stood, smoothing my sweating palms against my dress, wishing I had something to do with my hands, grateful when Everett thrust a bouquet of more of the sweet smelling, tiny, deep amethyst blossoms into my hands, their deep, dark green foliage striking against the cream of my gown.

"What are these flowers?" I asked her breathing them in, deep.

"Heliotrope," she said with a smile.

"I love them," I told her and she smiled bigger.

"Then you'll love what I got you for a wedding present."

I hugged her tightly and let go and she smiled broadly at me. "Come on, Dray is waiting." I nodded and tried not to get teary, slipping out the bedroom door in the old Victorian era bed and breakfast that Ashton had found and rented on such short notice so that my wedding could be held in the backyard.

It'd been decided that since Dragon, the president of the chapter was officiating, that it would be weird for him to walk me down the aisle, too. I had no one to give me away, and so Dray would do it as the chapter's vice president.

He gave a low whistle when I stepped out onto the staircase. Nox and Rush waiting with him with Ashton and Hayden, who they'd be escorting down the aisle.

"Wow, Mel…" Nox said, his voice trailing off.

"*Just* wow, Mel… there are no words," Rush said. I blushed faintly, and the professional photographer Ashton hired started clicking away as I came down the stairs. Everyone took position. Ashton with Rush, followed by Hayden and Nox and finally me, with Dray.

All of the men wore black slacks and black button-down shirts with their cuts over them, which I was fine with, I mean, I really expected nothing less. I swallowed hard, my pulse racing as we lined up at the back door, the music from the live string quartet striking up and playing the traditional wedding march.

Oh my God, I am really doing this! was my last thought before Dray took the final step and I was out on the back porch, then stepping off into the unknown which was an aisle made of the greenest grass, strewn with the whitest rose petals I'd ever seen.

"Look up, babe," Dray whispered, reminding me, and I did, my breath very nearly catching in my throat at the sight of Archer waiting patiently at the white archway trellis dripping with purple wisteria. His golden-green eyes seemed that much more rich and vibrant without the three or four day's growth he usually sported. The black of his shirt making the color pop all the way down to me. I felt wooden and drawn as if by strings as I automatically put one foot in front of the other.

Noah looked so handsome in his little black shirt and pants set and didn't fuss at all. He was held aloft by Trigger in the front row on what was traditionally the bride's side of things.

"Mamma!" he cried and reached for me, and I very nearly went to him, but Trigger gently put his arms down and Noah just stared.

All too soon, I was handing my bouquet to Ashton and Dray was putting my hands into Archer's. They were so clean, I noted. He'd managed to scrub away every last trace of engine grease and grime, though the warm calluses remained. I swallowed hard and met his eyes just as Dragon began to speak.

"We're gathered here today to join Melody Ann Beswick, and Charles Michael 'Archer' Turner together forever…"

I stared at Archer, and realized that it was today, the day we were getting *married,* standing *at the altar* that was the first time I had ever heard his name, his *real* name. The name I would be taking and would be known as the rest of my life. *Turner.* It wasn't bad as far as names went and I tried it on for Noah as well, *Noah Jeramiah Turner.* I liked it, so at least *that* was something.

"I do," I murmured, still almost completely on autopilot. I took the ring offered to me by Nox and with shaking fingers, slid it onto Archer's ring finger. I knew they were a gift from Dani, that she'd made them, because she'd told me the day before and had shown Archer's to me. She wouldn't show me mine, though, preferring that it be a surprise.

"I do," Archer said levelly and with no trace of regret. He slipped first a delicate wedding band in white gold, crusted with diamonds onto my finger and followed it with one of the most beautiful engagement rings I'd ever seen. It was white gold too, with diamonds on the band to either side leading up to the three larger stones. The center round stone was a deep purple and the two smaller stones to either side, also round, were purple but also green and blue, with hints of other colors, a veritable aurora borealis of colors that had me choking up and my eyes watering. It was beautiful.

"You may now kiss your beautiful bride!" Dragon declared and I closed my eyes, tipping my face up. Archer's lips landed gently on my cheek, the barest of touches to a course of "Awws" and a smattering of applause.

I opened my eyes and let my husband take me back down the aisle and off to the side where the judge waited with the marriage license. The photographer snapped photos while I signed my life away and took more photos of Archer, Noah, and I together. All of us managing to smile for the camera, my son seemingly happy as a clam for his mother and new father.

Before I knew it, I was in the back of a limousine and staring across at Archer, alone for the moment as it whisked us to the clubhouse for the reception.

"You didn't kiss me," I murmured and Archer frowned.

"When I kiss you, that's for me and no one else. I like to keep my private business private. You and me, we ain't a spectacle for the world, no matter what the occasion."

"Will you at least dance with me?" I asked.

"Depends," he said and I felt my heart sink. "Will it make you happy?"

I blinked, I hadn't quite expected *that*, but I answered him honestly, "It's our wedding, having my first dance with my husband? Yes, it would make me happy," I murmured. Archer nodded.

"Then I'll dance with you."

"Thank you," I murmured.

"Sure thing."

We finished the ride to the club in silence and the limo pulled around to the back to let us out by the white tent erected in the grass. The expanse under the tent was huge. I had wondered why the limo had taken so long to leave the bed and breakfast, and now I knew why. It'd given everyone time to get here and get settled for mine and Archer's big entrance.

The limo driver opened the door and Dragon called out, "Ladies and Gentlemen, Brothers of The Sacred Hearts, I present to you Mr. and Mrs. Archer Turner!"

Archer got out of the limo first and held out a hand to me, I took it, and stepped out into the sunshine to applause, whistles, and cheering, and felt myself blush. Archer took us to the bride and groom's table, set apart from the rest of the seats, on the edge of the dance floor. There was another table beside ours with these beautiful round hydrangea balls, that weren't hydrangeas at all, but rather our wedding cupcakes.

I smiled broadly at them and found Mandy's fiery red locks among the crowd, inclining my head in her direction in thanks. She waved at me and my smile grew bigger, all the while the clatter and clack of the professional photographer's camera shutter provided the soundtrack to what was supposed to be and had been achieved as my special day.

I took my seat, and Archer took his and I was surprised he kept his fingers wrapped around mine. I looked at him and he looked at me, his intense gaze searching my face. I mouthed 'thank you' at him and he inclined his head gently.

We were overwhelmed by guests coming and offering congratulations and to drop off their wedding gifts to us. Most of them small tokens and they were set aside on another table off to the side and behind Archer. Some were handed over with winks and a 'take it on your honeymoon' which made me blush, and really wonder what they contained.

Dani came up and I came around the table to hug her tightly. "Thank you so much, they're *beautiful*," I murmured.

"The center stone is Noah's birthstone," she said. "And these," she said indicating the two smaller, aurora rounds to either side, "are alexandrite, which is Archer's birthstone." I blinked and looked at her and hugged her tightly again.

"I can't believe you packed so much meaning into these rings," I murmured, and she had. Archer's wedding band was plain silver by all outside appearances, but inside? Inside the band, she had etched tiny musical notes, to remind him of me and my name, Melody. She'd explained that she knew Archer was a private man, which is why she'd etched the inside rather than the outside of the band.

"Of course," she murmured, and squeezed me back.

We ate a catered dinner, the bare electric lightbulbs coming on closer to dusk to illuminate the inside of the tent. At one point, Archer presented me with his rag, a vest crafted in my size, declaring me his property. I got emotional again then, the vest, more than any ring or ceremony, telling me how deeply his commitment ran where I was concerned. Not Noah, but me.

Finally, Dragon got up and announced our first dance and Archer surprised me once again, taking me into his arms as if I truly belonged there, no question, no hesitation. He danced with me, our first song as a couple *'Strangers in the Night'* by Frank Sinatra and I thought to myself someone had a sense of humor.

He kept his eyes on mine, his face unreadable, and I searched his, wondering, and not for the first time either, what he had going on behind that inscrutable gaze. I was surprised to find that I was disappointed when the song ended. That I wouldn't have minded staying right where I was.

Dragon cut in and danced the next song with me. The one traditionally reserved for the father of the bride but considering I had no father, just a stepfather who loathed me, and I him right back, this was a fair substitute; and Dragon was a gentleman. All of the brothers were, and the more time I spent with this chapter, the more *wrong* the Arizona chapter seemed to me.

My last dance of the evening was with my son, Noah. The photographer expertly capturing images I knew I was likely to cherish forever. It was growing on toward full night when Archer took me gently aside.

"We need to get going if we're gonna make it while it's still night," he murmured.

"Oh," I said. Noah was asleep against my shoulder, and Nox was just suddenly there, standing by ready to take him. I didn't want to let him go. I didn't want to leave my baby for a whole three days, it just didn't seem right. I hadn't left him for more than eight hours since he'd been conceived. I worried he would be afraid, I didn't want him to be scared, and I certainly didn't want him to feel as if I'd abandoned him.

"Melody, he'll be just fine, let Nox have 'im," Archer said and his tone was as gentle as I'd ever heard it. I reluctantly passed my son into his uncle's arms.

"You call me for *anything*, Nox. Promise me," I demanded, my eyes brimming with tears.

"I will, Mamma, I promise. He's gonna be fine. He'll have a total blast I promise. We'll facetime you tomorrow and you'll see."

I nodded and Nox took my sleeping child over to another group of the brothers and their ol' ladies.

"Come on, baby, "Archer murmured and with a final fleeting look in my son's direction, I let him lead me to his room in the club's outbuilding that was full of them. He ushered me through the door.

"Get changed so we can ride," he said and I nodded staring at the leathers and my 'property of' cut lying on the bed waiting for me. My riding boots were even there, lined neatly with one another on the floor. The door shushed shut behind me and I swiftly changed. I was scared of what experiences lay beyond the ride I was about to take, but thankfully, the ride was supposed to be a long one, about four hours or so. I always felt cleansed after a long ride and I hadn't gotten to ride since the short one I'd taken with Dragon to see Grinder.

When I stepped out into the hallway it was to find Archer changed and ready to go, his saddlebags packed and over his shoulder. I hadn't had to do a thing. The other ol' ladies had done literally everything for me. Archer looked a touch put out and I asked, "What's wrong?"

"Feels weird not packing my own bags," he said.

"I guess that's one of my jobs now," I murmured.

"Yeah, at least you'll listen to me," he griped.

I frowned. "What didn't they listen to you about?"

"Packed some of the wedding gifts, I said they could wait."

"Some of them *were* meant for our honeymoon," I said gently.

"Don't need nothin' for our honeymoon but me and you," he countered and I softened a bit.

"I would really like to go for a ride with my husband," I murmured, and Archer cracked a small smile at that.

"Yeah, well I'd really like to take my ol' lady for a ride," he said. I arched an eyebrow at him and his smile grew.

"Did you mean for that to sound as dirty as it came out?" I asked.

"You know it, honey."

Oh boy, I didn't quite know what to do with a version of Archer who joked. It was a totally new concept for me.

I followed him out to where his bike was parked by the tent full of guests, the music from the DJ's stand stopped and everyone gathered around while Archer put his saddlebags back on his bike. He got on and patted the seat behind him after starting up his bike. I got on to a round of rowdy cheering and whistling that was quickly left behind us and whipped away by the wind.

I loved to ride, and the ride to wherever we were going was definitely on my list of top ten rides I had ever taken. The wind was a living being that cleansed me of many of my misgivings. The road rushing beneath the tires my priest, as I silently dropped and confessed my sins, leaving them behind me. Archer was a solid warmth, my arms around his solid, rock hard waist as we moved through the warm night taking swoops and curves that made me feel alive again and not like I was simply going through the motions.

It didn't seem like it was a four-hour ride. Honestly, it felt like we'd only been on the bike for minutes. He motioned for me to get off, which I did and he backed into a space in front of the great old lodge's front porch and shut off the motorcycle. No sooner had the rumbling of his engine ceased, then the front door of the lodge swept open, letting out a rich, warm, golden glow.

"Are you Archer?" an older, portly woman asked. Her long, iron hair swept into two braids on either side of her head. She was short, and her eyes were in a perpetual squint as she smiled at us.

"Yeah, I'm Archer," he answered.

"Oh, good! I'm Contessa; José said you'd be coming. Congratulations to the both of you!" she cried excitedly and swept me into a quick squeeze of a hug in her excitement.

"Thank you," I said laughing lightly. Archer, in the meantime, had hauled his leather saddlebags up onto his shoulder.

"Everything's in order then?" he asked and Contessa beamed at him.

"Absolutely! You're in the honeymoon cabin, do you know where that is?"

Archer nodded, "That I do."

"Great! Here's the key." She handed him a key with an old-fashioned brass hotel key tag attached to it. "Breakfast is at nine, here in the lodge, lunch is at one, and dinner is at six. Would you like me to send someone to get you at meal times?"

"That'd be good, yeah. Might lose track of time." He cleared his throat and I felt my mouth go a little dry.

"Would you like to walk around or come through the lodge?" Contessa asked, motioning to the open front door.

"I think we're fine, I know the way. Come on, Mel." He held out his hand to me and I took the few steps toward him and took it. It was warm, his hands rough from the work he did with them on the regular.

"Have a good night, sleep well!" Contessa called after us, waving. I waved back at her over my shoulder and slid a bit on some loose gravel. I yipped in surprise and laughed and paid more attention to where I was going after that, following Archer down a steep, winding path towards a glimmer of what looked like water through the trees.

I held tightly to Archer's hand in the close dark, the sounds of crickets and somewhere an owl, very different from the rap music and general disorder surrounding the apartment. This was a welcome respite from the noise of a more urban setting.

We followed the winding path to a small, squat stone cabin that looked like something out of a fairy tale. The windows glowed with muted golden light, and Archer used the key to unlock the front door. He let us in to a very modern, very swank single bedroom, one other doorway leading into a bathroom and another standing open to a small closet.

He held the door open for me and murmured my name softly. I shook myself as if waking from a dream, and stepped past him, over the threshold onto a square, slate entryway.

A fireplace burned cheery in the stone fireplace and the bed took up the center of the room, which was odd placement but made sense when you realized that it *was* a pretty small room and it was to give the fireplace full advantage as well as all the little white tables and chests with candles on them the opportunity to do their thing. There was no electric lighting in the bedroom, it was all candles or oil lamp sconces on the walls. It was beautiful, and I didn't want to track dirt from outside onto the plush, cream carpet studded with white rose petals, so I stopped to take off my boots right there on the easily swept slate.

Archer looked down at what I was doing and tossed the saddlebags to the bed, leaning down to pull off his boots on the marble as well. I hated socks with no boots, in fact, if I could run around barefoot *all* the time, I would, so I stripped those off as well before stepping into the white foam that was just as soft as it looked.

"It's beautiful in here," I murmured and Archer made a noise of agreement. He went past me into the room and dug into one of the saddlebags, turning around with a wooden box in his hands that looked suspiciously like Rush's work, though simple in design.

"It was a long ride, why don't you take this and use it?" he said, and I frowned in confusion. My curiosity got the better of me though, and I took the box, releasing the little metal hasp and opening it up to an assortment of bath products and a folded note.

Hey Melody!

You should take some *time on this trip for yourself and relax! We hear the honeymoon suite has a killer bathtub. Feel free to lock Archer out and take some 'me' time.*

The Ol' Ladies.

I chuckled and handed the note to Archer who read it and frowned saying, "Better not lock me out, it's my honeymoon too."

I stilled and nodded, and thought to myself, *it's probably not his idea of a good time being ball and chained to me, either.* I wondered briefly what else we were going to do over the three whole days we had here, because sex couldn't and wouldn't be the totality of our stay… I mean, would it?

"Go on, it was a long ride, take a hot soak and try to relax. I'll put the rest of this stuff away." I looked up startled out of my deep thinking and tried a smile, nodding, and headed for the bathroom a few paces away.

I stopped in the door way and said, "Hey Archer." He looked in my direction, back over his shoulder. "Thank you for a lovely first dance," and I meant it. It had probably been one of the most perfect parts of my day.

"You're welcome," he said, and in a lower, husky voice that sounded like a closely held secret he told me, "I liked it too."

I softened marginally, and with a slight nod, took myself into the bathroom with my little wooden treasure-trove of a box. What I saw stopped me cold. It was like a fairytale in here too. The room was tiny, and the ceiling low, but instead of feeling claustrophobic it felt *right*; nice and homey and it was *definitely* beautiful.

The back wall, as you came through the door, was white with heavy brown wooden cross beams. The Tudor style is what I believed it was called, at least when it was the same effect on the *outside* of the building. I didn't know if it rang true for interiors as well.

There was a copper, yes *copper*, bathtub on a raised little platform against that back wall, the spigots for it coming out of the wall above it along the side, rather than to one end. The tub was big enough for two, and deep. Raised at both ends, and longer than your more modern bathtubs, which for me meant that I'd found the Holy Grail amongst women. A bath that I not only would fully fit in to, but that my boobs, stomach and knees would all be covered by the water at the same time.

There was a little table next to one end of the bath with an oil lamp burning on one corner. I gave the knob on it a little twist to raise the wick and the light level and admired the flickering flame inside the hurricane glass. I plugged the bottom of the tub with the little stopper on the chain and sat on the edge while I twisted the handles to get the water going, ensuring the temperature was just the other side of too hot for me. I didn't want it to cool too quickly.

I unwrapped a large bath bomb from the little wooden box and dropped it into the water, smiling to myself at both the heavenly aroma as well as the fact that it turned the water a milky white as it fizzed and fell apart.

One of the worst parts of this endeavor for me would be seeing the disappointment or revulsion on Archer's face when it came to my nude body. While I'd worked hard to regain my figure from before Noah's birth, there was only so much I could do. The scar from the cesarean not only remained, but my stomach, no matter how many sit ups and crunches I did, remained stubbornly flabby like a deflated balloon. What's worse? The stretch marks from having carried my son remained deep, pink furrows in my skin, wrinkled and less than attractive by anyone's standards, mine being at the top of the list.

I made it a point to keep my stomach hidden for just that reason and self-consciously checked over my shoulder before I undressed, relieved that Archer's back was turned and that he was making himself busy with unpacking and putting things away, which I found a little odd considering our short stay.

I folded my leathers carefully and set them on a bench below the lone round window facing out into the woods at the back of the little cottage. I stepped into the bath quickly even though it was a touch too hot and sank into the water to my chest.

There were washcloths and towels tucked under the little side table where the lamp sat beside the tub, so I had them in easy reach. I also had the little wooden box beside the lamp, and it was filled not only with bath bombs and bubble baths, but little bottles of shampoo and conditioner, massage oil and lotion. It had just about everything a woman would need for more than just a three day stay. The club's women really *had* thought of everything.

I leaned back and closed my eyes, letting the heat from the water work its magic, startling when the water shut off. I opened my eyes and Archer was perched in the wooden chair that sat beside the bathtub, across from the little stand with everything else on it. I glanced down at the water, grateful for its now milky appearance that hid all of me from the chest down. I just didn't know if I was ready yet... *You'll never be ready, even when it finally happens,* I told myself, *and it's going to happen.*

"You're going to drown yourself," Archer murmured and he was right, the water caressed my throat. Much more, and my mouth would have been covered. He slipped a washcloth off the top of the pile and set it on his denim clad knee.

When he'd changed, he'd left his black button-down collared shirt on, choosing to simply untuck it. He'd pulled on a pair of jeans and his motorcycle boots and had put his cut back on over his leather jacket. Once he had slipped that on he'd been ready to go. Now, his boots and socks were gone, and so was his jacket and cut.

He rolled the sleeves of the shirt back over his muscular forearms while he sat there with me and I watched in utter fascination as he did it.

"What are you doing?" I asked softly and he smiled a little and dipped the washcloth into the bathwater, soaking it thoroughly.

"I want to see you," he said and picked up a little bar of face soap, unwrapping it and sticking the wrapper in his pocket to dispose of later.

"I'm right here," I said confused and he shook his head gently, lathering the cloth.

"I want to see *you*," he repeated, emphasis on 'you' and when I shook my head he reached for me, gently smoothing the washcloth along my cheek. "This paint isn't you, Mel. Never understood why you put it on all the time; you don't need it," he said and I closed my eyes, wooden, holding stock still as he washed the makeup which I'd totally forgotten about, off my skin. He dipped the washcloth several times to rinse it and wiped at my face to remove all the soap, so that I could open my eyes.

"Thank you," I murmured and he tipped his head to the side, giving me a curious look. "For saying those things…" I said. "I don't think anyone's ever complimented me in such a way."

"That's a damn shame then," he uttered then ordered me gently, "Sit up."

I did, hugging my knees and splashed water on my face to rinse off any residual soap while Archer ran the cloth over my back, my skin tingling gently with every pass at the attention. It'd been a very long time since anyone had touched me and he was being so careful.

"I like your hair down, too," he muttered and hung the washcloth on the side of the tub, his fingers gently pulling flowers and pins from my hair, stacking them in a neat pile by the lantern on the table.

I closed my eyes and let him work, my scalp sighing in relief as the tight grip my hair had been in relaxed its hold. He went a step further, once all the pins were out, and deftly massaged my scalp and I swear I turned into a bit of goo. It did little to soothe my anxiety, but it felt wonderful none the less.

"Do... do you want in here?" I asked softly and Archer chuckled.

"Maybe another time, right now I'm just kind of enjoying this, right here." He braced his forearms on his knees and let his green-gold gaze travel over what damp skin there was peeking above the water.

I was silent, out of things to say, but I was surprised to find that the silence wasn't entirely awkward, but rather calming in its own way. Archer simply sat with me, making no move to do anything, and certainly making no demands. Eventually, it was as if his gaze had drank its fill and he straightened with a sigh. He stretched and stood up, a little stiffly.

"I'll grab your PJ's and you can get out when you're ready and join me. How does that sound?"

I nodded, and huddled in the cooling water saying, "Alright, that sounds good," even though my heart seemed to flutter erratically at the thought that my time was up, and this was the end of the line.

"Be right back," he murmured and went out into the rest of the little stone cabin.

He returned a moment later and laid a pair of peach satin sleep shorts with a matching peach satin and cream lace camisole on the chair. I blinked, stunned, I had never owned anything quite so nice before... like *ever*.

I looked up at Archer who was looking down at me, one brow raised as if challenging me to say something off about the gift. I wouldn't, I couldn't but I was curious...

"Was this you, or one of the girls?" I asked softly.

"Me," he said.

"Why?"

"Because I like you in those little shorts and that tank you wear around the apartment. There's something simple, and sexy as fuck about it."

I swallowed hard, I'd had no idea that he'd thought so, or that he'd ever even thought of me in that way.

"Thank you," I murmured, at a loss as to what else I should say, but if someone bought you a gift, that's what you said, right?

He gave me a nod, a simple inclination of his head, really, and he murmured, "Welcome. Take your time," and with that, he left the little bathroom shutting the door behind him so that I could get out and dress in peace.

I fished for the drain plug and pulled it, watching the milky water and bits of sparkle from the bath bomb swirl as it drained. I stood up carefully and plucked a towel from the pile, wrapping in it and stepping out of the tub onto the plush bathmat.

I huddled in the towel and dried my body carefully. My hair had somehow avoided getting wet, even at the ends, and I figured that was something. I didn't want to get wet spots on probably the nicest thing I had ever owned to wear.

Okay, I was as dry as I was going to get and had to admit to myself that maybe this didn't have anything to do with the sleep set but rather had everything to do with me procrastinating on going out there. I'd never been *scared* of sex before, so this was something new. I couldn't hide in here all night though, so I might as well bite the proverbial bullet, get out there, and get this over with.

Hell of a romantic way to spend your honeymoon, Mel.

I opened the door to the bedroom and tried not to gasp. He'd lit all of the candles and the room was not only warm but smelled lightly of vanilla and I think lavender. I swallowed hard and looked at him, naked from the waist up, sitting in the bed with the blankets over his lap. I didn't know if he was completely nude, but I figured I was about to find out. He patted the bed beside him and I forced my feet into motion, sitting gingerly on the edge of the bed.

"Nervous?" he asked in that low timbre that had me shivering for a whole different reason. Archer always had a really good bedroom voice, even when he wasn't anywhere near a bedroom.

"Scared," I admitted and he cocked his head to the side.

"Don't be, I promised you I would both honor and cherish you at that altar today, I'm a man of my word."

I bowed my head and let my hair, which was past my shoulders now, hide my face. He reached out and tucked the fall behind my ear, so he could see me.

"Come here," he said.

"Are you going to kiss me?" I asked.

"Do you want me to?"

"I… I really don't know."

"I don't think I'm going to do anything with you tonight," he murmured.

I felt stricken, like I'd done something wrong and it was out of my mouth before I could stop it, "Why not?"

"I don't like my women afraid, Melody. It doesn't do anything for me. I'd prefer it if you were willing—"

"I am," I said quickly, and he lifted the covers. I caught a glimpse of his hip as I brought my legs up to ease beneath them… he *was* nude. A lump formed in my throat and I wasn't sure I could speak past it if I wanted to.

"Straddle me," he ordered and I moved slowly to comply. He wasn't hard, at least not yet, and I still had my shorts on, so this was okay... I mean it *was* okay, right? I felt my breathing grow shallow and more rapid as his hands fell onto my hips. He smoothed them up my body, and around me drawing me down so my forehead rested against his.

My blood rushed in my ears, my pulse fluttering hard against the insides of my wrists. I had my hands buried in the pillows to either side of him and he sighed, breath warm against my lips; just another inch and they would touch.

"Touch me, Mel. I won't bite," he murmured and I raised my hands, placing them on his chest. His lashes fluttered against his cheeks and *he* sighed out – a strange mix of sounds, both erotic and contented.

"O... okay?" I stammered.

"Hmm, you're safe with me, just remember that; keep it in your mind, baby. You're *safe*," he said and before I could respond or think, or *do* anything he'd sat up with me in his arms and turned us. I felt like I was falling for one awful second before the soft bed caught me and my heart took up residence in my throat. *Oh God, he's on top of me* was the instant and panicked reaction.

"Shh," he whispered and kissed my cheek, trailing his lips lightly to my jaw, pressing them feather light there too, before moving again, this time to the throbbing pulse point in the side of my neck, that sweet spot that had me sucking in a sharp breath. He paused and flicked out his tongue lightly over the spot causing me to gasp.

"Hmm, right there, huh?" he asked and deepened his kiss in the same place. I closed my eyes and felt my body relax marginally.

The next kiss he pressed to my chest, his hands smoothing their way up from where they'd been fastened to my hips, rounding to the front of my body, my stomach, where he started to push up the camisole I wore. My hands jerked to his and I pushed them away.

"Don't," I said on a sharp inhale.

"Why not?" he demanded, freezing in place, his gaze boring into mine.

"I don't look like I used to," I said uncomfortably and he tipped his head to the side, his hands beginning their slow ascent to move the material out of the way. I felt tears gather at the corners of my eyes and he frowned down at me.

"This body did something amazing," he murmured. "This body did something mine could never do." He looked down and pushed the material out of the way. He smiled then, a slow smile full of appreciation and genuine awe. I was frozen and confused; he placed a gentle kiss against the cesarean scar and murmured, "This body carried my son and gave him life, nourished him; allowed him to draw breath and come into this world."

Archer raised his eyes to mine and said, "This body, *your* body, is beautiful to me. Dressed in these ribbons," he licked a wet line up one of the stretchmarks I found to be so ugly, "of sheer perfection... I love this body. Not only for what it's done for me by giving me a son, but for what it *will* do for me, by giving me another, or for giving me a beautiful daughter. I swore to you today that I was going to love, honor and cherish you. In front of my brothers, in front of my president, and that's just what I'm going to do. You see imperfection, I see life. I see something that, again, I could never do. I see strength, I see courage, and I admire you for it. This is my truth, this is my reality, and I really hope that you can get on board with that."

His words devastated me in all the right ways. I felt my walls and my fear crumble beneath the weighted gaze he held me pinned with. The only motion I could manage was the gentle rise and fall of my continued breathing as I stared in stunned silence. Tears slipped down my temples and cheeks of their own volition and when he realized I would make no further move to resist him, that I was capable of no further protest, he carried on with what he wanted to do; which as of right now was kissing all over my stomach. He kept on with those gentle, feather light caresses of his silken lips against my flesh which grew heated, awakening after its long dormancy.

The last man to touch me had been Grinder, and I was shocked to find that his much coarser brother touched me with more care and consideration than Grinder *ever* had. I didn't quite know what to do with that except to watch, fascinated, as he drew the beautiful satin and lace shorts down my legs, his fingertips skimming my flesh, leaving trails of tingling sparks in their wake.

My mind may have rebelled against the thought of Archer touching me, against the idea of doing anything remotely sexual with him, but he'd eased my fears and had taken the very edge off my concerns with his carefully chosen words. My mind was warming up to the idea of having him touch me like this, but my body didn't seem to care what my mind thought about it anymore.

My body certainly seemed to have a mind of its very own and it was all about having Archer's lips on my skin. It liked it very much, thank you, and it showed its appreciation for the attention by arching of its own volition very much *into* Archer's touch. I could feel him, hard and pressed against my throbbing pussy and I couldn't believe how much I ached to have him inside me. I wasn't sure I could completely chalk that up to biology, either.

He grasped the hem of my camisole and raised it up over my head. I lifted my arms to allow him to take it, feeling much bolder now that he'd made his position about the marks my body bore clear. He went back to kissing across my chest, exploring my skin, sucking one of my nipples into his mouth and tugging at it gently between his teeth all the while his green-and-gold eyes speared into the heart of mine.

He was so incredibly warm to the touch, and I let my hands do some of their own exploring, running them gently over his shoulders, tracing a weal of scar along his ribs, tiny pinpricks of white scar tissue riding above and below the rough mark where the wound had been crudely stitched back together.

"What happened?" I gasped and he stopped nuzzling my breast long enough to look at me and give me the truth, his voice rough with a cross between desire and annoyance at having to stop what he was doing.

"Got sliced pretty good around my second or third year with the Arizona chapter, a dispute with another club over wandering into our territory uninvited."

"Oh…"

"No more questions, I'm trying to make my wife feel good and I'd appreciate it if she'd let it happen."

I couldn't help it, what he said made me smile. A for real smile that he echoed faintly before he resumed trailing his lips and teeth in tiny nips against my flesh in an ever-downward trajectory. It took me a full minute for my brain to catch up to his intended goal and when it did, it was already too late. He had my thighs spread, using the breadth of his shoulders to keep them apart even as he fastened his mouth over my clit, his tongue teasing me carefully and gently into a fevered pitch.

I gripped the sheets and moaned, eyes squeezed shut as I just tried to concentrate on the feelings and shove the fact that this was *Archer* to the back of my mind which *still* didn't want to come to grips with the fact that – *This. Was. Archer.*

"Oh God!" I cried and it almost sounded like a plea, at least to me. Archer hummed in satisfaction against my body and it added a whole new dimension to what he was doing.

"Archer!" I gasped and he took it as an invitation, sitting up and licking the palm of his hand deliberately, the motion both erotic and slightly intimidating as he reached down and stroked himself between my legs.

"I'm gonna go easy, I promise," he murmured and placed himself at my opening, easing himself inside of me with restraint, letting my body adjust to take him comfortably.

I closed my eyes and let my head fall back, my breath escaping in a shuddering sigh. I hadn't expected to feel not *full* but more like... complete. His body met mine and he was fully seated, as deep as a man could go in a woman and my body lost some of the tension that it wanted to hold onto out of fear, suddenly going limp instead. He leaned over me, and smoothed my hair back from my face, his hands rough with callouses but his touch so gentle.

"Look at me," he said, voice rough around the edges with emotion that I couldn't place. I opened my eyes and sucked in a sharp breath when he drew back and surged carefully, but firmly forward again.

He captured my gaze with his own and I wondered, briefly, if this was what drowning felt like. While I could breathe and just fine, I might add, I still felt as if I were being drawn inexorably down into Archer's eyes. I forced my fingers to let go of the sheets, and instead, let them curve around his shoulder, drawing myself up, tucking myself into the shelter of his body even as he drove a slow, satisfied moan from some-where deep down inside me.

I couldn't ignore the truth, I couldn't deny what he was doing... Archer wasn't having sex with me, not one bit. Archer was as good as his word. With every slow and considerate thrust, Archer was making love to me, and I just didn't know what to do... if it was okay, this early on, for me to do the same.

22

A rcher...

I didn't want her to be afraid, any other woman and I probably wouldn't have cared, but this was Melody, the mother of Noah, who was now *my* child. She was *my wife* and would soon, hopefully, be the mother of more of *my* children. That deserved a level of respect that I'd never had the occasion to show any other woman.

I nearly came undone when she relaxed, her body accepting my cock, her arms twining around my shoulders and pulling me gently down over the top of her. I held her as gently as I could, as if she were more fragile than a baby bird in my arms even as I fought to draw this out. I didn't want to come too quickly, but it was hard holding off. For one, it had been a while for me, and two, I'd held a secret torch for my brother's woman for *years*. I could deny it out loud to my other brothers and to my club brothers all I wanted, but I couldn't deny it to myself.

I sighed out in both passion and contentment and kissed the side of her neck. I wanted to kiss her for real so badly, but I wanted to wait, I wanted her to take that from me. I didn't really have any other measure that she'd accepted me, so I figured that would be as good as any when it came to an indicator.

God she was fierce, so beautiful, and despite the rough go she'd been having, so solid. She needed to reach out though, she needed to understand I would protect her, just as fiercely as she protected Noah.

"Archer," she moaned, and my name on her lips in that breathy plea nearly made me completely lose my shit.

"Oh God, not yet, baby. I'm not ready for this to end," I groaned and she held onto me that much harder.

I knew she'd come at least once, her pussy gently gripping and releasing my cock in a rhythm that'd been hard to resist. I swallowed hard, pressed my forehead to hers and reached between us to tease her clit. I wanted to trip her trigger just one more time, just once more before I—

She cried out, her body gripping mine, pulling me deeper before she shuddered beneath me in every single fucking way that made a man feel like one. I lost my grip on my control completely and I came with her. I came with her, and I think, I came the hardest I ever had in my life. I let myself rest in her arms as we both fell back to earth, panting. Sweat cooled on my skin and my cock jerked in counterpoint to the little aftershocks that ran through Mel.

I looked into those true fuckin' blue eyes of hers from inches away, the candle light turning them a deep cobalt, and I told her, "You're mine, Mel. You know what that means to one of us." Her eyes widened and she nodded mutely. I held her in my arms and let my eyes sink shut, relishing the feeling of her so warm and close. "Good," I said and nodded, more to myself than anything else.

I had no doubts that she would take the oaths she pledged seriously. It was one of the things that had secretly pissed me off about my brother. I loved Grinder like no fucking other, but it fuckin' pissed me off *like* no other, him running around on Mel when she'd so clearly devoted herself to him. It wasn't right, which was why I hadn't wanted to believe that she'd chased Grind half way across the country, let alone that whatever she'd said or did had chased my brother right into his fuckin' death.

I never imagined the truth would be that Grind had chased *himself* to an early grave. That he woulda run *himself* to death runnin' from his responsibilities as a fuckin' man.

"Hey." Her voice was soft and just like her name to my ears; a melody beyond compare. Her hands gently cupped my face, drawing it forward so that I faced her again. I hadn't even realized I'd turned my head.

"What?" I asked her.

"What's wrong?" she asked and I swallowed.

"I've been meaning to ask you, and I need you to tell me... why'd you come runnin' out this way lookin' for Grind?"

I eased myself out of her and over her leg, stretching out on my side, head propped in my hand so that I could look at her. She looked like one of them paintings, hanging in a rich person's museum. The only thing that was missin' was some little fuckin' baby angel feeding her grapes.

She licked her bottom lip, and it was everything in me not to cover her mouth with my own; to suck that pink tongue into my mouth and let mine dance with it. I wanted her to have something, at least one thing that she felt like she had control over. I knew I was a controlling bastard. It was just my nature. I also knew it would take a special kind of woman, a strong one, to put up with my ass and Mel had done pretty fuckin' admirably the last several months on that account. I didn't have much to offer her, but what I had was hers... and I was not only impressed, but grateful, that she'd taken it.

"When Grind," she cleared her throat, "left..." she said diplomatically.

I shook my head, "No need to sugarcoat it for me, baby. When Grind ran out on you and the responsibility he owed you for being the half of the equation needed to make you pregnant with Noah—

"Ah, yes." She nodded, and didn't disagree with me, which was good. I was glad she wasn't makin' excuses for him. I damn sure wouldn't. "When he left, I held on for as long as I could with my waitressing job, but as you know – Grinder helped out a lot with bills and things when he'd been there."

"He should. I'da whooped his ass again if I caught him freeloading anymore."

She blinked, stunned into silence, "Excuse me?"

"You heard me."

She shook her head as if to clear it. "The doctors' bills, prenatal care, even with help and on a sliding scale... they stacked up quickly. I couldn't hang on anymore, and when I got into my sixth, almost seventh month, I had to move back in with my mother and Phil."

"Grind said something about them bein' some kind of piece of work," I murmured and pulled her protectively into me.

"That's putting it mildly. I spent the rest of my pregnancy being called a whore. When my water broke, I had to take a taxi to the hospital. They refused to stay for the birth."

I felt the darkness in her then, saw the despair and the fear. I'd never wanted to kill one of my own brothers before but if Grind had been alive, I would have put him in the ground. I smoothed her hair out of her eyes and waited for her to continue. It took her a minute to get her shit together enough so that she could, and it wasn't lost on me that she skipped over the rest of her hospital stay. It must have been bad, and it was something we'd have to revisit later.

"They were hard on me, but I figured I could withstand it, for Noah. They kept demanding that I move out, but in the next breath demanded

I pay rent. I paid them to stay in their basement with Noah, buy diapers and formula; I had trouble breastfeeding so I had to supplement it… took just about everything I had left.

"They wouldn't watch Noah at first, either. So, it was hard to get back to work at the diner. Finally, my mom agreed to watch him, and it was okay, for a while… hard, but okay. Except the longer I stayed, the more I tried to follow their rules…" She shook her head.

"It was like they would set down rules and I would follow them, but suddenly, midway through things, the rules would change. Then Noah started growing up, becoming more aware and I was afraid – I didn't want him growing up like I did. I didn't want him to grow up thinking the way they treated me, and him, was normal. Babies deserve to be loved. They deserve patience and kindness, but that was never what Phil was about. He was strict but it was *crazy*, Archer."

"Shh, it's okay." I smoothed a hand over that satiny, light blonde hair and listened to her, but I didn't need her getting worked up either. When she seemed calmer, I asked, "What made you run?"

"There was an argument. I was trying to work extra shifts at the diner to put away more savings, so that I could do what they wanted and get out of their house, but suddenly, that wasn't good enough anymore. They wanted *me* out, but they threatened to take my son away from me. They threatened to lie and tell the state that I was a drug addict and that I was sleeping around with all the brothers. They were going to keep my son and raise him right, they said, and I couldn't let that happen. They would have crushed his little spirit, and *I couldn't let that happen,* Archer. So when they went to church, I pretended I was sick and shoved as much as I could into the car. That night, I took Noah and ran. I had nowhere else to go."

She broke down and sobbed and I knew that she spoke nothing but the truth. I wasn't the best at comfort, but sometimes, women like Mel just needed to be held and just needed to be heard. So I tried that, and what do you know? It worked.

"I promise you, no one's taking our son," I said into her hair. "I'd make 'em fuckin' disappear first."

She clung to me and let it out, and I hoped like hell she heard the truth in my words, because I meant them. Melody and Noah were my property in the outlaw sense of the word. You touched a man's property upon pain of death. It was the way of my world and I wasn't changing it for no one.

We laid like that, the candles burning down, the fire in the fireplace too, and eventually, Mel slept and for once it was a role reversal; I couldn't. My mind turning over and over the possible ways her parents could either track her down or fuck with what we had going. I contemplated making a stop at their place when I went through Arizona, considered the best way to handle things and protect my new family.

Maybe this time it was best to let sleeping dogs lie? I didn't know. It wasn't exactly territory I'd been through before. I mean granted, I'd come up in the system, but I'd never done it from the side of being a parent and I was still pretty new at that part. I was hoping I wouldn't have too much trouble with the curve.

Eventually, I fell into a deep sleep. I'd meant it to be light, but it'd been a hell of a day. When I woke up, it was to light streaming through the windows, the gauzy white curtains not doing a hell of a lot to keep it out. I sat up only to find Mel wasn't in here with me, her new pajamas I had bought for her were neatly folded at the foot of the bed, but her boots were missing from the entryway.

I got up and went into the bathroom, getting my morning routine out of the way. I pulled my hair into a loose horse tail and threw on some jeans, a tee shirt, and because it was a touch cool, a flannel shirt I left open over that. I shrugged into my jacket and cut and pulled the front door open to see Mel striding up the path, one of those paper travel coffee cups with a lid on it.

"I brought you coffee, and some breakfast," she called softly. When she stopped in front of me, she handed the coffee over.

"Thanks," I said and took a drink. She pulled a banana out of one of her coat pockets and a muffin wrapped in a napkin out of the other.

"You were sleeping so hard, I didn't want to wake you."

"I wish you did, I don't like waking up and finding you not here. It just doesn't sit right."

She blushed faintly and stared at the ground. "Sorry," she said.

"S'okay, I guess." I took another drink of coffee which was perfect. I liked that she knew what I liked. "What do you feel like doing?"

"A walk would be nice," she said, and I nodded, the corners of my mouth turning down as I considered it.

"Not a bad start," I agreed. "Go where you want, I'll follow your lead."

"Okay," she said, and hands buried in her pockets, turned. I juggled the breakfast offerings a minute and got the door shut and latched while Mel looked on amused.

"Would you like me to hold something?"

"Nah, I got it."

I fell into step beside her and she strolled gently, giving me time to eat and drink my breakfast.

"Thanks for grabbing this for me."

"Oh, sure. I figured you'd get hungry without anything. Lunch is a ways off."

We fell into a silence that was more comfortable than not, and moved along at a sedate pace, towards the water.

"Mel, can I ask you something?"

"Of course." She side-eyed me curiously, as if surprised I'd asked her and hindsight being twenty-twenty, I guess I could have made more of an effort to talk these last few months. It was just hard for me to let anyone in; always had been. Once I did, though, for some reason it was like flipping a switch. Either you were out or you were in. There was no in between phase. I don't know… maybe some of my circuits were fucked up from getting the shit kicked out of me when I was a kid so much.

"This whole thing with your parents, is that why you freaked the fuck out so hard when Noah hit his head a couple months back?"

She pursed her lips and nodded. "I thought for sure the hospital was going to alert CPS, and that they were going to investigate and find that I'd bolted from Arizona with Noah."

I shook my head. "Mel, did your parents ever have any kind of *official* custody of our boy? I mean, was there any reason for 'em to?"

She shook her head. "No, I mean, I was living with them, and they told everyone I was on drugs and was whoring myself out to the club. I was even tested for drugs at one point. Not just my pee, but they tested my hair too. They didn't find anything. I guess I was lucky. I mean, I smoked weed before I found out I was pregnant. I stopped immediately once I found out I was though."

I huffed a little bit of a laugh at that. "Seriously? Weed? That was it? I thought sure you bein' with Grind he had you into some harder shit than that."

She shook her head. "I tried ecstasy once when Grinder and I first got together; it scared me so bad I swore never again."

"You and Grind were together, what? Three, four years?"

"About that long, yeah," she murmured.

"You stayed faithful to him the entire time, didn't you?"

"Yes," so quietly I barely heard her; I sighed.

"Always thought you were wasted on my brother. I loved him, don't get me wrong, but where you were concerned, I always thought he was a serious dumb fuck. You knew he was fuckin' around on you, why did you stay?"

"Because he said he loved me…" she smiled a little sadly. "No one had ever said that to me before him."

Aw, Jesus. That just about killed me. I swiped a hand over my face and turned down the dock. Melody following alongside. We reached the end and she sat down, letting her feet dangle over the water. I sat behind her, one leg to either side of her and snugged right up against her back. She gripped the edge of the dock tightly and squeaked.

"Don't push me in, I can't swim!" she said quickly and I wrapped my arms around her tight, frowning.

"I wouldn't do that to you, why would you even think that?"

She laughed, a bitter and incredulous sound. "Grind would have, and he would have laughed. No guarantee he would be the one to jump in after me though. He could be an ass like that sometimes."

I gritted my teeth. Man, I hadn't come up with Grind so he could be that way. I found myself wondering what else I'd been blind to. If maybe I'd made too many fucking excuses for his ass-tastic behavior.

"You don't think *I'd* do it though, do you?"

"I… I don't know Archer. I hardly know anything *about* you. You've always been the quiet one, until you weren't and when you aren't, you're always so *angry* all the time. I've seen you punch a brother in the face for as little as some *perceived* disrespect…"

"It can't be tolerated, baby. Respect isn't something that can be held onto from a position of weakness."

"Okay, but does it always have to be held onto through violence? Through fear?" she asked.

"They're effective tools," I countered.

"Okay, then what about Dragon?"

I frowned. "What about him?"

"Have you ever seen him raise a hand to one of the brothers?"

I thought about it… *Well shit… she has you there.*

"I'll take your silence as a 'no,'" she said gently. "Let me ask you this, how would you like to see Noah raised? Do you want him to turn out to be like his biological father?"

"No," I answered quickly.

"What about his father now?" she asked softly and I wished I could see her face, because her words sort of undid a hurt that'd I'd never speak on.

"I'd like to think I'm not so bad," I said with a wan smile.

"You're not, now… once you let someone in even the slightest little bit. Still, getting there, getting to a point where anyone can even *begin* to know you or even learn about you, you don't make it easy, Archer."

"Insightful," I murmured, nuzzling behind her ear. I pressed a kiss there and felt her shiver. I smiled, secretly to myself, glad I could elicit something other than a fear response out of her; that she was loosening up around me even just a little.

"Be that as it may, I would really like to break the cycle of hurt with my son. Grinder may have had his moments of being a complete asshole but, I think… no… I *know* there was good in him. I really do believe he would have come back to us or that if he were still alive, he would have let us in and lived up to the situation and been a father to his son at the very least. I don't think he left us in a bid to shirk his responsibility. I think he left out of *fear.*"

"What makes you give him so much credit?" I asked.

"You're angry, I get it. Do you ever stop to wonder though?"

"Wonder about what?"

I could hear her smile. "You hold yourself to a very high standard, Archer. I can see that now. Your word is your bond and you follow through with everything you say, no matter what."

"A man is only as good as his word," I said.

"That's just it; your ideals are sometimes superhuman. People have faults, and sometimes things happen outside of their control… failure is a part of the human condition but with you? It doesn't seem to be an option. You can't hold other people to the impossibly high standards you hold yourself to. It's simply not fair and it's the *one* thing that terrifies me when it comes to you raising Noah." I blinked, surprised at her forthrightness, and here and now of all places. When I didn't say anything, she continued.

"What happens when he doesn't live up to those lofty expectations? Are you going to be so disappointed, will it make you so angry, that you'll write him off? Will you continue the cycle of emotional violence against our son by withholding your love? That scares me so much, more than anything. You have proven yourself to be a good man, Archer, but I can't and won't let you treat our children that way. I grew up in a house of mental, emotional, and physical abuse. Everything I know about how you, Grinder, and the twins were raised tells me you come from much the same with maybe more emphasis on the physical abuse… I want better for our kids."

"I do too," I said quickly.

"You know my mom was an alcoholic right?" she asked.

"Yeah," I murmured, wondering where she was going with this.

"She met Phil when she started going to AA meetings in his church when I was seven. It was either the meetings or they were going to put me in the system."

"I didn't know that," I said.

"Well it's true, but the point I'm trying to make, is if it's one thing I remember from that time it was that in AA, the first step in dealing with the problem is admitting you have one. If you can recognize it's a thing, you can deal with it."

"Is that why you're bringing this up now?" I asked.

"Partially… partially because I wanted to talk to you about it away from Noah, and before we got pregnant with another."

"If you're so concerned about this, why did you marry me yesterday? Why not bring this up before getting hitched?"

"Because I made a commitment to you, too. I promised to love, honor, and cherish you in sickness and in health, and I think that's what this is. Not just for you, but for me too. We're sick. We were made sick by our parents and how we were raised, and you and me? We're the only cure for it. Each other, you know? Two people who have lived it and recognize it for what it is. There to hold each other accountable and to be able to stand up to the other one and say 'hey, you're slipping, you can't do that,' you know?"

I felt myself smile slightly. "You're brave enough to stand up to me?"

"Archer, these are my *children* we're talking about." I could hear her getting emotional and so I squeezed her gently. "If it came down to shooting you in the face to protect them from harm, it'd hurt, but I'd pull that trigger. You need to know that. I committed to you as much as you did to me yesterday, and I'm telling you, I never would have done it if I didn't believe for one minute you couldn't handle it. That you couldn't maintain your control and not repeat the same horror that we went through growing up."

"What are you saying?" I asked her softly.

"I'm saying *I do*, with every fiber of my being. I'm saying I believe in you, but that doesn't mean that this conversation didn't need to happen."

Well fuck me, swingin', I thought to myself. *Color me impressed.* I'd set out a couple of weeks ago to work hard at being a good man for her and Noah, to make her fall in love with me… and damn if she didn't go and just do it to me first.

We sat in silence for a really long time at the end of that dock, staring out over the water and soaking up some sunshine when the clouds let it through. I held her protectively in the curve of my body and thought real long and real hard about what she'd just said, and decided that she was right. That it was high time I got to work on my temper, and that I was out of excuses now that I was a father.

"You're a smart and pretty fantastic woman, Mrs. Turner," I finally said.

"I'll remember you said that," she said. "I might even hold it against you the first time we have a fight." I laughed at that and she leaned back, tipping her head back against my shoulder her body language eased considerably.

"Thank you for believing in me," I said and she smiled at me, the way she used to smile at my brother. I think my heart stuttered to a stop for a second in my chest.

"Thank you for really listening to me," she said.

"Eh, I might not always, although you're making a convincing argument right now for why I should."

"We're married, Archer. I'd be delusional to think we will never disagree, or that we will never fight."

"At least there's one thing I don't think we're ever gonna disagree on," I said.

"What's that?" she asked.

"That our children will always come first, come hell or high water."

"No, on that I don't think we will ever disagree," she murmured.

As ass backwards as this whole relationship thing had gone together for us, I think we finally clicked right there on the dock. Common ground was a pretty good starting point as far as starting points went.

"Come on," I said and scooted back so I could get up, "I got something for you back at the cabin."

She looked up at me with a slight frown. "What?"

"Come on and you'll see," I said and took her hand, hauling her up to her feet. I felt really good about the talk we'd had. Like a new man, with a brand-new direction. One that was hopeful, and maybe, even happy. I liked that, and I wanted to see if I could give her some of that feeling, so it was back to the cabin for a minute.

23

Melody...

"Okay, now I know this place is right out of a fairytale," I muttered when we reentered the cabin.

"What?" Archer asked, smiling.

"I'm putting money on furry little woodland creatures following Contessa around, cleaning up our mess."

Archer raised his eyebrows at me and I wrinkled my nose. "What?"

"Nothing, I'm just glad to see the woman I remember making an appearance."

I tipped my head and regarded him. "What do you mean?"

"I mean none of this has been ideal, for you, hell, for *either* of us. I don't think I've seen you smile, or be so light since you showed up at the club a few months back. It's like you're getting some of your sparkle and shine back. It's good."

"Oh," I murmured softly.

He shook his head and went to the closet, pulling out his saddlebags. "Come sit on the bed," he ordered in his gruff, typical Archer style. I kicked off my boots to preserve the nice carpet and went over to the bed as directed, hopping up on it and drawing my legs into an Indian-style sit.

"I got you this," he said and pulled out a wrapped gift from one of the bags, handing me the box. It was heavier than it looked and wrapped in white paper with brightly colored streamers, confetti, and balloons printed on it along with 'happy birthday!' all over. I raised an eyebrow and looked at him, smiling hard.

"Um, we just got married. Why does it say 'happy birthday' all over it?"

"Because, I didn't know when it was and you didn't say anything. I missed it, and I wanted to make it up to you now."

I blinked, surprised. "I didn't think you'd care," I said softly and he had the grace to look guilty.

"I'm not good with people, Mel; I'll be the first to admit that. I'm sorry you felt like you couldn't talk to me or tell me what you needed. That wasn't right, and as my wife, I want you to come to me with anything, big or small. I remember that Grind always used to make a big deal about your birthday and gettin' you at least *something* even when he couldn't afford it. I just never kept track of when it was. I felt like a dick when the girls told me I'd missed it."

"You know why, don't you?" I asked softly, staring at the paper-wrapped box in my hands, the bright, fabric yellow ribbon blurring.

"No, he never said."

"It was because when I was growing up," I had to clear my throat before continuing, "all of my friends at school had birthdays, but I never did. Phil didn't believe in celebrating them." Archer came and sat down next to me, putting a hand on my knee. "I don't know why that always hurt me so much, but it did. It bothered me, a lot, and when

Grinder found out about it, he always made such a big deal about it, you know? Always made sure to take me on a real date. Dinner, dancing, whatever I wanted, and he always made sure to give me *something,* always made sure to tell me he loved me. It was part of what made him so special."

Archer nodded and asked gently, "So you going to open it? You're killin' my nerves here, baby."

I laughed and dashed at the collection of moisture on my lashes. I took a deep breath and let it out slowly before tearing into the paper, edging the ribbon off around the corner of the box.

"No!" I gasped and looked at him. "Are you serious? Are you fucking serious right now?"

"Hey, language woman!" he said, laughing.

"Archer, this must have cost you a *fortune*!" I cried looking at the expensive, state-of-the-art digital camera; and I do mean *state-of-the-art,* like something a professional would use.

He shrugged and cleared *his* throat. "You like to take pictures," he said as if that explained why I had a camera in my lap that probably cost more than what my car was worth *when it was new!* Okay, maybe that last was an exaggeration, but still, it was certainly worth more than twice maybe even three times what my car was worth *now.*

"I don't even know how I would work something like this," I admitted hugging it and the box close to my chest.

"Well, it's kind of a two-part gift..." he admitted and pulled out an envelope from the inside of his cut. I had to set my beautiful new camera down in my lap to take it and I *really* had to blink at the return address on it.

"Art school?"

He nodded. "Photography lessons, from the ground up. You take some pretty good pictures with your phone, I kind of can't wait to see what you could do with this thing." I blinked, and just kind of stared at him open mouthed. "I can take it back if you hate it."

"Oh my God, no! I don't hate it, I *love* it... it's just... it's just..." I didn't have the words.

"It's not too much, I have quite a few birthdays to catch up on." He shrugged again. "Consider this me cashing in all at once."

"I don't know what to say," I uttered staring at the expensive gift in my hands. "Thank you."

He smiled and gave a nod. "I'm glad you like it."

"I want to try and play with it, even though I don't know what I'm doing."

"Sure," he said. "I made sure the battery was charged, and I figured there would be lots to take pictures of around here. Why don't you go for it?"

I gave him a sly grin. "You going to be my model?" I asked and he laughed.

"Fuck no. One shot of my ugly mug and I'd break the lens."

I bowed my head and took it out of the box. "I don't know," I said lightly. "I was thinking I kind of scored with a good-looking husband..."

"Yeah?"

"Yeah," I said and it must have shown on my face, or in the way I held myself, the nervousness because what he said next... it was the only explanation as to *why* he said it.

"I'm not like my brother, Mel. I won't cheat on you. I don't give a fuck how much free pussy walks through the club. I made a commitment so yours'll be the only one I'm fucking."

I smiled, blushing faintly and said, "Well when you put it *that* way."

"I mean it," he said and his tone was serious.

I nodded. "I know you do," I said softly, "and thank you for that, too."

"That ain't something you should thank me for, Mel. That's something you should just *expect.*"

"That's the thing about expectations though, Archer. When you have them, they're easy to get broken and when they do, it hurts, so I just try not to have too many anymore." I raised the camera to my eye and snapped a picture of him. I looked at the little screen and made a face. I hadn't adjusted the lens correctly, so it was all blurry. He put his head next to mine to look.

"You'll be giving Ansel Adams a run for his money in no time," he said dryly and I laughed.

"I didn't even know you knew who Ansel Adams *was.*"

"Sure I do, they were all those black-and-white pictures you had on your walls back in Arizona, weren't they? The ones of the desert and trees and shit, right?"

I nodded. "I like nature pictures, but I like taking pictures of people, too. I like black and white, but color is just as beautiful." I adjusted the lens and took another picture of him, smiling when I looked and it came out clear; his gold-green eyes practically glowing with some unnamed emotion I'd never seen come from him before.

He looked at it and nodded and I set the camera carefully on one of the table beside the bed, and the box and wrapping paper on the floor. I turned back to him and smiled, his hand finding my hip and sliding under my shirt.

"Happy birthday, Mel... sorry it was so late."

"It was worth the wait," I admitted, my breath squeezing from my lungs with the heated look he was giving me. He leaned forward and I closed my eyes, expecting the kiss to fall on my lips, but it didn't. Instead, his lips brushed over that spot on the side of my neck that left me jumping, an effervescent rush sweeping over the half of my body he paid attention to.

This time, the sex was even more slow and deliberate than it'd been last night. He took his time slipping me out of my clothes and let me give him the same consideration although I was a bit shyer when it came to my explorations.

It surprised me how patient he was being with me, I didn't think he had it in him to be honest. I'd never in a million years expected that Archer knew how to be soft, how to be kind, how to be gentle; but with every light touch of his lips against my skin, every caress of his roughened fingertips, the man was slowly stripping away my misconceptions as well as my clothes.

"Lay on your stomach," he murmured once he had me naked, and I complied, my curiosity at what he had planned having developed far more than any fear I'd held on to. He kissed my back, his teeth lightly scraping in these sensational little love bites, a sharp contrast with the tickling sweep of his hair that followed. His lips were warm and his touch made my senses wake up, coming alive until I was squirming underneath his attentions for want of a deeper touch. He pressed his hands to my ass cheeks and spread them. I stiffened for a moment, but he wasn't going there. Instead, he found the opening to my pussy with his cock, and pressing me into the mattress, slid inside. I groaned in pleasure, the angle sharper and deeper somehow. Archer swept my hair up off my neck and fisted it gently at the back of my head, running his tongue along the side of my neck as I grew impossibly wet, his cock slipping from me once or twice until with a curse he got up off of me.

"On your knees for just a second, baby," he said, voice husky and I complied, expecting him to just fuck me doggy style, less intimate than what he'd *been* doing but certainly still hot. He surprised me when he jammed a couple of the pillows beneath my hips and pressing me back down into the mattress by my shoulders, he found me again with little difficulty and slipped right back into me.

The satisfied, triumphant, pleasure filled groan he let out was almost enough to make me come, but what finally did it? The slight change in angle had him sliding right over that *spot* inside me. I felt the weight of my impending orgasm build twice as fast as it had been before, my pussy clenching around his cock. I wanted it, I wanted to feel good; I wanted *him* to feel good so bad.

He bit my shoulder and instead of the fire in my blood cooling, it was as if he'd doused the flames in gasoline. They overtook me and I lost myself in that pure, shining, burning light, all of my doubts and inhibitions burning away as I arched low to the bed, shoving my ass towards him in silent offering. Hell, I'd give him anything if he could make this feeling last, and he did, for as long as he could.

24

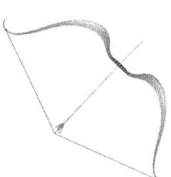

Archer...

Someday, I was going to take her ass. If she kept arching into me like she was right now, that someday might be today, hell it might even be right now. Her pussy was so hot, so wet, and so perfectly snug around me I almost couldn't hold back when she came.

She writhed so fucking beautifully when she orgasmed. Like some kind of mythical sea creature, which was funny considering she couldn't swim. Her passion-filled cries were definitely some kind of siren's call and when they rose an octave, when I found a particularly sensitive place inside her? That was it; I couldn't hold off anymore. I shoved into her tight pussy, hard and deep and spilled over the edge of my own orgasm.

I came back from the experience slowly, braced over the top of her, holding my weight off her body with arms that caged her protectively, despite their trembling. Her back touched my chest gently with every heaving breath she took, as she panted fervently, trying to catch it. I was gasping similarly, and wasn't really ready to speak yet myself, but I did press a kiss behind her ear, trailing them down the side of her neck, as I slid my limp dick out of the sticky mess we'd both created. I guess it was time we found out if that bathtub were really meant for two or not.

"I love it when you do that," she murmured.

"Mm?" I made the sound a question. I was pretty sure she was talking about the little kisses and nips I was laying against her skin, but I wanted to hear it. I wanted to know her exact meaning.

"*That*," she said, arching luxuriously like a well-fed cat beneath me just as I pressed my lips to another bare patch of pale silk that was her skin.

"Hmm, I'll remember that," I said, darting my tongue into one of the dimples at the small of her back. She sucked in a sharp breath and pretty much *melted* into the comforter and when I looked, she had her arms beneath her chin, and she turned her head *just so* to lay on them and the light was *perfect*. I snatched up her camera silently, and adjusted the lens carefully and, *snap!* Her eyes flew open and she stiffened, but it was too late, I'd captured my prize.

"There may be something to this whole taking pictures of *everything* that you do. I'm gonna have to have you print that one for me," I said showing her the result. She blinked and leaned up to take a better look, her face softening.

"Okay," she said softly. She couldn't argue with me on this one. There wasn't a damn thing wrong with that photo. It was tasteful, her tits were covered because she was laying on them and her ass was covered because the picture stopped before it went down that far.

"You on birth control?" I asked suddenly and she looked back at me over her shoulder, pushing herself up a little to do it which thrust out her perfect tits. Before I knew it, I was getting hard again.

"Yes, why?"

"I want you to stop taking it," I said frowning. "I'm not getting any younger and I don't want Noah and his little sibling too far apart in ages." She nodded, her eyes clouding with a faraway look that spelled trouble.

"I got another question," I said before she could get too far into her head and whatever she was thinking about spoiled her mood.

"Yes?"

"You ever try anal?"

"Once; it hurt and I didn't like it."

"Did he take his time?"

"Um, I think he tried."

"He use lube?" Her face was blushing a furious crimson by now and she let herself drop back to the bed with a huffed-out sigh.

"I don't really need to point out that if you're fucking me in the ass that you're doing it wrong, do I? I mean, that's not exactly how babies are made."

"No, but it fuckin' feels good, and I want you to try it with me at some point because I want you to enjoy it too."

"If I hate it?"

"Then that would suck, but I'd never make you do it again."

"Just once?" she asked uncertain, and it had that edge like she would let me do it, a sort of taking one for the team so she could say 'nope' and never do it again.

"Once is all it'd take, you don't like it, I'll never bring it up again. You do, it'll be kind of a regular thing."

"What *is* so appealing about shoving your dick in a woman's ass, anyways?" she asked and I could tell I was pushing her out of her comfort zone.

I fisted my cock and stroked it lazily but answered her question the best I could, "I don't know, maybe because it's considered dirty? Maybe because it's a totally different sensation? I just know I was willing to try anything once and that it *really* tripped my trigger."

"That's not really helpful for making me understand it, I mean… it is kind of gross, isn't it?"

"Meh, it can be messy, but I'm a grown ass man. I learned how to wash my dick a long ass time ago."

I could hear Mel roll her eyes. "Oh my *God*, Archer! Stop, your idea of romance is just killing me here."

I shoved my dick back into her pussy, her walls clenching in surprise as she cried out first in surprise, but pretty quick she bit it off into one sexy as hell moan. Oh man, she was still wet. I stroked in and out of her a few times.

"You were saying something?" I asked.

"Oh, yeah…" her voice was breathy.

"What were you saying?" I asked driving into her gently, I knew where that spot of hers was now, and I made sure I was going over it.

"More?" she asked.

"Fuckin' right," I growled and nipped her shoulder. I was a little more aggressive with my thrusting but made sure to stay inside her comfort zone. It took practice to read a woman's body language, to know where the boundaries were and to stay coloring inside the lines. I don't know what it was about Mel, but I picked up on hers pretty quick.

Maybe it'd been all those years watching her with Grind, as creepy as fuck as that sounded. Even if you don't spend much time interacting with someone, you spend enough time around 'em, spend a few months livin' with 'em, you pick up on some of their subtler cues. As much as I was enjoying keeping her pinned on her stomach, the delicate curve of her ass fitting the curve of my hips as I shoved inside her,

I was missing her legs and arms wrapped around me; I'd liked that, too.

I pulled out of her and thought that a bath would *definitely* be the next order of business when I was through with getting my fill of her lush body underneath mine.

"Turn over," I gasped and let her up enough so she could do it. She did, and immediately pulled me down on top of her, her legs going around my waist, her arms around my shoulders. Her nails dug into my back and I thrust into her a little harder than I'd meant to, but it turned out to be okay because she was *into it*. Like so into it, that she clamped her legs around me harder, pulling my cock into her further, her teeth setting into one of my trap muscles a little less than gentle.

I couldn't leave a challenge like that unanswered, so I drew back and thrust into her even harder. She arched and cried out, "Oh, yeah!" and it was pretty frenzied after that. I sailed past lovemaking right into some down and dirty fucking, and she kept pace the whole way. I was glad for it, and that it didn't always have to be slow, because I liked it a little on the rougher side some nights too.

"A little more! A little more!" she cried and I gave it to her, and she crashed to the bed, crying out in wild abandon as her body went deliciously haywire beneath mine. Oh yeah, it was just what I needed to tip *me* over the edge. It seemed we were compatible in the sack, which was a good thing. A very good thing.

We rested, catching our breath, finding our heartbeats and taming them into a more sedate pace. It was with more than a little reluctance and some regret that I pushed off of her and got to my feet.

"Where are you going?" she asked softly, and it made me smile that she wanted me to stay.

"Drawing us a bath, we're a mess and I'd rather not fuck up the sheets."

"It looks big enough for two, think we'll both fit?"

"We'll find out," I said and padded into the bathroom barefoot. I could have sworn I heard her hum with appreciation. I was glad she liked the view.

I started the water and looked at the box of bath shit that was still sitting on the little side table beside the tub. Melody laughed at me from the open bathroom doorway.

"What?"

"You're looking at it like it's going to bite you," she said, laughing so hard, tears sparkled in the corners of her eyes.

"I'm not rightly sure it isn't," I said.

"Want me to pick?"

"I sure as hell don't; I'd have to pull my own man card."

She dumped a vial of this and a bottle of that and pretty soon the water was foaming and swirling with sparkly shit in it. I stared at it, eyebrows raised, and Melody smirked.

"You need to get in first, if we're both going to fit," she said.

"You tell Rush or Nox about this, I'm going to spank that ass before I fuck it."

She giggled and I liked that she'd relaxed around me enough to do it. She got into the bath and I helped her sit between my knees and lean back against my chest. She hummed in appreciation and when the water was deep enough, reached up and shut off the tap.

"Like this," I said, head leaned back, eyes closed.

"Mm hmm, you?"

I chuckled, "I wasn't asking, I was telling, and I'm glad you like it, too."

She sighed in contentment and I actually cuddled her close. I couldn't ever remember a time I'd engaged a woman like this. Usually I fucked it and kicked it right out my fuckin' door. I'd never had a woman of any kind of real quality in my life before. I didn't have time for it, and it was kind of tough attracting any kind of woman with an understanding of this life that had the morals to live up to my expectations. I hadn't thought Mel was one of those women in the beginning... I thought I'd learned differently by watching her, but she was always tucked into Grind's side.

When he'd taken off out here, he'd said it was because of Mel, and hadn't wanted to talk about it at all. I'd figured she'd walked on him. I never in a million years thought it was my brother who'd walked on her. Grind knew he'd had it good with Mel. She kept takin' him back. Even after fuckin' around with no good club sluts because they were there and they were easy, Mel had taken him back.

"What are you thinking about?" she asked softly.

"Why'd you let him do it."

"Do what? Cheat?" she asked, and her sigh was heavy.

"Yeah."

"I don't know, to be honest. He said he loved me; said he was sorry, and I believed him. I could and would forgive him anything as long as he loved me."

"That's not love, baby."

"Closest I've ever been to it."

"No, it's not; it's really, not. Sit up for a minute, turn around, and look at me."

She did as I asked, slowly, and when she was at the opposite end of the tub, facing me, I pulled her towards me and into my lap. She was effectively straddling me and taller this way, so I had to look up, into those true-blue eyes of hers.

I had to sigh. "Walking out on your lady, putting her last, fucking some other skeeze." I raised my eyebrows and said, "Giving your woman who waits on you hand and foot, keeps your place clean, cooks your meals, and gives you freedom the fucking clap." Melody jerked like she'd been slapped and I was pretty sure she hadn't known that all of us guys knew but it just served to bring my point home. "I don't care how much you *say* to her that you love her, but that ain't love, baby. That's the furthest thing from it."

Her face crumbled and I didn't like it, in fact, I wanted to build it up right quick, so I told her the truth of it, "Putting a roof over her head, holding her when she cries, being her strength when she has none left, protecting her, protecting the children you have with her, providing nourishment not only for their bodies, but for their souls... *that's love.*"

She searched my solemn expression, her hands perched on my shoulders for the longest series of heartbeats my body had ever produced. Her eyes misted, and she wrapped my ponytail around her hand, tugging my head back as far as it would go. Her other hand resting on my forehead as her mouth crashed over mine and she kissed me as if she were a starving woman and my kiss would provide all the nourishment she'd need for the next thousand years.

I held her tight and kissed her back and it tasted sweet with relief and a lot like victory.

25

M elody...
  "No."

"Melody..."

"I said no, Archer!" I stared at him with disbelief over Noah's head, hitching my baby up higher onto my hip.

"I ain't exactly asking, Mel," Archer said quietly. We'd come back from our honeymoon just last night, and already he was standing here telling me that he was leaving again, on a run, to Arizona no less, and that he would be leaving in just three days.

"This is unbelievable," I uttered and he reached for me, I stepped back.

"Why?" I demanded. "Tell me; *why now?*"

Archer sighed and dropped his hand to his side, he hung his head and huffed a bitter chuckle. "That's club business, baby."

I frowned and demanded, "You swear to me, you *swear to me,* that it's legit club business and has *nothing* to do with my parents."

"I swear to you, it has more to do with the club than your parents, but I had planned on making a visit to them, too."

I felt myself pale. "Don't Archer. Please don't, you don't know what they're like and we don't even *know* how long it will take for you to legally adopt Noah. Please don't stir this pot until all is said and done. *Please!*"

"Hey, hey, hey!" He came to me and Noah both, and I was out of places to sidestep or back away, but I didn't feel like putting space between us anymore. I wanted the comfort he was offering. He took both me and our son into his arms and held us, kissing the top of my head. "No tears," he said and I nodded against his chest.

"We're leaving Friday, but baby, the Arizona chapter... the shit they're doing... Dragon won't have it. It goes against everything this club has stood for since Tilly died. They've had long enough to clean up and get on board."

"What happened to it being 'club business'?" My voice was muffled against his chest and the vibration of his chuckle made me want to cuddle a little closer.

"Somehow I don't think you're gonna rat me out, but I've got a vested interest in seeing Dom's face, looking him in the eye, when I ask about the way he treated you."

I nodded, my eyes riveted to the floor and the scuffed and worn toes of Archer's motorcycle boots. Heat rose in my cheeks, and I felt the blush bloom against my skin. I don't know why it still humiliated me so much, but the sting of embarrassment was still pretty sharp. Archer touched my face with gentle fingertips that smelled of orange hand cleanser and beneath that, worn metal.

We'd both gone to work that morning and my feet ached from having been on them all day and then some. One of the girls hadn't shown up for her shift, and I had called Revelator to see if I could take half of her shift and get a few extra hours in. He'd been happy to keep Noah, and so I'd stayed, picking up dinner for Archer and myself and a little dessert for Noah as Rev had said he'd feed our son dinner.

Noah was tired, his little head against my shoulder and I figured Rev had successfully worn him out for us. That made mine and Archer's life a touch easier, at least for tonight, so I reminded myself to thank him when I dropped Noah off tomorrow.

"Put our son to bed, Mel, then come to bed yourself, k?" Archer asked in that low, soothing, husky voice of his that I was becoming so accustomed to.

I nodded gently and told Noah, "Say goodnight to Archer, baby."

Noah fussed and rubbed one eye with a tiny fist before throwing himself at Archer who swept him up before I dropped him.

"G'night, Little Man," Archer said hugging him.

"Ni Daddy Atcha." Noah hugged Archer around the neck and we exchanged a look.

"Noah," I asked, having my suspicions, "did Rush and Nox tell you to say that?"

He nodded. "Unca Atcha kissed Mommy in her white dress and that makes Unca Atcha Daddy Atcha now," he said and it was a *mouthful*. I was proud of him, but I was also grateful to Rush and Nox. Archer and I had no idea how we were going to explain it to Noah, now, it seemed we wouldn't have to.

"Uncle Nox tell you that?" Archer asked and Noah nodded.

"Remind me to thank Nox," I uttered and Archer hugged Noah, bouncing him a bit and moved over to our son's crib to put him down.

"Yeah, no shit," Archer said and winced before I could say it. I closed my mouth and smiled raising an eyebrow. "Go on, I got this," he murmured and I nodded.

"Ni ni Mommy!" Noah called and I waved at him.

"Night, night, baby!"

I went into the bedroom and swung the door closed enough to hide behind it while I changed out of my uniform. I wanted to shower, but my tired, aching feet had other ideas when it came to me standing around. I hung my head and Archer, who could still see me through the crack in the door called out, "What's wrong?"

"I need a shower but I'm really tired and my feet are *killing* me."

"Shower," he ordered and I sighed.

"Yeah…"

I made it quick, resisting the urge to live under the siren's call of hot water for longer than it took to wash my body and hair. Stepping out onto the bathmat, I knew regret and with a reluctant sigh, I toweled off and slipped into the gorgeous satin and lace pajama set that Archer had gifted me the first night of our honeymoon. Of course, I hadn't had occasion to wear it since then.

I slipped out into the bedroom and raised an eyebrow, Archer had the wedding gifts piled on one side of the bed. The other he patted and told me, "Get over here."

I sat down next to him on the edge of the bed and he lifted my feet into his lap. It was an awkward position for me to maintain sitting up, so I lay back against the pillows. We'd opened the few gifts that had been labeled for the honeymoon. Aside from Rush's simple box filled with bath accessories from Hayden, there had been massage oil scented like the little heliotrope flowers from our wedding, that had been from Nox, and a little matching bottle of perfume from Everett. Mandy had sent a box of chocolates infused with things considered in some cultures to be an aphrodisiac.

Rush had sent along a tube of lubricant called 'anal eaze' which made me blush brightly and had Archer suggest we would definitely be using it in the near future, which we hadn't yet; I was still warming to the idea. The last honeymoon gift from the wedding had been from Blue and had been another of Rush's simple wooden boxes that had contained a blindfold, as well as a whole bunch of sensation causing implements. From a set of wicked metal claws Archer could put on his fingertips, to a spikey little needle-sharp wheel on a metal handle, to silk and velvet scarves as well as a little page of instructions that had been beautifully written in calligraphy.

We hadn't precisely gotten to that box either, and I'd been impressed at how much these little boxes had held, and that Archer had fit them into his saddlebags. Now, I looked dubiously at the small pile beside us and sighed.

"You insisted on the 'thank you' notes." He smiled and handed me a notepad and pen and I arched an eyebrow at him.

"It's been a long day," I said.

"Yeah and I put that frown on your face, it was the only thing I could think of to turn that frown upside down." He started to rub my aching feet which he'd placed in his lap and I let my eyes drift shut.

"That's a really good start," I said faintly and he chuckled. We lapsed into a few moments of silence and eventually, I broke it with, "Are you sure *you* have to go?"

"Melody…" his tone held an edge of warning.

I gave him a look and he almost softened in reaction to it. He raised an eyebrow in a silent bid for me to speak.

"If your word is absolute in everything, this probably isn't going to work. I'm allowed to have misgivings and feelings about this."

"No one said otherwise, baby," he said pressing in a painful spot on the sole of my left foot that very nearly made me yelp. He instantly eased up on the pressure with an apologetic look.

"You may not be saying it, but you're certainly toeing the line of you're going to do it because reasons and fuck what I think," I said unhappily.

Archer frowned. "Hey, did I say that?"

I searched his face. "No," I admitted. He hadn't, not in so many words, but the feeling came across just the same.

"I'm doing this for me, but also for you and for Noah," he said softly. "The shit ain't right, it's in our by-laws and they're fucking up big time. It's as much for the good of my brothers and holding their chapter of this club together as it's anything."

I could see the war in his eyes, his loyalties divided. On the one hand, he had ties with the Arizona chapter, ties that were forged in blood, tears, and *years* spent with them. He'd served time with them and had done countless things with them and for them. They were his brothers, but so too were the brothers here, in his new chapter, where he now lived.

"So what you're saying, without saying it, is that the club is the thing and the Arizona boys are straying too far from that?"

"Yeah, that's what I'm saying, but I won't go into any more detail than that."

I nodded, pressing my lips together. "That I find to be fair."

He nodded and looked thoughtful. "I promise to work on some things; I don't need you feeling like you can't talk to me, or that I'm completely unreasonable. I know I can be bull headed, Mel..." He looked down at his work roughened hands where he pressed his thumbs gently into the aching, tender flesh of my foot. "I'm working on things."

"I know you are," I said and felt my eyes grow glassy. I think I was beginning to love Archer for real. This welling and sudden outpouring of emotion at his fragile words of truce were certainly evidence of that. "I appreciate it, more than I can possibly express, and I guess I'm just having a little separation anxiety is all."

He looked at me, freezing, and searching my face carefully. "I didn't think about that, I'm sorry."

Archer wasn't the kind of man to apologize lightly, so that, more than anything, told me just how much he had changed and was trying since coming out to the mother chapter. I spoke it out loud as much for me as for him, "It scares me. The last time a man I loved got onto his bike and drove away, it was the last time I ever saw him."

"I promise you, I'm coming back."

"In one piece," I demanded and he smiled.

"All my pieces intact," he agreed.

"Good."

He smiled and moved on to my other foot saying lightly, in a much-needed change of subject, "Grab that one over there; I'm almost afraid of what Rush went and gave us."

I smiled and pulled one of the largest wrapped boxes across the bed toward me. "If it's something insane, I reserve the right to smack him without getting penalized for disrespecting a brother."

Archer laughed, and I tore into the paper, eyes growing wide. The tube of anal lube had been addressed to me, this, however, was addressed to Archer and it was a *beautiful* wooden chess set, raised with little drawers on all four sides. Two sides held the light and dark pieces, and the other two, carved light and dark checker coins. It was beautiful, and so detailed. I looked up at Archer.

"I had no idea you played chess," I murmured.

"Used to play with Grind. Nox has been upping his game though. Dragon and Doc both play too. I'll be teaching Noah, but I'll start with the checkers." I smiled and thought about the photos I would certainly be taking of the biker and the small boy playing over the beautiful wooden board.

"That one is from Rush, too, addressed to Noah."

I pulled it closer and unwrapped a handmade Jenga set that'd been put together from many different shades of woods. For a simple stacking game, it was awfully sophisticated looking and beautiful. Rush didn't do anything half assed when it came to his craft.

"I see a game room in our future," Archer uttered.

"What else could he possibly make?"

"Backgammon, cribbage, Chinese checkers; hell, I've seen him make a wooden battleship board and he was still building a Monopoly board; he was just trying to figure out how to get the cards and money to match the classier wood setup."

I laughed. "Seems like it's an awfully expensive use of wood."

"Most of this was made from scraps, believe it or not. He doesn't let anything go to waste and he has a lot of wood in his shop that he literally just went out into the woods and picked up random chunks and fallen limbs to make shit out of."

I shook my head. "He's wasted as a mechanic," I murmured. "He should be making a living at his woodcraft."

"I've said the same thing, but you know Rush." Archer lifted a shoulder in a shrug and I nodded.

I smiled, a lot of the rest of the gifts were things that belonged in a house, not the small one-bedroom apartment we were in. From Ghost and Shelly, we'd received a beautiful full set for a bathroom –shower curtain, bath mats, towels, soap dispensers, toothbrush holder – you name it. It was all very beautifully done in varying shades of purple and lavender and I couldn't wait to have a place to put them all. For now, I simply piled them neatly on top of one of the bins that had things in it that Noah and I weren't using daily.

"Oh, hey, this one is from Nox to you."

I opened it to find a beautiful little box, maybe twelve by fourteen or sixteen inches. Nox did some woodcraft with his twin, but I could tell. This may have come from Nox's mind but it was Rush's execution and more than made up for the honeymoon gift. It had little pockets and places and they were for things like Noah's first tooth along with jewelry or what have you. There were places for other, subsequent children's milestones and the whole thing was a bit overwhelming to me. I set it down in my lap and Archer rubbed a gentle hand up and down my shin.

"You okay?"

"Your brothers certainly know how to do it, don't they?"

"Yeah, yeah they do."

"Okay, I don't know that I should do anymore tonight, I'm gonna cry for real if I do."

Archer chuckled. "You're tired. You get more emotional when you're tired, I've noticed that about you."

I nodded, I couldn't be mad at him for making astute and accurate observations. Even if the way he said it did come off as just a little bit sexist.

We went to bed, and even though it wasn't our first night sharing the bedroom in the apartment, it still felt strange. I was so used to sleeping in this bed alone. I had to admit, though; I felt a million times safer and slept at least one hundred times better wrapped in Archer's arms.

There was something to be said about that safe, protected feeling I got from being with a man. I know, I guess I could be sexist too, but that didn't stop it from being any less true.

26

A rcher...

Dealing with my old chapter had been tough for a number of reasons, one of which had been the loss of all respect for my former chapter's president. A dude, I had erroneously, but seriously looked up to before my time spent with Dragon's chapter. After a little more than a year under Dragon's roof, I'd picked up pretty hard that the old Arizona chapter had been doing a few things wrong.

In the beginning, I hadn't thought anything of it, chalking it up to being a dog-eat-dog world and the fact that we'd all pretty much been raised in a shitty environment. Running guns across the Mexican border didn't make no never mind, and under Dom, we'd taken his version of 'no women, no children' to mean something vastly different than what the original charter now did.

We'd figured it'd just meant *leave the women and children of our enemies out of it.* Now I knew different; after that whole mess with Dani, I'd been schooled in the actual meaning. Still, it wasn't until Melody that I fully came to appreciate and understand it.

Dom hadn't been too happy when we'd showed up. He'd been even unhappier when he'd come out of a closed-door conversation with Dragon, Trigger, and Data. It'd been agreed upon, with my personal stake on all sides, that even as road captain for the first SHMC chapter, I needed to wait this one out.

When they'd come out of the room, Dom had looked pissed, his steely gaze falling right on me.

"You fuckin' serious, bro?" he demanded.

"Yeah," I answered him grimly.

"You went and married that snatch, and now it's a big fuckin' issue how we do things? Shit, she's just a goddamned club whore! Whatever happened to 'bro's before ho's'?" he demanded. Dragon made a disgusted noise and Trigger looked like he'd just plain smelled something bad. Data remained stone-faced.

I felt my blood start to simmer and took a slow deep breath, letting it out and counting to ten like they'd made me learn in some anger management class I'd been ordered to take after an assault charge some years back. What I really wanted to do, was punch Dom in the face, but there were some things that were supposed to be left to the SAA. Throwing punches was one of 'em. I wasn't SAA, either here or back in my new home. Dom was disrespecting me, sure, but he was also hotheaded and not thinkin' too straight right about now.

"I'm gonna let that slide, but Dom, I'm telling you right now, that's the *last* time you talk about my wife an' Ol' Lady that way. You get me?" I shook my head. "Mel deserved a hell of a lot better that what you fuckwits gave her. Did you even know she had a kid?" I demanded.

"What the fuck are you talking about?" Dom demanded.

I pulled out my phone and lit up the screen to a picture of Melody and my son, Noah, playing on a picnic blanket in the park. We'd gone right before I'd left, and I'd been calling her every day, surprised to find how much I missed them both.

I used to think that Dray and the rest of them were fuckin' whipped. That the pussies on their women must have been made out of gold or some shit. When Mel had hit town, I'd learned quick that it wasn't their vaginas, but rather their hearts, and I definitely now knew the difference. It was a humbling experience.

Dom was staring at the screen like he'd never seen it before and demanded, "Who the fuck's is it?"

"Mine," I uttered and he raised his eyebrows.

"You were diddling Mel behind Grind's back?" he asked shocked.

"You ain't a dumb motherfucker, Dom. Grind is gone; that makes the boy my responsibility." I shook my head. "You knew Mel was head over heels for my fuckin' brother, when he ghosted on her. Did you think for one minute with anything other than your fuckin' dick? Did the fact that she was Grind's woman mean a damn thing to you?"

Dom had scoffed. "Grind never made nothin' official," he said.

"Maybe not," Dragon intoned, "but the last I checked, when a brother went astray, or didn't live up to his responsibilities as a man, it was his *brother's and president's* responsibility to fuckin' help him. To get him back on the path to success, not to leave him on the side of the fuckin' road. This ain't what we're about, Dom, and you fuckin' know it. I don't think there's really anything else to be talkin' about here. Archer, you good?"

"No, P. I'm not, but you know what? That's just the way it's gonna be." I turned back to Dom. "Brother, do me a solid, pull your head out of your fuckin' ass."

With that parting shot, I took myself out of my old fucking clubhouse, straddling my bike and resisting the urge to punch something. Dragon, Trig, and Data came out a few minutes later and got on their bikes. I glared at the closed door of the club from behind my sunglasses and Dragon asked me, "Any other business you got to attend to while we're here?"

"Yeah," I uttered. "Shit that should be done solo, though."

"You know that ain't how we roll," Trig grunted and I nodded.

"Yeah."

We started up the bikes and rolled out, the guys giving me the lead, seeing as I was the one who best knew where I was going. It was a small enough town that just about everybody knew where everyone else lived, they just didn't give enough of a shit to bother to go over there, except this time? I did.

It was only something like five turns to get to the street I was lookin' for and when I pulled up to the curb in front of the house, it was to Mel's mom coming out onto the front porch. I guess the noise from the bikes had gotten her attention.

"What do you want?" she called out before I could take so much as three steps in her direction.

"Just letting you know, Mel and Noah won't be coming back here; *ever*," I told her. She drew herself up, chest all puffed out and I felt myself quickly losing my temper. I bit the inside of my cheek and shook my head, saying, "Just save it, bitch. You're so damn stuck up that you lost your daughter. You missed her wedding, you're going to miss out on your grandson growing up, and you're going to miss out on more grandchildren being born. That is what it is. You did it to yourself, you and that loser judgmental bastard of a husband of yours."

She gawped at me open mouthed for a second, high spots of color on her cheeks as she drew breath and I cut her off again, "They're my family now. Mel's my *wife*, Noah's *my* son, and you come near my family, try to fuck with them in any way, it's not going to phase me none."

"Are you threatening me?" she demanded and I again shook my head.

"Nope, I'm telling you that you got two options, you can either leave us alone and maybe someday Mel will come around and let you be a part of her life again, or you can try to fuck with us and kill any chance you have at *ever* being a part of their world except for a distant bad memory. I'm not playin' and I mean what I say. I won't let you or that asshole hurt them anymore. She deserves better than a self-centered narcissistic cunt for a mother; it's just too bad you couldn't be that for her."

She really started squawking then, but I didn't give a shit. Someone needed to stand up to Mel's parents. The more she'd opened up about them, the more I wanted to just beat the shit out of something, so rather than listen to this shit, I got back on my bike and rode away. My three brothers at my back hadn't said a damn thing, the whole exchange, but they knew. I'd talked to them about it on the way here.

We stopped for a bite at the old diner Mel used to work at on the way out of town, the three of us agreeing that our business here was concluded, and it was time to go home. I think all of us were irritated enough that we just wanted to put this place as far in our rearview as possible before we crapped out for the night. Maybe it was just me, or maybe I was just projecting. Who the fuck knows?

What I do know, is that it was fuckin' late when we stopped and that we hadn't quite crossed into the next time zone, so it was later still where Mel was at. It didn't stop me from calling her though. I was beginning to worry it'd kick to voicemail when she picked up, her voice dusky with sleep as it slipped over the airwaves and made the miles left between us seem like just some kind of cruel illusion.

"Hello?"

"Hey, baby. Did I wake you up?"

"Yeah, but it's okay… wait… are *you* okay?"

"Just fine, how's our little man?"

"A holy terror today but sleeping like an angel now."

I chuckled. "What was his problem?"

"He's a toddler, heading into those terrible twos, does he need any other excuse?"

"What happened?" I asked her. "One of those – why is my kid crying? – moments?"

"He threw a full on fit at the grocery store, no reason why. Just threw himself on the floor, screaming, crying; the whole nine yards. I had to take him out, leave the cart and finally leave the store all together. It was so embarrassing! I felt horrible for the people in the store that had to listen to him, let alone the employees who had to put all the stuff in our cart back on the shelves."

"Woah, hey, that *is* bad, even for him. You get anything out of him on what the meltdown was for?"

"No. We came home, he went into his crib, screamed for like an hour while I told him 'no' that his behavior was awful, and I was having none of it, but you know, putting a one-and-a-half-year-old in time out... they don't really get it and I'm not about to hit my kid."

"No, I know, I hear you, babe. I'm sorry you had a hard day."

"Actually, the day wasn't so bad except for that."

"Hmm." I sighed, and I asked her, "You miss me?"

She was quiet for a time, and I heard her draw breath through the line. "Yes, yes I do," she said quietly. I replayed her words from our last argument in my head, *the last time the man I loved got on his bike and drove away...* I don't think she'd realized she'd slipped, but I had.

"Okay, baby. I'm sorry I woke you up. I love you and I'll let you get back to sleep."

A long silence on the other end of the phone before a tremulous, "I love you, too. Hurry home and ride safe, please?"

"You got it."

I hung up and stared into the star-scattered sky up above. I was stretched out flat on a picnic table at a rest stop. The rest of the guys were laying across the spines of their bikes, but I wanted a little distance and, at the very least, the illusion of privacy for making my call. I closed my eyes, the hard and flat surface of the table giving my muscles a good stretch, even as I felt like my bones still held a hum from the long day spent riding.

"We crashing here or we finding a hotel?" I called.

"Fuck it, why spend the money?" Data called.

"Out here suits me just fine," Dragon muttered, the coal on the end of his cigarette flaring bright.

"Might as well make it unanimous," Trigger's deep baritone filtered out through the dark.

"Right, night then," I said and settled in for a nap. We had until dawn or until some state patrol pigs rolled up on us. Either way, we weren't doing nothing illegal.

27

M elody…

"I can't wait to actually find a place and move," I was saying. We were all gathered in what we affectionately called the club's backyard, which was really just the mammoth swath of grass set inside the circular track of asphalt out back. It was *all* of the club's ol' ladies. Mandy and I were keeping a solid eye on Noah and Eden who were playing on a blanket nearby, while we all lounged in a semi-circle in the sun on chairs constructed by Rush.

The guys had, for the most part, gone on a leisure ride and we were all content to have some girl time, and to stay behind with the kids and Shelly, who was due quite literally, *any day* now.

"I am so ready for this baby to come out!" she complained for like the thousandth time and Mandy and I laughed, but it was more in solidarity. We knew *exactly* what she meant. Hayden stuck out her bottom lip and pouted.

"Doesn't look like it's going to happen for me and Reaver, but you know what? That's okay because it's still a hell of a lot of fun trying."

Every woman, from Ashton to Dani, mother and non-mother alike had to laugh at that. Ashton wrung out a washcloth and helped lay it on the back of Shelly's neck to try and keep her cool. The boys had staked a large table umbrella in the ground to give her shade, but it was still hot out, being the middle of August.

Archer had returned from his run to Arizona something like two weeks before and we hadn't spoken on it since. What we *had* been talking a great deal about was finding a house, both of us agreeing that we were totally over the apartment. One, it was too small, two, it was falling apart, three it was in a *really* shitty part of town, and four, the level of dealing, gang violence and domestic disputes surrounding us were off the charts. We didn't want Noah around it, hell *I* didn't want to be around it. It was becoming a harrowing experience just going from the front door to my car and vice versa.

"Trust me, honey… a few more months and I'll be right there with you," Mandy said patting her distended tummy. She was moving right along in her pregnancy, too.

"I don't know what's worse," Shelly complained, "the heat, the swollen ankles, the weight gain, or the having to pee because this kid wants to use my bladder as a trampoline."

"All of the above?" I suggested, adding, "I can't imagine being as pregnant as you are in this heat, I mean, it's so muggy compared to the dry heat of Arizona. I may be a sun-worshiping fool, but this is seriously taking some getting used to." I fanned myself with the catalog that Hayden had brought me full of housewares and the like. She and Reaver had gotten me a gift certificate to it for mine and Archer's wedding and I was daydreaming about filling our future house with things from it, even though we had yet to find something suitable.

"I'll be right back," Shelly said and Everett had to help her up out of her lounge chair. I winced in sympathy.

"You look so uncomfortable," Dani said with a similar look on her face that was on mine.

"This is the pits," Shelly agreed, took two steps and *sploosh!* She looked down between her legs and back up, fear and panic on her face.

"Yep! That just happened," Mandy said and pushed herself to her feet.

"Shelly, don't panic honey; it's okay," I said and was the first one to her.

"Did my water just break?" she asked, a little stunned, and looked down at her soaked sundress.

"It sure did," Mandy said.

"Oh, God! Somebody call Ghost!"

"On it," Everett declared, her cell pressed to her ear.

"Oh no, this is bad," Shelly said and I let Ashton and Hayden take her from either side to walk her to Ashton's Jeep which she had conveniently parked here out back just in case of this eventuality. Everett had her finger in her other ear as she spoke quickly to someone on the other end of the line. Mandy and I were making beelines for our kids. Dani was already there helping to pick up their toys, tossing them into a plastic bin and marching it to her shop for safe keeping.

"Shelly, I need you to calm down," Hayden was saying with some authority. I ran the blanket that Noah and Eden had been playing on ahead of them and put it on the passenger seat of Ashton's Jeep before they could help Shelly into it.

I ran back to Mandy who had Eden on her hip and was holding Noah by the hand, walking him along.

"Why Auntie Shelly scared?" he kept asking, over and over, and was getting increasingly upset when he wasn't getting an answer from any of the grownups.

"Auntie Shelly is having her baby!" I told him and he just kept craning his neck in the direction of the Jeep as Mandy and I made for our cars and the car seats.

"Why Auntie Shelly scared? Where the baby? Mamma I wanna see!"

"We gotta go to the hospital with Auntie Shelly. I need you to be a good boy and let me get you into your car seat, okay?" I started to buckle Noah in but he kept twisting and fighting to turn around and see.

"Why Auntie Shelly scared? I wanna see Auntie Shelly!"

"Noah Jeramiah Turner, sit down!" I said in my no-nonsense mommy voice after a full, almost five minutes of struggling to get him strapped in. His eyes as wide as saucers he complied and I finally got him buckled in.

Mandy was similarly having troubles, Eden crying from her car seat, her mind firmly made up that she didn't like all of the hullabaloo. Not one bit.

"Thank you," I told Noah and kissed the top of his head quickly.

"See you at the hospital!" Mandy chirped over the roof of her car and I smiled.

"See you there!"

"I hope she isn't in labor long," she said and I shrugged.

"Always hard to tell when it's the first, it felt like forever when I was in labor with Noah."

"Tell me about it!" she called getting into her car. I got into mine but our windows were rolled down, she called out, "I was in labor for something like thirty-six hours with Eden."

I winced. "Okay mine wasn't quite *that* bad, but not going to lie, my birthing experience was just awful."

Mandy's face crumbled and we started our cars. "I'm getting that story over margaritas!"

I laughed and waited for Dani who came trotting out the front of the club and got into my passenger seat. Everett climbed in with Mandy.

"Okay, I got it, we're ready to go."

Ashton and Hayden were long gone with their precious cargo when we pulled down the drive. When we were through the gate, Dani turned around and clicked the remote. The gate trundling shut smoothly behind us.

She immediately got onto her cellphone. "Yeah Aaron, you might want to head to the hospital. Yeah, her water just broke. Uh-huh. I'm sad you missed it, too! Boo for late practices. Okay, yeah. Do you need to be picked up? No? Great, okay. See you there."

Dani and I had become good friends in the beginning, secretly commiserating about what an ass Archer could be, bonding over our less than ideal encounters with the private, stubborn man. She grinned and said, "I can't wait for this."

"What?" I asked.

"Disney is like Shelly's BFF. He and Aaron are supposed to be in the birthing suite, Aaron has camera duty and he told me a long time ago that he's *always* been gay, as in he's never even seen a vagina."

I started laughing. "And his first encounter with one is going to be during the miracle of childbirth?"

"I know, right!?"

We both laughed hysterically over that for a minute, and I thought to myself, what I wouldn't pay to see the looks on their faces at the same time that I prayed for Shelly that what happened to me with Noah would never happen to her. Although with the lot of these men and the ol' ladies of the Sacred Hearts present, I didn't think there was an icicle's chance in hell.

"I'm so happy for her I think I could die," I confessed.

"So am I, but I'm *dying* to know if it's a boy or girl."

"Me too! I can't believe she and Ghost literally waited to the last second."

"Me either."

We chatted about it all the way to the hospital, and when we parked, we got out to the sound of the far-off thunder of rapidly approaching motorcycles. I got Noah out of his seat and he was twisting this way and that calling, "Daddy! Daddy! Mamma, I hear Daddy!" which made me smile. Everett and Mandy had Eden out of the car in equal time and we all headed inside.

We met Ashton, Hayden, and Shelly just inside the door. Shelly was sitting in a wheelchair panting, a light dew of sweat on her upper lip as she squeezed her eyes shut and groaned.

"Okay, here we go!" a nurse declared.

Hayden said, "I hope you have a waiting room big enough for all of us."

"How many of you are there?" she asked.

"A lot!" Dragon called, striding through the sliding doors.

"Where's my wife?" Ghost called and Shelly started screaming for him.

"Ghost! Ghost, I'm right here, oh God it hurts!"

Ghost and Disney blew past us and took up post to either side of Shelly's chair, holding her hands.

"Aaron's on the way!" Dani called and Archer found me and Noah.

"Daddy! Auntie Shelly scared." Our son reached for his father and Archer picked him up.

"She's gonna be okay, buddy. You'll see," Archer said and Noah hugged him.

"Poor Auntie Shelly!" Noah declared to a round of laughter from all of us, brother and ol' lady alike.

"Waiting room is this way, folks! Come on!" Another nurse had taken charge of the lot of us and we followed her down to a waiting room.

Noah and Eden ended up in a corner with the toys, sliding those wooden beads along the metal twisty and curvy wires. Those strange toys for infants and toddlers that just about every waiting room in every hospital or doctor's office had.

Nox was sitting with them and Archer and some of the guys had gone to raid the vending machines. We'd been sitting here a good long while. Like going on nine hours now and finally, Mandy broached the topic.

"So, what happened when you gave birth to Noah that made it so awful?" she asked.

I sighed. "First off, I was alone. My parents had me take a taxi to the hospital. So as if that wasn't bad enough, I couldn't afford anything like birthing classes, so I had no idea what to expect. First, I was told by one of the nurses that I looked too young to be having a baby. She was the *worst*. I can't even begin to describe how awful this woman was.

"I was in a lot of pain, because first time giving birth, and I kept asking her if that was normal and she basically told me to quit whining."

"Oh my God!" Dani decried.

"Yeah, if I'd been there, I would have hoofed her right in her front butt and told her to quit whining and walk it off, see how she liked it," Everett said darkly.

"Then, the doctor decided that he wanted to be home in time for dinner and that Noah wasn't coming on his schedule, so that meant I needed a C-section, which I *didn't want*."

"Are you serious?" Mandy asked.

"It gets worse. So, I'm screaming at these people, *no* I don't consent, that I don't want a Cesarean and the doctor looks at me point blank and says, 'I don't care what you want, I can write whatever I want in your chart. If I decide it's medically necessary, then it's medically necessary, now we're doing this, so I can go home.'"

Shocked silence rang out from not only the women listening, but several of the men nearby, too.

"Oh, please tell me that that shit didn't fly," Reaver said.

I nodded. "I was alone, I didn't have anyone there to look out for me, so it did... but wait; it gets worse."

"How could this *possibly* get worse?" Rush demanded, looking up from where he was playing with Noah.

"They wheel me into the OR crying and pretty much hysterical, right? They dope me up and they put up the drape and they start to cut, and I'm screaming at them that I can *feel it*, but they ignored me. I could feel just about everything. I don't know if the epidural didn't take or whatever, or if they didn't wait for it to take effect. I just don't know, but I could feel them cut me open and I could feel them pull Noah out of my body and I could even feel every poke and pull of the needle and thread as they stitched me up."

Stone cold silence, a bag of chips dropped and hit the floor and I turned to meet Archer's equally horrified and downright angry gaze. If he had been turning that look on me, I would have been terrified, but the fact that he looked that way on my behalf, it warmed something inside of me and gave me back a piece of confidence I hadn't known I was missing.

"It gets *worse,*" I uttered and Dray threw up his hands and said, "Oh come on! That's seriously not enough?"

I shook my head. "So they pull Noah out and then, they wouldn't even let me hold him. They just whisked him away without a single word. I kept crying and demanding to see my baby, but no one that was left in the OR would speak. They wouldn't even look at me. I passed out, and when I woke up, it was to find out it was six hours later and I'd basically missed every first milestone bonding moment with my son. I had no skin-to-skin contact, that I was conscious for, and I guess a nurse had helped him latch and at least get the colostrum he needed, so I even missed breastfeeding him for the first time, too."

"Oh my God," Mandy said, tears in her eyes and pulled me into a fierce hug. I hugged her back and tried not to get teary eyed myself.

"No one, not a single fucking person stood up for you? I mean, where were your parents? Your *mom?*" Revelator asked.

"My parents were furious about me getting pregnant out of wedlock, let alone pregnant by a dirty criminal biker." I held up my hands, before anyone could chastise me and said, "Their words, not mine."

Archer made a disgusted noise and came to sit down on the floor at my feet, resting his back against my chair. He put my hand on his shoulder, but not before kissing my fingertips. It was a gesture that both comforted me and lent me strength. I saw it for precisely what it was, a silent promise that nothing like that would ever happen to me again. That he wouldn't let it.

"You straight got robbed," Red-Thirteen said and pulled Dani close into his side.

"Man, I wish I knew who was who, that story totally makes a trip to Arizona worth my while. Put some fear into those heartless bastards," Reaver said.

"You're not leaving me again," Hayden said and Reaver gave her a sad sort of smile.

"I promised, and I keep my promises, but if ever there were a band of happy bastards…" he said, letting his words trail off.

"I don't disagree," Hayden murmured. "You're still not leaving me."

Reaver smiled and leaned down from where he sat on the back of her chair and kissed his wife.

"I'm not going anywhere, Doll," he said with a sort of solemn reverence and my heart ached a little for them, and their story. Hayden was still having such a hard time with what had happened, but she and Reaver were totally committed and were making it work. Sort of like Archer and me, but with far more drama involved.

The conversation turned to other things after a long, quiet, reflective and introspective lull. Archer threaded his fingers through mine where my hand rested over the warm leather of his jacket and cut and I sighed with some contentment.

I hadn't told my story fully before, and I couldn't say why now, of all the times, it had felt right to do so, but it had and I felt almost cleansed for it.

I had had one or two lessons with my camera since the return from my honeymoon at a local photography studio. Just some of the basics, a free class given by a photographer by the name of Antonio Franco.

I couldn't wait to get into the classes that had been paid for at the art school, but they didn't start until fall. This was still summer break, it being only August. Still, I had my camera with me, Nox having gone out to my car to get it for me when I'd forgotten it in all the excitement.

I took pictures in the waiting room. Candid shots for Ghost of his brothers and of the ol' ladies for Shelly. At one point, Aaron came out into the waiting room as pale as a ghost.

"How's it going?" everyone asked looking up expectantly.

"Oh, man. I don't know how you ladies do it! She is in *so much pain*."

"They give her an epidural?" Mandy asked.

"They're doing it now, which is why I'm out here, I can't stand needles."

Rev laughed. "You can't stand needles when your ol' man is a tattoo artist? You picked great there, fruitcake!"

Aaron laughed nervously. "Tattoo needles are fine, big fucking needles as long as my finger going into sensitive areas that could paralyze you for life? Not so much."

Several of the guys were laughing at Aaron, Archer among them, chuckling lightly. Even I had to smile and laugh as I snapped away, capturing his discomfort. Shelly would love it.

"Okay, they should be done. They say a few more hours yet. She's dilated but not enough. No crowning or whatever. I don't have the first clue about anything they're talking about."

"Go on, don't come back until there's a baby!" Duracell cried and a rowdy cheer went up throughout the group. I snapped a picture of Trigger cradling Ashton adoringly in his lap.

A few more hours dragged into almost eight or nine more before Shelly gave birth. We were all notified by Ghost coming out in his green hospital gown covering his tee shirt, cut, and jeans, paper booties on his feet and a surgical cap over his hair. He whipped off the cap and cried, "It's a girl!" and the waiting room erupted into rowdy cheers and applause.

I took pictures of him handing out cigars and the guys hugging and congratulating him before Everett piped up over them all and said, "What's the stats?"

"Seven pounds and nine ounces; twenty and a half inches long with all her fingers and toes and her mamma's gorgeous eyes and a full head of her daddy's hair!" he declared proudly and more cheering and applause went up.

I smiled and thus began the long procession of visitors, my camera earning me a VIP pass to the front of the line, so I could take pictures of everyone getting to meet Harmony Rose Pauley for the first time.

Shelly looked beautiful, all glowy and exhausted but just beautiful. Reaver was the first one she wanted to see.

I took all of the pictures as Reaver bent over mother and child and kissed Shelly's forehead. "You did so fuckin' good, Baby Cuz," he said, tears in his blue eyes, a match for Shelly's.

"Thanks, Big Cuz," she murmured and looked down at her beautiful baby girl. I was surprised to find that I held no bitterness or jealousy in my heart, just a pure shining happiness for her happiness.

Archer was one of the last to come visit and I had to smile as I took photos of him meeting the tiny baby, her little fingers curling around one of his thick ones as she dozed in her mother's arms.

The look of sheer longing on his face spoke to just how much he wanted this for himself, and it made me want more than anything to give it to him. Enough so, that I vowed to throw away the birth control pills I had secretly been taking as soon as I got to them. I hadn't been ready for another child. I guess I'd just needed the assurance that if I were to get pregnant again, that I would be protected, and the next time it wouldn't be anything like the horrific experience of before. I had that assurance, I had it in spades, and I couldn't help but promise with my smile when Archer looked at me over the baby's head, that our turn would be coming soon, just as soon as I could get pregnant.

I was ready now.

28

A**rcher...**

"I got him," I whispered and laid our son in his crib. Noah hadn't gotten any real sleep or naps in the hospital while we'd waited on Shelly to give birth. I was amazed at how good he'd behaved, too. As long as he'd had someone or something to play with or food, he'd done okay. He'd racked out a few times on either me or Mel, but for the most part he'd been awake, thriving on the thrum of excitement that'd been coursing through all of us since Everett had reached out with word that it'd started.

I still thought it was cool that Doc had been allowed to bring Shelly and Ghost's child into the world. I mean, he was the hospital's emergency doc, not a baby doc. I guess he'd delivered plenty of babies in his time in the emergency room though, so the hospital had allowed it. I was kind of looking forward to a day when he delivered mine and Mel's first child, but right now, something apparently needed sorting because Mel was looking down at Noah with an almost guilty expression on her face.

Her true-blue eyes glassy with unshed tears, she turned to look up at me and murmured, "I have something to tell you."

"Uh-oh," I uttered quietly, drawing her into my arms. "Nothing good ever came of a conversation that started *that* way." I was trying to be a goof, to inject some levity into the situation, pretty sure that I had a good idea of what it was she was gonna say but the expression on her face almost full on crumbled. I kicked myself and figured I should just stick to being a solid bastard, that humor had never been, and would never be, my strong suit.

I tried something else instead, having been paying more and more attention to the guys with women, trying to learn how to best handle these kinds of things, even going so far as to ask 'em questions on occasion.

I asked her, "If I promise not to be mad about whatever it is, would that help?"

She nodded, her mouth drawing down and her eyes squinting up as she tried not to cry, and I pulled her lightly into my arms, wrapping them around her and thinking to myself just how much I hated to see her cry.

"Shh; it's okay baby, whatever it is, we'll get through it. I promised, didn't I?"

"Promised what?" she asked with that heartbreaking warble to her voice.

"For better or worse, in sickness and in health, all of it. I promised and I ain't going back on that promise. I swore it, I swear it, and I mean it. Now how can I fix it?"

Melody sniffed and motioned towards the bedroom and I nodded. It wouldn't do to wake our little man up, so I struck out in that direction with my wife carefully tucked into my side. Once in the bedroom I sat down with her beside me.

"I haven't exactly been holding up my end of the bargain," she said miserably and I raised one eyebrow, pretty damn sure I knew *exactly* what it was she was talking about now.

"Oh?"

"I've been keeping on my birth control," she said miserably and I nodded carefully.

"I think I kind of knew that," I murmured. "I think I understand why, too. After that story, who would wanna get pregnant again?"

"You're not mad?" she asked, voice tremulous and I pulled her tight against me again and kissed the top of her head, choosing my words carefully.

I sighed. "Not mad at you, baby. Disappointed, maybe, but I don't think I'm disappointed with you either. I think I'm more pissed or disappointed at me."

"Why?"

"For makin' you feel like you can't be open with me for one. For two; that you had to go through something like that all alone... I can't even imagine what that was like."

"I wanted to come clean, say I was sorry. After today, I think I'm ready now."

I nodded carefully. "That's good, baby, but I'm realizing now that it was pretty unreasonable for me to just expect you to carry a child into this world when you weren't ready. I never realized how much of a commitment that was, or how much of a toll it took on your body until I saw Shelly today."

She looked at me and smiled faintly, almost carefully. "Who are you and what have you done with Archer?" she asked and I laughed lightly.

"Guess I'm just a man who finally gets it," I said, caressing the side of her face, drinking in the sight of her.

"Gets what?" she whispered, and it was like she'd stopped breathing for a second. I knew the feeling pretty well.

"What real love is; what it's supposed to be."

She nodded carefully, never breaking eye contact with me. I leaned forward and pressed my lips against hers and her eyes drifted shut. It was something else to feel the tension drain from her shoulders as she almost melted into me. I thought to myself it was high time I made this woman feel appreciated for everything she did, and being the man that I was, I really only knew one way to express myself and that was physically. I broke the kiss and said, "Let me make love to you."

Her eyes flicked open and she nodded very carefully, watching me as predator watches prey. I started at the front of her short-sleeved blouse, plucking buttons free, carefully and lightly while she breathed shallowly, watching me; waiting to see what I would do. After every button popped, I bent and placed a kiss against the newest bit of exposed flesh.

Her bra was one of those front clasp deals, so I undid that, and pushed the whole mess of fabric back off her shoulders. I was right there, so I took a nipple into my mouth, biting gently, Mel's body jerking toward me, fitting more of her breast in my mouth, her breath leaving her in a shuddering sigh, her fingers finding the ponytail holder Dani had made me to remember Grind. With deft fingers, Mel pulled it out of my hair, gripping it so it wouldn't pull. As I lavished her chest with attention, my hands found the real prize of the globes of her ass, giving them a squeeze, before I was forced to put one arm around her back to hold her to me.

I didn't remember doing it, but I was on my knees at the side of the bed, drowning in Melody, and her sweet smell of those flowers from our wedding. I watched her daub the perfume, a gift from one of the girls, behind her ear every morning and I think I was beginning to understand why. It did my heart good to know that she *wanted* to remember our wedding day. That it was, for her, a happier memory than it wasn't.

It renewed my vigor in kissing down her body, her fingers threaded through my hair and holding it back, so she could watch me. I hooked fingers into the waistband of her denim shorts and slid them around to her front, so I could work the button free and the zipper down. She kicked off her shoes for me and arched her hips, so I could take the material down her legs, sweeping her panties off right along with them.

I pressed her back to the bed, palming one of her breasts, and braced her knees open with my shoulders. I licked her pussy, sweet and musky with her arousal and let my tongue play against her clit. She arched and moaned softly and I smiled against her body, sliding one finger inside her, teasing around until I got the same response from her from my attentions to her inside.

She gasped out this beautiful little pleading moan that took the shape of my name and let me say, the struggle was real to not just get my cock out and in her. I wanted her so fuckin' bad, but this wasn't about me. It was about her, and she needed this. Needed my reassurance that I wasn't pissed at her, which how could I be? I'd let Dom and even Grind pollute my head with a bunch of garbage for far too long where women were concerned. What Melody had said on our honeymoon, about breaking cycles, and the chains of our upbringings, let's just say it applied to more than just my childhood with coked-out parents and more time spent in the system than anywhere else.

I kissed her pussy lightly, drawing on her lips, sucking at her clit like my life depended on it, but honestly, I just wanted to get her through her first orgasm so that I could play a whole other way that had every-thing to do with making her melt, and relax. I'd had to ask Blue what the fuck was with all the weird shit in the box he'd sent along on our honeymoon and he'd laughed at me, but he'd told me today, in the waiting room in his weird, quiet way and now I couldn't wait to try it out on her. See what reactions I could get.

I could tell she was getting close, her body arching provocatively, her voice a breathy gasping plea. She had this adorable habit of when she was getting ready to come of saying 'higher' as if she were being launched into the sky. I knew the feeling, but I thought it was cute as hell that she said it, probably without being aware she said it, instead of something way more traditional like, 'almost' or 'so close' or even 'yes'.

"Oh God, Archer, higher! Just a little bit higher!"

She cried out and crashed to the bed, her body shuddering, and I sat back, pleased with myself, wiping a hand over my mouth while I fucked the shit out of her with my fingers. She grabbed my wrist, to get me to stop, crying out, "Mm-mm! Mm-mm!" completely unable to form coherent words.

Jackpot! That'd been a good one. I slipped the box out from under the bed and opened it up, pulling out a length of black silk while she lay panting.

"Middle of the bed, baby. I want you face down." She groaned and complied and I used the silk to tie her wrists together above her head, securing her to the wrought iron headboard.

"Archer, what are you doing?" she asked, and I soothed her.

"Shh, you trust me, right?"

"Yes."

"Then let me do this for you, please?"

"O-okay."

She trembled slightly and I slipped the satin sleep mask out of its spot and put it over her eyes. She sucked in a breath but didn't protest or say anything. I admired the line of her body, laid out in my bed, and slipped the claws onto my fingertips, doing what Blue had suggested, and taking up a scrap of velvet in my other hand.

I lightly traced a line with my four fingertips down the length of her back. She pushed her body into the mattress, faint pink lines raising on her pale skin, a wash of gooseflesh radiating out from the marks. I glided the velvet over her flesh in the wake of the sharp sensation and watched her shudder... oh yeah. This was going to be fun.

For the better part of an hour I played with Melody, using sensation as a means to excite, torment, and soothe her until she was limp, relaxed, and just about putty in my hands. Soft things, sharp things, prickly things, cold things, warm things, the touch of my calloused fingers, the prick of the spikey wheel thing, the glide of silk, the catch of velvet; all of it coming together to titillate and inflame her senses until she was wet and ready, begging me to be inside her.

I took my time, slipping out of my clothes and laying kisses all over her body before laying myself over the top of her. I quested for a moment or two for her opening, and only when I was sure I had it, did I slip inside her, between her thighs. She was incredibly warm and close and taking her this way was tighter than any other way I'd taken her to this point.

I took my time loving her, probably way later into the night than either one of us should have been up, given that it was Sunday night leaking into Monday morning, but I didn't care. It would be worth it to be tired the next morning.

I cradled Melody close in my arms and made love to her until we were both exhausted. It was needed, it was wonderful; it most definitely brought us closer... Best weekend ever.

29

Melody…

"Yay!" I laughed with Noah and he giggled and we both clapped. It was moving day and we were picking up Noah's toys and packing them away in yet another cardboard box. The door to the apartment was open as Archer and the rest of the guys were coming and going, fixing things around the dingy one-bedroom apartment and loading out furniture, so when a shadow fell over the door, I didn't think anything of it.

"Melody Beswick?" a woman's voice, authoritative, called out into the gloom of the apartment. I looked up sharply.

"Turner, its Melody Turner… can I help you?"

"I'm Carina Washington with the Department of Children's Services, may I come in to talk to you?" My heart sank and I felt myself nodding.

"Yes, of course." I opened up my hands and Noah threw himself into my arms like he always did. I picked him up and stood. "Oof! Good Lord, Noah, you're getting too heavy for this," I uttered.

He laughed that beautiful high baby laugh and declared, "No!"

To Ms. Washington, I said, "Please come in. I apologize for the mess and lack of furniture, we just closed on a house and we're moving in today. What can I do for you?"

She stepped across the threshold, this regal, curvy black woman in a grey business suit. Her long hair flowed down her back in elegant tiny braids and her deep brown eyes sparkled with intelligence. Her quick assessment of the apartment left me feeling hollowed out, self-conscious, and pretty much gutted, but we hadn't had a choice when we'd arrived and now we did. Archer had found us a home with plenty of room and now we were moving.

"We received a call from a Mr. and Mrs. Phillip Whitmore—"

"That'd be her mother and stepfather, what sort of crazy are they spouting now?" Archer demanded from behind her, as he came through the open apartment door.

She startled and looked really unhappy about that and demanded, "And you are?"

"That would be Mr. Turner," I said and Noah reached for Archer.

"Da da!" he cried and Archer plucked my son from my arms settling him against his side before using his free arm, tucking me against his opposite side and holding me close.

"Well, Mrs. Whitmore claims that you threatened her and that Melody here is both on drugs and an unfit mother, who kidnapped Noah out from under their care."

Archer laughed, a genuine, jovial laugh and I looked up at him, blinking. "Well if it makes you happy," he said, "I'm sure Mel would be willing to submit to any drug tests you might want her to take, as for any accusations or threats? I did have a talk with Mel's mother a few weeks back and I have three witnesses that were there with me, all of 'em upstanding citizens, who will tell you I was downright civil given my history."

The woman shifted her stance and asked, "And what might that history be?"

Archer glanced down at me and his gold-green eyes radiated *'trust me'* and I did, implicitly. How could I not? He had been nothing but good to my son and I knew in my heart of hearts he would be devastated if we lost Noah. I nodded and he turned back to Ms. Washington and he told her that he was a felon, that he hadn't been in trouble since his twenties, that he loved me and my son and that he hadn't when we'd gotten here, running from the mental and emotional abuse of my family.

He told her everything and it was simply amazing, just how much he'd grown as a person, because Archer was *intensely* private. I had fully expected him to tell anyone that even remotely hinted at 'government official' to fuck right off, but here he was, trying a lot of diplomacy and I had the distinct feeling that Dragon had a hand in that.

"So, all that being said, would you like to follow us over to the new place? See where Noah will be staying and that it's a safe environment? I mean, Nox and Rush – excuse me, Landon and Logan, my twin foster brothers growing up and Noah's uncles, should actually be putting the finishing touches on babyproofing the place. I had them installing socket covers and child locks on all the cabinets before I came over here to grab Mel and the baby."

The woman blinked, an 'are you serious?' look on her face as she furiously scribbled notes onto a yellow legal pad balanced on one of those metal clipboards meant to house paperwork.

"I somehow get the feeling you were expecting me to call," she said and I nodded.

"Like Archer said, it was the reason I ran and tried to find Noah's biological father. I didn't know he'd died and when I got here and explained the situation, Archer didn't want to turn us away. He made it work, and we've worked very hard to get us out of this one-bedroom as soon as possible."

"And the getting married?" she asked still looking flummoxed.

"It was the best thing for Noah. This way, I could put him on my insurance and Mel, too. Plus, the tax breaks and the like weren't going to hurt for getting us into a house sooner rather than later."

"There were more reasons to, than to not," I murmured.

She nodded, noting things down as we said them, and it was Archer who said, "Never counted on falling in love with her for real, but I did. I'm glad I did, too. Noah needs a father and I want to be that guy." He looked down at me and I raised myself up on tiptoe to kiss him, a quick kiss that was heartfelt and not at all for show.

"This the last box?" he asked gruffly and I nodded. "Okay, Little Man! I gotta give you back to your mom, you ready to go?"

"Yah!" I took our son from Archer and he hefted the box.

"Go on, ladies, I'll be right behind you."

Ms. Washington followed me down to the car and spoke to me while I strapped Noah carefully into his car seat.

"Truthfully, I'm a little blown away," she was saying. "I've never in my twenty-three years of social work, come across a case like this. Usually, I get a call like this and I come out expecting the worse and find it."

"Well, there's a first time for everything," Archer said, shoving the last box into the back-hatch area of my car and shutting it tight.

"I guess so! There is one thing, can you tell me about this emergency room visit back in —"

"Oh, you don't have to look for the date, I remember *that* all too well," I said darkly.

"Scared the hell out of her," Archer said laughing.

"What happened?"

"I came through the door on my way home from work, just in time for Little Man to run smack into the strike plate on the bedroom door."

"I was in the kitchen trying to get some dinner ready and Noah was just being a big ball of energy running around the apartment. I told him to stop, but he was being a willful little boy and sure enough, he tripped over his own feet and went head first into the door jamb."

"We took him right to the emergency room, and he got two stitches. If he's anything like Grind, there will be a lot more than that ahead of him just growing up."

I groaned. "Please don't even put that out there."

"Eh, Grind was always active and doing stupid shi- 'cuse me, stuff when we were growing up. Almost got bit by a diamondback when we were nine, the damn fool."

"Right, well, I'll follow you," the social worker said and we both nodded. Archer rode, I drove, and Ms. Washington followed us in her much newer state vehicle over to our new home.

It was a two-story, three-bedroom with a large family room and a garage. It was painted a lovely shade of blue, bordering on lavender with white trim and a grey shingled roof. The front porch was broad and a wrap-around style without actually wrapping around, and the front lawn was so green, a large oak taking up a good sized chunk of it where Rush and Nox were busy stringing up an old tire.

"Oh my God, you guys, no!" I called out as I was getting out of the car and they both looked over grinning like they'd just been caught with their hands in the cookie jar.

"What?" Rush called. "He ain't gotta use it now, we just thought it'd add character to the place!"

"No!" I called back and they were laughing at me, their laughter dying when Ms. Washington came walking up the sidewalk. The twins exchanged a look. They knew a social worker when they saw one.

Both of them came slinking over and Nox asked, "What's the deal?"

"My parents," I muttered darkly. "They called to let child services know I'm a drug addict and a horrible mother."

The twins couldn't help themselves, they started laughing, and I'm pretty sure Ms. Washington heard the whole thing.

She went on a tour of the house with me and Archer, noting things down, and nodding. She seemed impressed with the childproofing and Noah's room which had been unbelievably kitted out thanks to Rush's amazing wood working skills. Our house had a long way to go, but Rush had nearly thrown a fit when we said we were going to buy furniture, saying he'd much rather build it. The only thing he would hear of us buying furniture wise, was a couch, mattresses, and lamps.

"You built this?" she asked of Noah's bed, the crib having been tossed in the dumpster out back of the apartment.

Rush grinned with pride. "Noah's gonna be a car guy, just like his dad, huh?" Rush asked and Noah shouted "Yah!" Rush had built Noah his very own race car bed, and it was nothing short of amazing and as safe as could be.

"It's all one piece, no screws or nails for him to get scratched on and no joining pieces to crush little fingers or toes."

I rolled my eyes. "I'd better have another boy at the rate you guys are going," I said.

"Nah, we can totally turn your girl into a race car lovin' – and I'm not going there," Nox finished at my spectacular mommy death glare.

"I already feel like I'm on my own here, but if she likes race cars then far be it from me to say otherwise, still, I will hold out for mermaids and princesses like when I was growing up."

The guys chuckled and laughed and Ms. Washington was even smiling. I took that as a good sign.

"I think I've seen everything I've needed to. I'm going to make a note in your file that it appears your mother and stepfather are attempting to use the system to harass. I'd like to make one additional follow up visit in the next three months, if that's alright."

"Of course," Archer and I agreed at once.

"Okay, y'all have a nice night then, and congratulations on your new home."

"Thank you," we both said in unison again and laughed at each other.

"Noah say buh-bye?" I asked and he grinned his cheeky grin and waved bye-bye to the woman. We saw her out and the moment she was gone, I very nearly sagged with relief.

"Do you think we're going to be okay?" I asked apprehensively.

The three guys all looked at each other and Archer sighed. "I think so, but with these government types, it's always hard to tell."

"All you can really do is jump through their hoops and do everything they tell you to do and hope for the best," Nox said and tried his best to smile. I sagged and sighed deeply.

"I'm terrified," I admitted and Archer pulled me into him, wrapping his arms around me.

"Don't be, doesn't matter what it is, we'll get up and over it. I promise."

"I wish you would have just left them alone," I said, breathing in the smell of clean laundry and Archer through his soft tee shirt.

"Wasn't happening, I drew a line in the sand and they've crossed it. Now it's seriously war. I don't want you to contact them, I don't want them to ever see our children again. They had one shot, they fucking blew it. Now let's see how they like dealing with the consequences of their actions."

"That's just it, they *don't*. They turn their consequences into *my* consequences. I'm the one that has to deal with the fallout."

"Not anymore, baby. I promised I'd protect you and our family and that's exactly what I'm going to do."

"The only thing you can do is try not to think about it," Rush said and I nodded.

"Let's try to put as much of our house together before people start getting here, huh?"

I nodded. There was supposed to be a barbecue celebrating our first house and there was supposed to be more things moving in from various other places. Most of it purchased brand new. Archer had actually saved quite a bit of money for the eventuality that he would one day buy a house, and when he'd made an offer on this one, it was almost too good to be true. He'd had well over three quarters of what was required to purchase, but had offered them half down, that way there was money to furnish the place.

Well, that had mostly been the plan, but then Rush happened when it came to things like headboards, dining room tables and chairs, coffee and end tables, dressers, curio cabinets, and whatever else you could think of. Except it turned out that he actually had almost all of it made... it was just sitting in storage.

"Okay, I gotta go meet up with the guys with the truck, we'll see you soon."

Rush gave me a quick hug, squeezing me between himself and Archer and I nodded. Nox was supposed to keep Noah entertained while I fixed up the master bathroom off what was supposed to be mine and Archer's bedroom.

"See you on the other side of this mess," Archer told me and kissed me quickly.

The social worker had been a setback, taking up a good two hours that were meant to be devoted to actually moving, but it couldn't be helped. Not if I wanted to keep our family together. I had the bathroom done with everything Shelly and Ghost had gifted us at the wedding in practically no time. I moved on to putting the majority of mine and Archer's clothes away in the walk-in closet.

Rush had let us pick whatever furniture we'd liked out of his dragon's hoard. He was paying a ridiculous amount for storage at a place and it was now Dragon's mission to clean up the central bay out at the shop so that Rush could, in effect, expand. It was spring cleaning for The Sacred Hearts' home chapter, just a few months too late for spring, but it was time for a new beginning.

In more ways than one... I thought to myself.

30

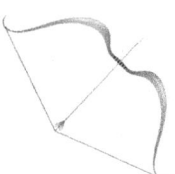

Archer...

"I thought he'd never go down," she murmured and sighed, collapsing back against me lightly. I put my arms around her as we watched our son in his brand-new bedroom, sound asleep in his very first big-boy bed.

"A lot of excitement," I said and knew contentment.

"Mm," she hummed, a noise of agreement.

"Think you've got it in you to christen the bedroom?" I asked and she laughed lightly.

"I think, maybe, I can manage."

I chuckled and lightly nipped the side of her neck which caused her to giggle. I turned her out into the hall and lifted her in my arms. She kissed me, and I made quick strides to our new bedroom.

I stripped her quickly and shucked out of my own clothes double-time. I wanted skin on skin, I wanted inside of her something fierce, and I wanted to claim her body in every way possible as completely, one hundred percent *mine*.

I captured her mouth with mine as she crawled back up onto the bed, kneeling on it as I stood beside it to reach my mouth, kissing me with a fierce passion that told me that what I had in mind was going to work.

She wrapped her hand around my shaft and stroked with a firm grip, a slow steady rhythm that'd like to drive me nuts; my hips unconsciously rocking into her grip. She broke our kiss, a glint in her true-blue eyes that I recognized by now and I voiced my pleasure at going right along with what she had in mind, "Oh God, yeah baby; do it."

She lowered her mouth to my dick and sucked me and I tilted my head back, closing my eyes; just concentrating on the feel of her mouth on me. She felt un-fucking-believable, hot, wet; silk, wrapping me in soft-ness, her tongue a gentle velvet caress along the underside of my cock, her fingers gentle where they massaged my balls. I lowered my head and swept her hair into a ponytail so I could watch her. The sight of those blue eyes, a deep, dark sapphire with her arousal as she looked up at me, my dick disappearing between those peaches and cream lips… I almost lost my load right then and there.

It took everything I had in me to hold still and not face fuck her; I wanted to thrust so bad and eventually the need overrode my good sense to the point that I pulled gently back on her hair. She disengaged her mouth from my dick with a sexy little pop and I let go of her only so I could order her, "Turn around, on your knees, I want that pussy."

She gave me a sexy as sin, carnal look, and turned around, shaking that ass at me, bending low to the fucking mattress, face down, ass up and I loved what I saw. Her pussy was glistening with her desire, wet and ready, and her little asshole was begging for some attention too. I glanced to the nightstand, to make sure it was in reach and satisfied we were close enough to it, I gave my woman my full attention.

I shoved my cock into her, hard and deep, pulling back on her hips and groaned when she ground herself tightly against me.

"Fuck me, baby," I said and stood still, letting her work herself back and forth, sliding along my dick, the sounds we made, full on porno quality.

I'd been getting into ass play with her slowly over the last few weeks. Starting out easy by teasing the entrance to her forbidden door with my thumb. Then breaching her entrance with it, I'd successfully worked my way up to two thick fingers, then three but tonight I think I was going for the gold.

I snatched the tube of anal lube off the nightstand and squeezed some onto my finger, teasing her ass with a gentle touch, distributing the half cream, half gel consistency generously. Melody moaned and I smiled. I didn't give her as much lead time before I slipped a finger past the first, tight ring of muscle, but I waited patiently for her to get used to it before I started thrusting again, so she didn't have to do so much work.

I slid that one finger in and out of her ass carefully, gently, getting her ready to take the second and she was like a cat in fucking heat, loving it, arching her back, her pussy strangling the hell out of my cock as she got ready to come for the first time.

When I introduced the second finger, I could tell she was really, really fucking close, and by the time I started to work the third in, she was coming all over my dick. Snatching a pillow from the head of the bed on her left, biting into it to muffle her cries so she wouldn't wake our sleeping boy.

I rode out her orgasm and fought not to come myself as she milked my cock with her muscle spasms, when she fell limp to the bed with satisfaction, I pulled out of her pussy. I laid a strip of lube along the top of my cock with my free hand, my other hand still working back and forth and when I thought she was ready, I took out my fingers and pressed myself at her tight hole.

She cried out, and I soothed her, "Shh, it's alright, baby, do what I told you honey, push out. Oh yeah, that's it!"

She did what I told her and the resistance eased. I slipped into her slowly, inch by inch and when my body met hers and I was totally inside her, only then did I take my eyes off her shoulders and look. I never fucking lasted long when it came to this, it was just so fucking *hot*.

"You good?" I asked and she nodded.

"Yes!" she gasped.

"Good, good. I'm gonna move, baby. Slow and easy. You tell me if I need to stop, okay?"

"Mm-hmm!"

I pulled back slowly and eased back in, until I was able to pick up speed. Mel had gone silent, her face pressed to the comforter and pillow, her eyes glazed, and I could feel why. I'd found that sweet spot, had done things right, and I could feel her pussy pulsing along the underside of my dick as she came, one long almost continuous orgasm. Her body fluttering, her pussy flooding wet. Made me almost regret not putting on a condom. I could have stripped that shit off and gone back to fucking her pussy for my finish.

Fuck it though, this was heaven and I didn't want to give it up so soon, but when she started to moan and gasp like she was in the throes of the most desperate pleasure she'd ever experienced in her life, at my hands, I couldn't hold off if I wanted to. I thrust into her deep and felt myself spill, shooting jet after jet deep into her ass. I groaned and tilted my head back as the sensations wracked my whole fucking body, withdrawing from her gently, and slowly, careful to do it before her system ran out of endorphins.

"Oh my God," she gasped out. "I should have let you do that a lot sooner."

I smacked her ass, rubbing away the red handprint as soon as it started to form and grinned. "I told you."

"Okay, but I'm not done, we need to clean up and go for a round two. I want more of you," she said and I laughed a little to myself.

"You can be as greedy as you want, baby. I love fucking you."

"Good," she sighed and straightened up slowly, "because I love it when you fuck me."

She turned around and wrapped my long ponytail that was resting over my shoulder around her hand, tugging my mouth down to hers and I fucking loved it when she got demanding. Wasn't long before I was hard again, but I needed to wash up before I could tap that pussy again.

"Shower, now, you little minx," I growled against her mouth and gave her another playful slap on her ass, urging her in the direction of the bathroom.

"Yes, sir!" she exclaimed and I almost liked the sound of that so much I considered making it a regular thing. Right now, though? Right now, I wanted to clean up, clean my woman up, and as tired as we both were, I wanted another round.

31

Melody…

Archer led me into the bathroom and started the shower. We spent almost as much time making out as we did cleaning up, and boy was it necessary to clean up. I was drenched from the waist down and as amazing as the sex felt, the aftermath? Not so much. While I didn't feel gross or dirty, I just felt… messy. I don't know how to describe it.

Archer let down his hair and held it back from his face as we kissed. He soaped his body quickly and rinsed, washing between his legs thoroughly and twice. I stepped under the spray to take my turn and found myself bent over, hands pressed to the shower wall as he introduced himself back into my vagina.

I was so not complaining, the only thing I feared was slipping on the wet tub bottom, but Archer wrapped one strong arm around my waist securely and promised, "I've got you," so I let go. I let him have me and soon, the feral sounds were pouring from my throat in carefully choked off whimpers, so I wouldn't wake Noah.

Archer was much more controlled, much less frenzied this time around and eventually, he ordered, "Touch yourself, baby. I wanna feel you come around my cock."

I let one hand slip from the wall and found my clit with pruning finger-tips, slicking them in wetness that had nothing to do with the water pouring down my back and over my body. It didn't take me long to start coming around Archer and when I did, I felt him come with me. I could always tell, he lost his rhythm when he did, thrusting in deep, hips jerking as he tried his best to keep both of us rolling. I shuddered hard in his arms and we both stood gasping, seeing stars.

"That's my girl," he murmured proudly and kissed my back. I straightened slowly, his arm clamped across my body tightly to make sure I was solid, that I was good. We washed up for real this time and shut off the water, just as it started to grow tepid.

"You okay?" he asked gently as we were toweling each other off.

"Yeah, sorry. Mind just wandering back to the social worker lady," I confessed.

He sighed and pulled me into the cover of his hard body, kissing the side of my neck. "I have a good feeling about it. I think she was suitably impressed, plus, they ain't got no grounds to take Noah away from us. We ain't doing everything but what's right by him."

"I know, but I'm still scared."

"Don't be, we've got this."

I huddled into his embrace and nodded, taking comfort from his stoic strength where the matter was concerned.

"I love you, Melody. I love Noah, too. I'd fight to the bitter end for the both of you," he said against my hair and I closed my eyes.

"I love you, too," I said. A deep, welling of emotion filling me out from the center.

"It's going to be fine, baby. I promise you."

I nodded against his chest and looked up at him.

"Let me braid your hair?" I asked.

He blinked and nodded, the request taking him off guard.

"Sure."

I grabbed a hair brush and we went back to the bed. I knelt up behind him and began to brush. It was a favorite thing of mine to do. Something simple and mechanical, something that was enough to concentrate on that the disquiet in my mind would settle. I brushed out Archer's long, long hair, longer than even my own now, until it was very nearly dried. He sat so patiently, and I realized that his eyes were closed, and he was almost in as a meditative state as I was.

I smiled, and simply let myself feel good, to take pleasure in giving a simple pleasure to this man who worked hard to support his family; who had taken my son and me in without a second thought. Did we have a rough beginning? Sure, but we'd found each other in the chaos, and I wouldn't trade that for anything. I felt stronger than I ever had before, and that was because of Archer. That was because I felt *supported* for probably the first time in my life.

"I love you," I uttered quietly as I used the special hair tie at the end of his braid, the one he'd said Dani had made for him, to remind him of Grinder. I loved it, the simple gold disc set with a tiger's eye semi-precious gemstone at its center.

Archer chuckled, easing himself onto his back and pulling me down to lay on his chest before saying, "I told you I'd make you fall in love with me, didn't I? I guess I just never figured you'd make me love you first."

We kissed and I sighed, settling against him, letting my fingertips trace patterns across his super warm skin. I loved that about him, that he was always warm to the touch. I closed my eyes and felt more centered than I had before, finally able to let my worries go for a night. Despite the setback that morning, it really had been a perfect first night in our new home. A little sour, to enhance the sweet... wasn't that almost always the way?

32

A rcher...

The new house still felt new, despite having lived in it more than a couple a weeks, hell, it might have even been a couple of months now; I'd lost track. When I pulled up and into the garage, it was with a bit of a sinking feeling. The state social worker woman's car was parked at the curb, and I felt irritation rise to the surface. A feeling I pretty quickly shoved back down so that I could face what was coming.

Very rarely, when the state got involved, did good things happen. In fact, with the way I'd come up? I can't ever remember *anything* good coming of it.

"Archer?" Melody called and I rounded the corner into our dining room to find her, along with the black social worker lady, and Noah sitting at the table. Noah was in a high chair that Rush had built for us when it was obvious that the new dining room table and chairs wasn't going to work for our little man until he put on another growth spurt or two.

"Hey, baby." I kissed my wife. "Hey, Little Man." I kissed the top of his head. "Ma'am," I greeted the social worker with a nod. She smiled at me, and I took off my jacket and cut, hanging it from the back of my chair.

"As I was telling Melody, neither one of you have anything to worry about. You are both exemplary parents from everything I have seen, even given the somewhat unorthodox lifestyle," she said, indicating my jacket and cut with an inclination of her head. She seemed regal, but what was more, she seemed respectful, which was a fuck of a lot more than I could say for Mel's parents.

"That's good to know," I said dropping heavily into my seat. It'd been a long day and I felt like cutting to the chase. "So what happens now?"

"Now, I finish my report, which will be nothing short of glowing, and my supervisor contacts the complainants and tells them rather politely to go fly a kite." I blinked and laughed, I couldn't help myself. She'd just caught me well off guard.

"Oh yeah? How's that?"

"Well, for one, we'll be telling them their accusations have been found to be boundless, but I warn you, with people as zealous as your mother and stepfather seem to be, this might not be over. They have the ability to file a complaint through family court, but it will, more than likely, get tossed right out. I can't imagine a judge granting your parents' custody when there is absolutely *nothing* suggesting that it would be in the best interests of the child."

Melody sank into a seat across from the lady while I sat in stony silence… *and there it is,* I thought to myself, *the other shoe just dropped.*

"You mean that even after you've investigated, after you've come out here twice and seen for yourself that Noah is perfectly healthy and happy, they can still try to take him away from me? Drag me to court, and make us go through legal proceedings?"

"Yes and no," the woman said. "They can file suit in family court, in effect, suing you for custody of Noah, and there will be a hearing, but they have absolutely no grounds and the judge will most likely toss it out right on its ear. I would be happy to testify on your behalf, too. They don't have any legal leg to stand on. Noah is your son, and you've done nothing but what's in his best interest since the day he was born according to everything I have both seen for myself and read. I wouldn't worry, Melody."

"Think we should get a lawyer?" I asked.

"Couldn't hurt," the woman said, "though I doubt you would need one. If your parents were serious about this, they would definitely have one."

Mel got up abruptly and went into the kitchen, bracing herself against the counter by the sink, looking out into the backyard. Everything about her hunched shoulders said how painful this was for her. It made me doubly if not triply determined to do everything in my power to protect her and Noah both.

"Honestly, at this point, I wouldn't borrow trouble. I would just wait and see what happens."

"We're not borrowing trouble, trouble is already here," I said with a tired sigh. "Thank you for warning us, I'll make sure we're prepared."

The woman nodded and stood up, "You all take care, now. Hopefully, I never see you again, but if I do, know that I'm on your side." She bent down and shook Noah's hand. "It was very nice to meet you, Noah."

He grinned at her and she and I shared a chuckle. I heaved myself to my feet and saw her out. She gave me a couple of her business cards at the door.

"I mean it, if trouble comes up, don't hesitate to call. You have a very sweet family you've built for yourself, Mr. Turner."

"Thanks again, Ms. Washington," I said and let her out our front door.

I tucked the cards into my wallet and went back into the kitchen. Mel was still at the counter, head bowed, shoulders shaking with silent tears. If she were so dead certain that this was going to be the course of action her parents were going to take, then I needed to find us the best family lawyer I could. It just seemed like good sense.

I held my wife in our kitchen while she cried bitterness and hurt onto my tee and I didn't do anything to stop her. I just stood there, impervious by all accounts, when secretly, all I could think to myself was how much I'd grown to hate it when my wife cried.

If anyone causes one of these little ones – those who believe in me – to stumble, it would be better for them if a large millstone were hung around their neck and they were thrown into the sea.

I don't know what made me think of that particular bible verse right then, but I knew one thing… it may be an old-fashioned form of retribution, but I damn sure had a few ideas on how to modernize it. I may not be God, but I damn sure was a force to be reckoned with.

Just try it, I thought at Mel's wretched bitch ass mother. *Just try it and see what happens.*

33

Melody...

Two weeks had passed since Carina Washington's last visit and I was walking on eggshells every time I went and checked the mail. Today wasn't exactly an exception to that. I was with Dani, Everett, Ashton, and Hayden and we were all painting my living room. Sheets covered all of the furniture and carpets and when I bent down to put my roller through some paint to finish attacking the wall, I stood up and Dani burst out laughing.

"What did you do!?" she cried and I frowned.

"What do you mean?" I looked down at myself and what she was pointing at and found the entire front of my tee shirt wet from my right breast.

"Oh my God!" I cried.

"What's the matter?" Ashton asked and Hayden frowned.

"I think I leaked," I said in disbelief.

"*Leaked?*" Dani asked.

"Leaked," I reiterated and had to roll my eyes at the three of them. "Leaked! As in my boob just leaked as in I need a pregnancy test!" I cried.

All three of them started screaming excitedly and began to jump up and down while my mind started to work furiously.

"Nope, no dollar store pregnancy test, we're taking you to the doctor and are having it done right!" Ashton declared and I felt myself blush.

They did, too. They made me drop everything and took me to the doctor, but unfortunately they were so close to closing all I could do was pee in a cup for them.

"No worries, honey, a day or two and you'll have the results in the mail," the nurse assured me and I smiled, said thank you, and tried to put it from my mind. I couldn't believe it would take a day or two to get results from a pregnancy test! I guess gone were the days of same day results… *Thank you ever so much, Obamacare.*

Now, here it was, three days later, my living room was done and I was sitting at my dining room table waiting for Archer to get home. Two letters in front of me… both the best and the worst possible news on the same frickin' day.

I watched Noah play in his playpen nearby and listened to the front door open. When Archer came in, he frowned, and asked, "What's up?"

"You want the good news or the bad news first?" I asked softly.

"Gimme the rough stuff first," he said and tearfully, I handed him the letter stating we were indeed being sued for custody of our son. Archer read over it carefully and gave a one shouldered blasé shrug.

"This is why I got that lawyer on retainer. It's going to be fine," he said tossing it on the kitchen counter. He opened the fridge and got out a beer and looked over to me. "What's the good news?" he asked.

I stood up and went to him, looked him in the eye, took a deep breath and said, "I'm pregnant."

Crash! His bottle of beer slipped from his grasp and hit the floor shattering, before I could even jump he had me up in his arms and his mouth fiercely pressed over mine. My tears borne of fear and frustration disappeared, instantly replaced with ones of joy at just how happy Archer was. He sat me on the counter and started working at my jeans.

"Noah!" I gasped quietly.

"Is in the living room, can't see us, is safe in his playpen, and baby, I'll only take a minute – or wait – can we still have sex or do I gotta wait nine months?"

I laughed and dragged his lips to mine and kissed him, he worked at the front of his jeans and sprang free of them almost instantly. I raised my hips so he could get mine off and when he dragged me to the edge of the counter, I parted my knees willingly.

His reaction to the news made me love him even harder, despite how nearly frozen with terror my heart was. I knew, I just *knew*, that this time would be different. That this time I wouldn't be alone in the delivery room. That this time, if I said something about my body, that Archer would defend me to the last, and that he would only sway if my life or the life of our child were in danger.

He slipped into me and I arched, wiggling my hips to take him in all the way. It was a slightly awkward angle, against the counter like this, but we made it work, and God did it feel good. He was right, he didn't last very long, but then again, he didn't need to and I didn't need him to either. The timer was about to go off for Noah's chicken nuggets.

LATER THAT NIGHT, we lay in bed together and Archer asked, "If it's a girl, what do you want to name her?"

"I don't know, honestly... I'm only a couple of months along according to the letter. I hadn't really thought about it."

"Did you get sick? Is that how you knew?"

I laughed slightly. "No, we were painting the living room and I leaked."

"What? Like pee?"

I laughed, high and bright. "No, that comes *much* later," I said, "Breastmilk, I leaked breastmilk. I bent over and the next thing I knew, my whole bra and shirt were wet."

"Huh, more fun things I should try," he murmured, copping a feel.

"You can be so crude sometimes," I laughed.

"Mm, you like it."

"Like it better if you'd put your mouth to work doing something other than talking," I both teased and hinted.

"Why, Mrs. Turner, are you horny?"

"Hmm, a little bit," I confessed.

"Yeah?" he asked, kissing along the side of my throat, his hand drifting up along the outside of my thigh.

"Mm-hmm, quickies are nice and all, but I kind of figure that was just a preview of coming attractions," I murmured.

"Oh, you'd be right on that account, baby. You'd be so right..."

He kissed me for real then, and I pulled him close. I loved how his powerful arms caged me, how his warmth filled me, and how his body fitted to mine. I loved how he loved me, and how no matter if it was a five-minute quickie in the kitchen, or an hour-long lovemaking session in the bedroom, Archer gave it his all.

I giggled, and wrapped my legs around his hips, kissing the side of his neck, holding him close, until the laughter faded into desperate moans and I gave over to simply feeling and being in my husband's arms.

"I love you," I whispered in his ear as we both came, and he kissed my shoulder reverently and murmured, it back.

"I love you, too, Melody. God, I love you, too."

34

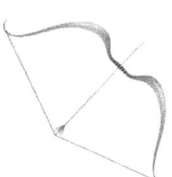

A rcher...

"Dude, why didn't you tell us about this sooner?" I sat back in my chair and sighed.

"I probably should have, but you know how I get," I said frowning.

It was Friday, and we were all sitting around in church, Dragon was nodding and looking thoughtful.

"So you think it would help, having some of the more upstanding guys without records there?"

"Yeah, I figured it couldn't hurt. They might not even be needed. Just dress nice and sit behind us kind of a thing."

"I think this is a job for our Wonder Women, don't you?" Ghost asked and I nodded in his direction.

"Carina Washington, the social worker assigned to us says that the more of a support network we have behind us, probably the better we'll fare."

I swept eyes around the table and honestly didn't expect any of them to offer up. I mean, I'd at least rubbed every single last one of them the wrong way at least once in the last year, but I guess the lessons were just going to keep on coming, because Doc was the first one to speak up.

"Count me in," he said.

"Long hair might throw 'em off but my record as a Marine won't. May have a history of drug use, I admit that, but nobody really knows about it. It ain't on paper anywhere. I'll be there, too," Trigger said.

"Count me in," Ghost said.

Rounds of 'yeah', 'yep', and 'I'll be there' went around the table, the only brothers bowing out being the ones who had a record or wouldn't do much if anything to support the cause with their lifestyles or tattoos on full display. We were in the heart of Bible belt country, so that eliminated Disney and Aaron, as well as Blue and Duracell with their criminal histories. Zeb bowed out with no way to hide the tribal tattoos all over one half of his face, and Dragon on account of his past, said he'd run the shop for the day so Dray could go with us as my boss.

"Add the women, you'll have a pretty good showing," Dragon said judiciously.

"Hayden will go, but I'll hang back. The judge might know me from years past and battles over Connor." Reaver made a face and I nodded.

"I'm sorry 'bout that, Bro."

Reaver shrugged, "It's my own damn fault, but the good news is, Connor's getting older and is wanting to spend more time around me, not less, so there's that." Nods went around the table like a wave.

"Anybody got any good news?" Dragon asked with a little bit of a huffed laugh and I grinned.

"Actually, I got that covered, too, P."

"Oh yeah?"

"Yep, Mel's pregnant. I'ma be a daddy again."

Cheers erupted around the table and guys started slapping me on the back. Hugs were traded with the twins, and I think Nox even may have had something in his eye; I know I did. It was kind of a surreal experience. I never in a million years expected to be one of the guys that would have this. At forty-three, I felt like some kind of an old dog, and I'd pretty much believed that you couldn't teach an old dog new tricks.

"Just letting you know, I got the whole diaper change thing down to a science, you need help with that, I'm your man," Ghost said.

Rev raised his fist. "I second that."

"Man, you guys have no idea. I used to change these motherfucker's diapers when they were kids, first dropped off in our home," I said, jerking a thumb at Rush and Nox.

Rush nodded. "It's true, it's true," he agreed.

"This calls for shots," Disney said and set a tray of 'em down.

Every man helped himself; Dragon saying over the rim of his, "This better be the good shit."

Disney grinned. "Glad you said it that way, 'cause it is."

"To Archer! Brother and now father. May it be healthy, whatever it is, boy or girl."

"To Archer!"

We pounded shots and glasses hit the table. Cheers went up and more congratulations went around. It was a better day than not, especially when Rush gave a shrug and said, "I better go get started on a crib and shit, I ain't got one of those in storage."

"I'm surprised you got *anything* left in storage," I said after he'd literally kitted out my entire fucking house.

"Meh, gives me an excuse to build more and work on some new designs I had ideas for," he said and slapped me on my shoulders where I remained seated, gripping them tight and giving me a shake back and forth in my seat.

"Nox, you comin'?" he called out.

"Yeah, be out there in a minute, but you know I gotta watch the hands."

"I know, you pussy!"

Chuckles went around the room and Nox shrugged. "I actually like what I do. You have any idea how many hot women come across my table?" he demanded.

"Not enough," Rev said and Disney and Trig laughed.

"That is true, but I still get enough to make it worth my while," he said and stretched before getting up and sauntering out toward Rush's shop. We never did figure out what'd possessed my brother to become a massage therapist, but apparently the money was good, and it'd given him the benefit of a hell of a grip which came in useful sometimes.

Reaver dropped into a seat next to me and bounced his eyebrows, the creepy fucker. He grinned and I raised an eyebrow.

"You lookin' to get into some trouble?" I asked.

"Maybe a little," he said and bobbed his head.

"Let's not and say we did," I uttered.

"Oh, come on! We could totally make it look like an accident," Duracell said jovially, dropping into the seat next to Reave's.

I thought about it and looked around to make sure we were still estrogen free. "Non-lethal?" I asked.

Reaver pouted and Duracell grinned. "Sounds like a job for me and Blue!"

"Dammit!" Reaver pushed to his feet and went over to where Trig and Rev were standing.

"What's his problem?" I asked.

"Think he's having Reaver-specific issues," Duracell said, and leaned back in his seat.

"Yeah, well, hopefully he can keep a lid on that shit," I said eyeing the crazy enforcer.

"Meh, we all go through it," Duracell said with a shrug and I turned my attention back to him, the grin on his face more than a little disconcerting.

"So, what did you have in mind when it comes to a little retribution?" I asked.

"Well, they have to be at the court date if they want an icicle's chance in hell of actually getting custody; that means that their house'll be empty, yeah?"

I nodded. "Yeah, sounds about right."

"Excellent! Then Blue and I, we'll head down and give good 'ol Karma a helping hand."

"Yeah, y'all should see if she needs some help with the heavy lifting."

"Don't worry, Bro. It'll totally look like an accident, or better yet, negligence on their part." I glanced at Blue who winked and shook my head, chuckling, letting a little bit of my own evil out to the surface.

"Remind me never to cross any of you fuckers," I said dryly and they both exchanged a look, lighting up like it was the best compliment they'd been paid in a while. I looked over to Reaver who had his lip stuck out in a childish pout.

"What is his deal?" I wondered out loud without realizing it.

"Frustrated, I'd imagine," Blue murmured.

I frowned. "Yeah?"

"Yeah, he and Hayden have had like zero luck getting her knocked up, looks like his past caught up to him. His little swimmers just ain't up to the job. Another wonderful side effect of junk use," Duracell said with a sour face.

"Oh, shit. That's real fuckin' rough."

"Hayden doesn't mind, I think it's just really bothering Reave," Blue said and I looked at him.

"Ain't you talkative today?"

He shrugged. "It happens sometimes."

I laughed and looked up as Melody slid her hands along my shoulders, I looked up at her and she smiled down at me, but ever since that damn letter had come, every time she managed one it held an edge of sadness.

"Babe, what're you doing out here? Church ain't been declared over."

"I know, I'm sorry, but Noah has some kind of a bug. He's running a low fever so I was going to take him home."

"Oh, shit. Okay, thanks for coming out and telling me but you best go on and git before —"

"Everything okay, Mel?"

She winced. "Um, I needed to tell Archer that Noah's sick and I'm taking him home."

"Next time you find a prospect or make yourself known before comin' in here, sweetheart. Them's the rules."

"I'm so sorry, message delivered and I'm gone," she said and backed out of the room. I looked over at D. and he gave me a wink.

"We were done," he said. "You pretty much missed it when I called it."

I sagged with relief. "You fucker," I said smiling and he shrugged.

"Hell, lesson learned on her part. Best to get in reminders like that done when it's small and as gentle as possible, like."

I nodded and thought about that, adding it to the stack of lessons learned that I might be able to put to use with my own family in the future.

I saw Doc slip off out of the corner of my eye and had to smile to myself. I got up and went after the older biker and found him in the hall with Mel who was holding Noah. My boy looked a touch poorly, laying his head on his mamma's shoulder, thumb in his mouth; spots of color on his cheeks. Doc was murmuring to Mel and put a hand to Noah's forehead.

"Get him home, give him some Children's Tylenol and see how he does. If he gets any kind of worse, gimme a call and I'll come look in on him. I'm sure it's just one of those bugs kids get."

"He wasn't sniffling, or coughing," Mel said concerned. It was about then Noah pulled his thumb out of his mouth and hurled all over my wife.

"Oh, God!" Mel cried and I went over to help.

"That's because it's a stomach bug," Doc said and started laughing.

"Oh no, he really is feeling poorly isn't he?" Ashton asked, coming out of the media room we pretty much affectionately had nicknamed the she-shed.

"Doesn't look like." I held Noah, who had started crying, and said, "Mel go get cleaned up, can one of you ladies gimme a hand with the floor?" I asked.

"I'm already two steps ahead of you, fella," Everett said in her rich Irish brogue. She'd popped open the janitor's closet with one of them floor sinks and was filling a mop bucket.

"Oh, poor guy get sick?" Aaron asked.

"Yeah." I bounced Noah trying to get him to stop crying or feel better and it was the worst thing I coulda done. He unleashed another torrent of throw-up that drenched my coat sleeve. I gagged but held my shit together.

"Right, family cleanup it is," I said making strides for the back door to get to one of the shower rooms near my room out back. Mel and I had clean clothes here, and I was hoping she had something for Noah, too.

"Oh no, did he get you too?" she asked, face sour.

"Yeah, let's get cleaned up and get him home, yeah?"

"Oh, yeah."

It was an awkward family shower time, but we managed and I realized that this was something that was pretty new to me. I mean, on the outside I was calm about it, but on the inside? Fuck, man; I was afraid. I wanted to know what was wrong and I almost didn't want to believe Doc.

"You think he's gonna be okay?" I asked and Mel nodded, smiling wryly.

"What?" I asked.

"Welcome to true fatherhood, you have officially arrived," she said.

"What?"

"You aren't really a parent until you get thrown up on or peed and pooped on," she said cracking up. I looked at her and grinned.

"Bonus points that it was grape juice?" I asked and she winced, nodding.

"Oh yeah."

I went from fuckin' worried, and scared as shit, to glowing with some kind of absurd pride at reaching such a stupid and ridiculous milestone.

"You're gonna be okay, Little Man, I promise." I hugged my son and felt awful for him, but we'd go home and get him squared away and he would be okay. He had parents who loved him and a doctor that made house calls. He was one lucky little boy, and I was probably the luckiest son of a bitch alive to be his daddy.

35

Melody…

My hands shook as I smoothed down my white, fitted business blouse before tucking them into the neat, grey slacks I'd found among the clothes I'd evacuated from Arizona. I suppose I should just be grateful they still fit. I was definitely heavier after bearing a child and with another on the way, even though it was still so early in the pregnancy, only slightly snug was better than *oh my God, what am I going to wear to court?*

"Hey, look at me," Archer ordered from behind me and I turned away from the full-length mirror that had been part of the bedroom set that Rush had built.

Archer leveled me with his calm, gold-green gaze and said, "It's going to be fine. Noah's not going anywhere."

"I know, I guess I'm just worried about seeing them, you know?"

"You ain't gotta worry about that either, babe. I'm gonna be right there with you."

"I don't like that they're making me bring Noah with us, he shouldn't be there."

"He won't be," Archer soothed, standing up from where he'd tied his shoe. He was in an honest to God suit. A dark blue one, with a light blue shirt, and tie. It looked wrong on him, even if he did look good. I'd braided his hair tightly at the back, so from the front, it gave the illusion that he had short hair.

My hair I'd put up into a French twist, a light fringe of bangs over my eyes. My makeup was understated, but there, and all I wanted to do was throw up – but that would make my mascara run. Additionally, I didn't think this nausea had anything to do with morning sickness. None at all. I sighed and let Archer pull me into his arms.

"Everything is going to be okay, baby. Your parents are crazier than a shithouse mouse and everyone knows it. Just give 'em the rope to hang themselves."

"I know, I mean, you're right, but I'm still afraid."

"I know, now come on; let's get this done."

I followed him downstairs to where Revelator bounced Noah, holding him up high above his head. My sharp-dressed little man, with his blue slacks, white shirt, and little red and blue striped clip-on tie. He was dressed just like his daddy, and it was adorable.

"Thank you for helping us out," I murmured to Rev, taking Noah from him. He was likewise dressed for court in black slacks and a white button-down. He'd forgone a tie though, and the shirt material strained across his shoulders, and around his arms. Mandy had even tamed his hair, however the gauges in his ears, even tasteful and not stupid huge as they were, still stood out.

Mandy held Eden on her hip, her belly swollen with Dante, their boy, who was due very soon in November.

"It's no trouble, you guys are family." She smiled and said, "Even my daddy is coming. Imagine the look on their faces when they realize you have a preacher of your own on your side!"

I sighed and nodded. I felt a keen sense of dread the entire drive to the courthouse, grateful that Archer was the one behind the wheel. Rev and Mandy followed us in her economical car, and I closed my eyes and just tried to remember to breathe.

"Feeling sick?" Archer asked.

"Yes."

"Think it's the baby?"

"I don't know, it could be either or," I said bleakly.

His response was perfect. He reached over the center console and gathered my hand resting atop my thigh in his and gave it a squeeze, and he held it the whole rest of the way there, even when he parked.

We got Noah out of the car and met Carina Washington on the front steps. She smiled warmly at us and waved at Noah who smiled broadly and waved back. A lot of the club and their ol' ladies were here, too. All dressed professionally and respectfully for court.

"Hey, Little Guy!" Rush held up his hand for a high five and Noah hit it. He flung himself at Rush and Rush grabbed him. I relinquished my son to the track of laughter around us. That was Noah, when he liked something, he was all in; often times leaping before looking, and whether or not Mom or Dad were prepared for it.

"How are you doing?" Carina asked.

"Ready to fall apart at any second," I said honestly.

"Don't be, we're on your side and good news, we pulled Judge Mathers."

"Why is that good?" Archer asked.

"Judge Mathers is a straight shooter and has a *very* low tolerance for bull pucky. I think that will definitely work in your favor."

Archer looked down at Carina with a faint, amused, smile on his lips. "*Bull pucky?*" he asked.

"Ohhh! You know what I mean." She swatted him lightly in the arm and they both laughed and I just wanted to scream at them. *This is not funny! How can you both be so blasé about this!? They're trying to take our son away from us!*

I didn't though, I simply held myself rigid and as stoic as I could manage, because if I opened my mouth, I really was going to start screaming and I wasn't going to be able to *stop*.

"There he is! Hi, Noah!" I stiffened and turned slowly, a man I didn't know stepping between my mother and my son, putting a hand up.

"That's far enough," he stated. "You'll be able to see him pending the result of the hearing, and that's *if* his parents permit you to see him."

"Who are you?" my mother demanded coldly. "That is my *grandson!*"

I took a step forward, incendiary rage building and threatening to spill from my mouth, but Archer stepped in front of me, a wall of muscle in his off-putting suit; he looked down at me, eyes solemn and murmured, "Easy, baby. Don't let 'em rile you up. Not now; now is the worst possible time to lose your shit and show your ass."

I nodded, and breathed slowly, in through my nose and out through my mouth, tuning back into what the man was saying to my mother.

"...name is Jonathon McNulty and I'm your daughter's attorney."

"Here, Logan. It's about time we went inside. I'll take Noah for the time being," Carina said to Rush, and Rush nodded grimly and handed Noah over to her while Phillip, my stepfather, was reading into my lawyer about what an awful, godless mother I'd been to Noah. How I'd never been home after he'd been born, and how he and my poor mother had done the Christian thing and had cared for my son when it'd become obvious that *I* had had no interest.

I was so angry I couldn't speak, and I could tell my lawyer was nonpulsed by what they had to say. Even Carina was looking at Phil like he was off his nut, behind his and my mother's backs as she went up the steps. Noah was looking at Phil as if he were troubled, and I wondered if he remembered my stepfather. If he remembered the yelling, and screaming, and the threats.

I closed my eyes and drew strength from Archer and did the hardest thing I have *ever* done in my life. I kept my mouth shut and walked past my parents as if they weren't even there. I kept my mouth shut, when what I really wanted to do was burn down their whole world around them.

We filed into the hearing room and the first three rows of Archer and my side of the hearing room was packed; which made my parents exchange a look when it was just them, and one or two people from Phil's congregation, just as stringent and hateful as the man himself behind them.

I stood beside Archer, our hands entwined, as he introduced me to Mr. McNulty, the family lawyer that he'd hired.

"We have Judge Mathers, that's good," he assured me. "Just stay calm, and keep looking like a deer in the headlights, Mrs. Turner." I felt my eyes widen and Archer suppress a chuckle, and again I suppressed the urge to just scream at them. I'd never experienced anxiety like this before in my life. Never, ever.

I opened my mouth to speak but was interrupted before I even had the chance to get started when the courtroom clerk said loudly, "All rise!"

I faced forward as an older gentleman in stately black robes appeared from a doorway in the back.

"The Honorable Judge James Mathers now presiding."

The older man sat creakily into the big leather chair behind the court bench and banged his gavel. "Sit down, the lot of you," he ordered and sounded annoyed. I sank into my seat, my hand automatically groping for Archer's. He gripped it and I felt my heart go into my throat.

"Not very often I preside over cases quite like this," the judge drawled, polishing his glasses on the sleeve of his robe before putting them back on, "and I have to say, after reading through everything presented, I am most heartily disturbed."

I felt my heart sink, and saw my mother and Phillip sit up straighter in their seats. The Judge's mouth set into a thin line as he looked from my side to my parent's side. He looked over to the little box off to the side of the older courtroom where Carina Washington sat bouncing Noah. The judge smiled fondly over at my son and I felt some of the tension in my chest ease. The very real, very kind look that he bestowed on my son telling me silently, that this man did, indeed, have my child's best interest at heart.

"I'm not usually one to drag things out unnecessarily in here, but I am curious, so I would like to hear character witnesses, starting with you," he said indicating my mother and stepfather's lawyer. Phillip was, of course, called up first.

He had a lot to say about how difficult I'd been in high school. How I'd been caught skipping class, sneaking out, and how the one time I'd been dragged out of a party drunk and reeking of marijuana when I was seventeen, which was *ten years ago*. He went on to say about how reckless I was, getting pregnant in the first place and by a biker and felon, no less.

I sat biting my lips together, eyes glued to the judge who had his glasses perched on the end of his nose, holding a file out in front of him, scanning what was written there, half listening to what Phil was saying. He dropped the file flat to his desk and peered down his nose at me.

"Mrs. Turner," he said.

"Yes?" I asked and my attorney gave me a gentle shove. I got to my feet, awkwardly, and felt like I was gonna faint.

"Now I know I'm not supposed to ask a lady her age, but how old are you ma'am?" I blinked.

"I just turned twenty-eight this last April," I said.

"Twenty-eight," he said thoughtfully, nodding to himself. He turned to say something to Phil, and turned back to me. "You can sit down now," he said and I dropped like a stone.

"Do you think you can get to anything she's done *lately*, sir? I do believe I said I don't like dragging things out unnecessarily."

Phillip stammered, and a lot of what he had to say after that was just so unfair that it was just about everything in my power to stay seated and keep my mouth shut. I gripped Archer's hand under the table and was squeezing it so hard my knuckles were mottled red and white. He didn't protest, or pull his hand away, he simply endured my panicked GI Jane Kung Fu grip in silence as if nothing at all were amiss.

The judge listened to everything Phillip, my mother, and her cronies had to say and sat back, fingers set in a steeple in front of him.

"Right, okay, Mr. McNulty, I think I'd like to hear from your character witnesses now."

"Of course, is there anyone in particular that you'd like to begin with, Your Honor?"

"You said the child's current physician is on your roster?"

"Yes, Judge."

"Let's start there," the judge leaned back and Doc went up and was sworn in.

"When did you first meet Noah Beswick?" the judge asked.

"He was brought into my emergency room with a minor head laceration," Doc answered and the courtroom on my parent's side broke out into murmurs. It was like every bad courtroom television drama and I felt my gorge rise.

"What did Mrs. Turner say happened?"

"She was in her kitchen making dinner, and Noah was running through the apartment they lived in at the time. She was tending hot food on the stove and before she could get to him, Noah tripped and his head hit the sharp corner on the strike plate of her bedroom doorway. You know, the thing that the little tab on the doorknob's side fits into."

"I know what a strike plate is," the judge grumbled. "Thanks for explaining anyway. How bad was the injury?"

"It required two stitches."

More murmurs and I was terrified that as well-meaning as Doc was, he was making the situation worse and not better. I started to pray.

"And you don't consider stitches serious?" the judge asked, scribbling notes.

"No, not in my line of work."

"Fair enough. How was Mrs. Turner behaving?"

"Honestly, she was a right mess. Crying, scared for her son, and carrying the weight of the world on her shoulders. She was frazzled, like any good mother would be."

"Objection." The lawyer on my parent's side stood up. "The doctor can't judge whether or not someone is a good parent based on one emergency room visit, let alone one where the child was clearly injured due to his mother's negligence."

"Well now," the judge said, tapping his name plate on the desk, "I do believe *I* will be the judge of that. Mrs. Turner?"

I stood up. "Yes, Your Honor?"

"Were you being negligent on the day in question?"

"I… I honestly don't think so, Judge. I was home alone with Noah and trying to make sure he had dinner. I told him to stop running, but how do you get a one-and-a-half-year-old who is excited, laughing, and having a good time to stop doing something that makes them happy?"

The judge huffed a laugh. "I'm not the one whose parenting is being called into question." *Ouch. God damn it, Melody.* "I'll assume you were being rhetorical though, and answer your question, and the answer is – you don't." I nodded and he gave me a nod indicating I should sit down.

"You didn't report the incident as abuse or negligence, did you doctor?"

"No, I did not."

"Why is that?"

"Because, in my professional medical opinion, there was no negligence or abuse. Mrs. Turner, who at that time was Ms. Beswick, was beside herself and completely distraught. That's not how an abuser, or negligent mother acts."

"And what do you base that opinion on?" the judge asked.

"Over thirty-three years of being a medical professional, fifteen of which have been spent in one of the area's busiest emergency departments; I've seen a lot of negligence and abuse cases in that time, and I can tell you right now, Melody Turner's case wasn't one of 'em."

"Okay, thank you. I think I've heard everything I need to. Mr. McNulty, who's your next witness?"

"Carina Washington."

The judge looked over to where Ms. Washington held my son who'd fallen asleep and said, "Well, I don't see a problem with you giving your testimony from right there, Ms. Washington. I've had you in my courtroom before, why don't you tell me how you became involved in this."

"Your Honor, my office, the Department of Children's Health Services, received a call from the plaintiffs in this matter stating that Noah Beswick had been kidnapped from their care and was currently with his mother, Melody Beswick, who was supposedly negligent, abusive, and according to the call, a substance abuser."

"And you went to investigate I imagine?"

"I did."

"And for the record, what did you find?"

"I found Ms. Beswick and her son moving out of a one-bedroom apartment that very day. Ms. Beswick informed me that she was now Mrs. Turner, and not only offered to take any drug tests we asked for, but asked me if I would like to see the home that she and Mr. Turner were moving their son Noah—"

My mother got up shrieking, "My grandson is *not* that man's son! That boy's father died! How dare you, madam!"

Crack! Crack! Crack!

The judge banged his gavel and glared at my mother. "How dare *you*, madam. Sit down! Mr. Price, one more outburst like that from your client, I'll hold her in contempt. Do I make myself clear?"

My parent's lawyer stood up hastily. "Understood, Judge. My apologies to you and the court."

He sat down and started whispering furiously to my mother who practically wailed into my stepfather's shoulder. Archer gave my hand a squeeze as Phil just glared at me like this was somehow all my fault. My mind, not for the first time, was absolutely boggled.

"You were saying, Ms. Washington?" the judge asked.

"Yes, Your Honor, as I was saying, I took them up on their offer and I have to say I was suitably impressed. Not only had they completely babyproofed the house by having child locks on every cabinet, they also had socket covers installed in every electrical outlet. The boy's uncle, Logan Fisher, had even constructed a rather impressive race car shaped bed from one solid piece of wood citing that there would be no nails or screws for the child to become injured by, nor were there any parts of the bed joined together to pinch little fingers or toes."

"Ha," the judge said in disbelief, "now that's dedication."

"Yes, Your Honor. There should be photos included in that report of the steep measures taken to keep Noah safe in the home. Quite frankly, I wish every household adhered to the same example."

The judge swept through the files in front of him and took long moments pondering over both notes and photographs.

"So, I take it you found the allegations the plaintiffs alleged to be false in one visit?"

"Yes, Your Honor, however, to be safe I asked Mr. and Mrs. Turner for a return visit inside a three-month window."

"And how did they respond?"

"Favorably, Your Honor; they invited me to come into their home whenever I liked."

"That's different," the judge muttered.

"Agreed, Judge."

"And you made a return visit?"

"I did, Judge."

"And how were things then?"

"Much the same if not further improved, Judge. Mr. and Mrs. Turner maintain a beautiful home, and I found Noah to be one healthy and very happy little boy."

"You have anything you'd like to add, Ms. Washington?"

"Yes, Judge. In all my time as a social worker in this county, I've never seen anything quite like this. I truly believe that the plaintiffs in this case are using the system to terrorize Mrs. Turner with the threat of taking her child away as a form of some kind of twisted punishment because Mrs. Turner doesn't hold the same family views as the plaintiffs. I see absolutely nothing wrong with how Mrs. Turner is raising her child, and I feel sick watching the fear and agony she has had to go through as a result of this debacle."

"Alright, thank you, Ms. Washington."

"You're welcome, Judge."

The judge sat back and I swear, I felt the first ray of hope peeking through the clouds since I first took Noah and ran from Arizona. He turned to my lawyer and said, "I think I might like to hear from Mrs. Turner herself, now." His steely gaze shifted to me. "Mrs. Turner, would you come up here please?"

I rose, shaky, and with feet that felt like lead, I plodded to the witness box, and climbed the two steps. I woodenly went through the motions of swearing in and what have you and sank into the chair, focusing on Archer and studiously ignoring my parents. I was giving it everything I had just trying not to hyperventilate.

"Mrs. Turner, why did you leave your parent's house?" he asked me. "Why did you pick up in the middle of the night and drive all the way here, across several states, without having any assurance that you'd have a place here for you when you got here?"

I looked over to my sleeping boy and the fractured ache in the center of my chest throbbed anew. "Because I could see it," I said and sniffed, unable to stop the tears from slipping free. I looked up at the judge, and said, "Because they were killing my little boy's spirit just like they did mine and he wasn't even out of diapers yet. He still isn't. Because I realized the longer that we stayed there, the more they would just keep emotionally beating me down and keep stripping my little boy's sparkle and shine away."

"Was there something specific that happened to make you leave?"

"Phillip hit me, in front of Noah. It was bad enough they were screaming at me in front of my son, but when he backhanded me, I was done. I didn't want my son raised in an environment where he thought that that was *okay* or *normal*. I want my son to grow up to be like his father now, like Archer – excuse me, Charles Turner, my husband."

Archer's look softened as he gazed at me from across the room and I sighed. The judge asked me *a lot* of questions, and I told him everything. About how I'd been trying to save money. About how my parents kept changing the rules mid-game and how it was impossible to keep up. I told him how I'd brought Noah into this world alone, and how I realized that if I could do *that*, that I could take care of him myself too.

I told him about how when I arrived, it was to find out Noah's biological father had died. I told him the truth, all of it, and then I tearfully begged him not to give those monsters my baby.

The judge thanked me quietly and let me get up to go back to my seat. When I got there, Archer stood and pulled me in tight, kissing the top of my head while I bawled all my bitterness and fear onto his nice but so-wrong-on-him suit. He got me into my seat and rocked me back and forth while the judge called a recess to deliberate.

It took me the whole fifteen to twenty minutes to calm down and get ready to hear his decision. When he came back, it was with a grim expression on his face. He sat down and waved all of us down to sit, too. I sank into my chair and watched him.

He scoffed and took off his glasses, rubbing a hand over his eyes and then the rest of his face. He sighed before saying, "I've been in family law for almost fifty years, and I've been sitting on this bench for more than thirty-five of 'em and I have *never* seen anything come across my desk like this right here."

He looked over at my parent's table and leaned heavily on his bench in their direction. "First off, your case for kidnapping has no legal standing whatsoever as your daughter is your grandson's custodial parent. Always has been, and to put her mind at ease, I'm telling you right now, she *always will be*." I sagged into Archer, the wind sucked clear from my lungs, gasping to reclaim it.

"Second of all, I quite agree with Ms. Washington. Your blatant attempt at using the system to terrorize Mrs. Turner and her son, are quite probably, the most disgusting abuse of the legal system I have ever seen and that is saying a lot. I don't think you realize what could have happened and it horrifies me that one of those things that could have happened would be that your grandson landed in your care.

"I can tell you straight off that that *isn't* going to happen today, or any other day for that matter. I am denying your petition for custody, and what's more, I am issuing an order of protection against you in favor of Mr. and Mrs. Turner, that way your attempted abuse of the system is on record."

The judge shook his head. "I don't know where you people get off," he said and turned to me. "Mrs. Turner, I am so very sorry that you had to be here today, and that you've had to live with your fear for this long. You have, by all accounts, been doing a marvelous job as a mother and I wish you and your family all of the best."

"Thank you, Your Honor," I said faintly, still in disbelief.

"I will leave it up to you, on if you want to show your parents the love, mercy, and compassion they have seen fit to withhold from you by allowing them to be a part of your life and your son, their grandson's life. I am still going to put forth this no contact order against your parents. If you wish to have your parents be a part of your life again, you will need to have that vacated before any visitation can take place, lest you find yourself in violation of the order. Restraining orders, no contact orders, orders of protection – whatever you would like to call them – are a two-way street. Am I understood?"

"Yes, Your Honor. Thank you, Your Honor," Archer said for me. I was too stunned. My mother was howling and wailing. Her church ladies trying to console her, and Phillip was whispering furiously with their lawyer.

"My decision is final, so entered, so ordered, this hearing is adjourned."

He banged his gavel and my side of the courtroom erupted in whoops and cheers, along with applause.

"We won?" I asked stunned, it hadn't quite sunk in.

"We won," my lawyer confirmed. I held tightly to Archer and stared at my son who Ms. Washington was bringing to me.

"I don't understand," I said. "Good things just don't happen to us without something going horribly wrong."

Archer barked a laugh. "That may have been the way of things before, but not anymore, baby. I promised you that I'd protect our family and I meant it. You, me, Noah, and our little bean you got growing in there. Now let's get out of here."

I took Noah from her who was just out, slept through the whole damn hearing, which I was so grateful for.

"You have a beautiful family, now go on and get out of here, Melody. You have much better places for y'all to be."

"Oh, you wretched girl!" my mother cried when I turned around to leave. The judge was long gone and I didn't even remember him leaving.

"Me?" I asked incredulous. "Take a look in the mirror, Mother. Jesus, I can't even with you," I said and let Archer lead me out through the gallery. His club brothers, and my club sisters forming a human blockade between me and my former family.

"Head to the club," Revelator called out and I marched right out to the parking lot and my car, my son in my arms. I put him carefully in his car seat and strapped him in.

"Come on, baby. I'm driving," Archer declared.

"Good, because I'm so not fit to do it."

Without a single backwards glance, we left this whole damn nightmare behind.

36

Archer...

The party was in full swing back at the club and Rev and Mandy had been kind enough to take Noah for the night so that I could try to destress my wife. She hadn't wanted to let him go, which I got, but I'd explained to her that one night wasn't going to kill her and that she needed a rest.

We were sitting around a fire out back, Melody sharing one of the lounge chairs with me, lying on me, staring at the flames, a blanket over the both of us. She had lemonade in a glass on the ground next to us, and I had a beer perched on my knee. I sort of felt bad I couldn't get her drunk.

Summer had hung on into fall and it felt like it was *finally* starting to wind down, the night air holding that crisp edge to it, hence why Dani had laid a blanket over the both of us. I'd nodded my appreciation and had murmured thanks for the both of us, but Mel just wasn't here with me. A million miles away with her thoughts, which hey, let's face it, that was okay.

"What 'cha thinking about," I asked her and she roused a bit, her hands caressing her stomach, her baby bump starting to show but not really, probably more wishful thinking on my part.

"What do you want to name it if it's a boy?" she asked me, her voice holding that dreamy quality.

"Well, I kind of would have liked to name my first boy after Grind, but you took care of that for me." I kissed her hair and she swallowed hard.

"I don't like the name David," she murmured.

"I don't either. I always kind of liked the name Chandler for a first name."

"Chandler…" she murmured, hypnotized by the flames. "Chandler," she murmured again and closed her eyes.

"Yeah," I said.

"I like it," she said. "It fits, I mean, he did bring us together."

"Yeah?"

"I named Noah, you should name your first son, especially if it *is* a son."

I snorted and took a drink of my beer. "Noah *is* my first son, Mel. Always will be."

She dragged herself up so she could look at me, searching my face. "You really do love him as your own, no difference, don't you?"

"No difference," I agreed.

She pulled herself up so she could straddle my hips, both of us still in our court clothes which was slightly awkward, and she kissed me. I set my beer down on the cinderblock next to the chair where her alcohol-free lemonade sat, getting watered down by its melting ice. I let my hands gently frame her face as I teased the seam of her lips with my tongue. She opened her mouth to me, plunging her tongue past my lips and I moaned slightly.

I loved how her lush, soft curves molded into my body, how she melted against me, boneless, liquid, and graceful. She whimpered into my mouth and I swallowed the small sound. I felt my cock stir between us in the fancy slacks I wore.

Melody adjusted herself, rubbing her body along mine and setting me on fire with a desire to be with her. The light from the flickering firepit didn't help me one damn bit with that. I wrapped my arms around her and let the warmth spread from my crotch, through the rest of my body.

"My room?" I asked her and she answered me without stopping her kiss.

"Mm-hmm," she moaned past my lips and I hauled her up my body, sitting up with her in my arms.

"Hold onto me, baby," I uttered and she moved her mouth to the side of my neck, kissing me, lightly flicking her tongue over the spot in the side of my neck that gave me shivers.

I made quick strides across the grass and the asphalt track to the outbuilding that housed my club room. I took one of my hands off of the taut globe of Mel's ass just long enough to twist the knob and kick the door open before plunging into the room and it's blueish, deep shadows.

I didn't need to switch on a light when I held the light of my life in my arms. This woman, *God*, this woman who was so tolerant and giving. This woman who was so fucking brave to marry my cantankerous ass, when by all rights she could have laughed in my face for even suggesting such a thing.

I'm glad she didn't. I'm glad her crazy at the time matched my crazy so well. I'm glad she saw the same wisdom in it that I did, and that she held on and went through with it. I kissed her again, lying over the top of her across my bed while she deftly unbuttoned my shirt and jerked the wife beater under it out of my pants.

My hands were a match for hers, popping buttons free of their holes on her blouse, shoving her camisole she wore underneath it up out of my way, so I could get skin on skin. I paused only long enough to pull my shirt off the rest of the way for her, peeling the cotton back off my shoulders and down my arms. Ripping the tank off over my head and tossing it carelessly aside in the deep gloom.

"I want you," she breathed.

"I need you," I confessed right back.

It was a quick frenzy to divest each other of our clothes the rest of the way and it was pure fucking bliss when I sank balls deep into her waiting wet heat, her pussy grasping around me firmly, pulling me in further. She wrapped her arms and legs around me and I drew back, surging forward, her voice painting the night with her pleasure, splashing across my sense of hearing like rich paint, coloring me alive.

"God, baby, I don't want to know what my life would have been like if you hadn't come into it like that," I told her. "I love you so fucking much, you incredible, brave, beautiful fucking woman."

She moaned and stroked the side of my face gently, I turned my head and kissed her palm, closing my eyes and breathing deep the scent of her delicate perfume on her wrist. She was everything to me now, and I couldn't believe that I could be so lucky. She almost made me believe there was such a thing as God, because if there were, she surely had been sent from him.

37

M elody...

I arched beneath Archer, and reveled in his slow, arduous slide in and out of my body. It was so *different* when there was true love involved. It felt like he reached places inside of me that couldn't be touched any other way. It was new, unique, and I don't think I'd ever experienced anything like it before – nor did I want to experience it with anyone else.

I carefully took down his hair at one point, and now it caressed my body like warm silk, if silk could be a living thing. I loved how it enshrouded our faces as we kissed, and I couldn't help but close my eyes, to concentrate wholly on all the feelings I was having at once.

I felt the warm weight of orgasm, deep in my womb, and I loved how Archer simply held me on that edge where I felt so good; my consciousness drifting beautifully, like there wasn't a care or concern in the world except how we felt right now, right this minute, with each other.

I didn't want to come, afraid that if I did, that this would all end so quickly, but eventually, I wasn't given a choice. Archer reached between us, teasing my clit with his thumb and I felt like a star, falling right out of the sky. I shuddered beneath him as I reentered earth's atmosphere and crashed, plunging deep into the liquid pool of pleasure when I'd fully expected to be dashed upon the rocks.

He held me so sweetly, and loved me so completely, I didn't ever want to come up for air.

I came back from wherever I'd gone slowly, tucked warm and safe against my husband as he kissed each individual fingertip on my right hand. He'd somehow gotten us tucked beneath the covers and I didn't remember that happening either. I worried about that, but he stole my worries away with a well-placed kiss against my forehead.

"Sleep, baby. You've had a hell of a day... we both have."

I nodded against his chest and sighed. "Am I wrong for never wanting my mother to see our children again?"

He snorted. "Hell no. Don't worry about it too much, babe. Karma's on its way to town and it's going to bite those fuckers but good."

I felt my forehead wrinkle in a frown. "What did you do?" I asked suspicious.

"I didn't do shit," he said and I knew Archer, if he said he didn't then he didn't... but I also knew that didn't mean that one of his brothers hadn't.

"What's going to happen to my parents?" I demanded.

"Nothing is going to happen to them, baby. They're going to get back to Saguaro Flats just fine."

I thought about it... *just fine.* "They're getting back to the *town* just fine, but not *home*?" I murmured, the pieces falling into place.

Archer gave an evil little chuckle and the pieces that'd fallen right into place cemented together. I hadn't seen Blue or Duracell, and while both of them worked on a road crew, Duracell was a demolition's expert by trade. A rather specialized field of work.

"I'm not sure how I feel about that," I confessed.

"Make you feel bad?" he asked curiously.

"No," I murmured, surprised.

"Well there you go," he supplied.

A long silence stretched between us and finally he asked, "You wanted to know what I wanted to name our baby if it were a boy, same question, if it's a girl, what do you want to name her?"

I thought about it and finally sighed out, "It's a moot point, it's going to be a boy," I said with certainty.

"How do you know? Doctor say something already?"

"No, I just know. I just feel it all the way down to my bones, when we were out there, staring at the fire. It's going to be a boy, I can just feel it, I just know it. Women's intuition, okay?

"Hmm, you know I don't ascribe to all that mystical bullshit, right?"

"No, I know you don't, but mark my words, I'm carrying your son, Archer."

He gave a little shiver under me and I smiled into the dark. "Okay, you need to go to sleep 'cause you're seriously giving me the creeps right now."

I smiled and laughed a little. "So much for not subscribing to all the 'mystical bullshit,'" I said and laughed hysterically, jolting when Archer went after the ticklish spot on my ribs.

"Don't you go calling me out, Woman!"

I laughed and settled down, the day's events settling over me like one of the blankets on the bed. It'd been an extremely long day. I closed my eyes against the pervasive dark of Archer's room and sighed, beginning to drift off.

Archer kissed my forehead and asked, "You're sure it's a boy, huh?"

"Uh huh," I murmured.

"Sweet," he uttered and I was out, sound asleep.

LIFE RETURNED to normal for us so quickly I could almost convince myself that the hearing had been little more than a bad dream. Archer worked as much as he could at the shop, but he'd quit his job as a doorman and bouncer in the evenings. It'd become important to him to be at home and we really didn't need the money that bad.

I carried on waitressing, and about three or so days after the hearing, Duracell and Blue had come into the diner, sitting in my section and ordering lunch. I'd gone by to refill their glasses and Duracell said nonchalantly, "It's a cryin' shame about your folks' house, burning down like that. I hear the insurance company isn't going to pay out, either. They don't, you know, when it's a clear-cut case of negligence."

I blinked, stupidly, and Blue opened up his cut and pulled a book out from the inside of his jacket where he'd been holding it under his arm. He set it on the table and slid it towards me and my eyes misted. I set down the pitcher of water on the edge of the table beside the book and picked it up with shaking fingers.

It was Noah's baby book, the one that had been given to me by the hospital with his teeny tiny footprints, his birth certificate, and his very first picture. It even had his tiny knit cap in it. I looked at Blue and he nodded at the book, saying with his mouth full, "Important stuff."

"Thank you," I whispered, and hugged the book to my chest.

"Hey, uh, Blue wants to know, who's that chick over there?"

I looked over and asked, "Who, the waitress?"

"Yeah."

"That's Hayley," I said and the kitchen rang the bell for pickup. I retrieved my pitcher and said, "That's me, I've got to go."

I'd set Noah's baby book somewhere safe and had gotten wrapped up in the lunch rush after that. I'd pretty much stopped seating Duracell and Blue anywhere but Hayley's section after that. I couldn't tell which one of them had the crush on her, maybe it was both? I was always too busy to really think about it.

I had been spending time catching Noah's book up the last few weeks off and on, and that's where Archer found me today. He came home and knelt, first kissing me then kissing my swollen stomach before the patter of Noah's footsteps came in from the living room.

"Daddy!" he cried and it never failed, no matter how tired Archer was, he caught our son up and hugged him and kissed him.

"How you doing, Little Man?"

"Good." They wandered into the kitchen, having their talk while I pressed my favorite photograph of them into Noah's book. The candid photo I'd taken of Noah sprawled across Archer's chest in the morning gloom of that dreary, sad, little apartment.

"How was your day?" I asked when Archer had set Noah down so Noah could go back to his scattered toys in the living room.

"Good, how about you?"

"It was alright, the car started to overheat on me. I hate to say anything about it since you just got home, but at least it happened as I pulled onto our street and I got it in our driveway."

"Ahh, that piece of shit," Archer grumbled, and I gave him a reproachful look. He smiled and leaned back in his seat. Dinner was in the oven and had about ten minutes more to go on the timer.

"Well, I guess it at least had the good timing to do it now," he said.

"Why?"

He got up and held out a hand to me. I frowned and took it and let him pull me to my feet. He led me to our front door and opened it wide. While it wasn't brand new, it was considerably newer than my old rust bucket. A minivan sat in front of our house at the curb. A light blue, with a red Christmas bow on the antennae.

"You bought me a car?" I asked incredulous.

"Naw, I just bought a transmission for it. Customer brought it in last week and when he saw the price tag, decided to get somethin' else. Signed it over to the shop. I picked it up, dropped a new tranny in it, and it's as good as new. Only has eighty thousand miles on it. You like it?"

"Are you kidding me? This is fantastic! I've been so scared that thing was going to leave me stranded somewhere, I've had Ghost on speed dial right underneath your number!"

I hugged him tightly and he smiled down at me. "Cool deal. Feed me and you can give me a ride back to the shop, so I can get my bike. Test out your new wheels."

"What doing?" Noah asked and we turned to look in the open doorway.

"Lookin' at your mom's new car, you wanna see it?"

I let the boys play, Archer showing Noah all the cool new things in my new van while I set the table and dished up dinner, all the while thinking to myself that *this* was perfect. *This* was what I had always secretly dreamed of, and because of love, and more than a little perseverance, it was finally mine.

38

A rcher…

"Archer! Archer, wake up!"

"Huh, what?" I demanded and sat up, rubbing the sleep from my eyes. Melody was sitting up in bed next to me, distress drawn in every line of her body. "What's wrong?" I demanded.

"My water just broke!"

"Ah shit, hang on, baby. I'll get us going."

She sat in bed and breathed while I woke up Noah and got him dressed. I put out a call to the club, while she whined through a contraction, probably one of the more heartbreaking noises I'd ever heard. I helped get her up and dressed while Noah watched us and moved around with as much efficiency as I could muster juggling my very pregnant wife and two-year-old son. I got everyone into the van, and Mel's bag in the back and started for the hospital.

"You're doing good, baby. Just breathe."

Mel looked at me, the fear in her eyes very real and alive and it was all I could do not to speed. Didn't matter either way. When I pulled up outside the hospital a bunch of brother's waited outside. Aaron took my van keys and said, "I'll bring up her bag, stay with your ol' lady."

"Thanks, kid," I grunted and before I could get Noah, Rev was there, getting him out of the back seat.

"You're gonna stick with me, okay, kiddo?"

"Is Mamma hurt?"

"No, son. Mamma's coming with me to go get your baby brother."

Noah perked up at that one and started talking Rev's ear off while I picked up Mel and took her through the hospital doors.

"A little help, please?" I called.

"Oh boy, do you know who your OB is?"

I explained to the nurse that Doc was going to be making the delivery as I set Mel into a wheelchair. We were whisked back into a room and they started helping my wife into a gown. I felt helpless and I didn't like it. She was hurting and I couldn't do a damn thing about it, which sucked, like epically and royally sucked.

"It's okay, I'm okay," Mel said breathing through her pain and I balked.

"You're about to squeeze a human being, the size of a fucking watermelon out of your snatch which is a hole the size of a lemon and you're trying to reassure *me*?" I demanded.

Melody laughed, the nurses right along with her, and I took her hand in mine now that they were finished putting an IV into the back of it.

"God damn, nobody told me I married a total badass!"

More laughter and Mel moaned out, "I love you, I love you so much."

"No way that you love me more than I love you, baby. You just hang in there, okay? When can we get her something for the pain?" I demanded.

"Gotta see how far along she is, just a minute," the nurse said and thank fuck, that's when Doc breezed into the room.

"Hey, girly. Someone told me you were ready to have this baby."

"I hope so," she cried. "I really hope so!"

"Okay, let's have a look…"

SEVEN GRUELING and agonizing hours later, I was holding Melody's hand as she looked over and said, "No pain, no gain, right?" I pressed a cool cloth to her forehead and shook my head. I was scared, and I knew she was too, but she was trying to keep *me* from being afraid, too which was nuts.

Doc was looking at some kind of read out shaking his head. "Mel, I'm sorry, honey, but we gotta take this to the OR. I gotta give you a Cesarean."

Mel dropped her head back to the gurney and groaned. "Ohhhhh, no. What's wrong? What's wrong with our baby, Doc?" she asked but Doc was already getting my woman ready to move.

"I think the cord is around his neck, honey. We gotta do this and we gotta do this fast, come on Papa; you're going too."

"Well, no shit, Doc!" I cried. I hadn't left Mel's side. Not even once, and I wasn't about to now that one of her biggest nightmares had reared its ugly head.

"Oh! I don't want to do this again! I don't want to do this again!" she cried as she was wheeled down the hall, clinging to my hand for safety.

I held it tight and told her, "I'm right here, baby. I'm not going anywhere, you just hang tight."

"What's going on?" Dragon called from up the hall.

"Emergency C-section!" I called back and we were through the doors, everything happening so fast after that.

The nurses let me stay by Melody's side as they gowned me, and I kept talking to her as they put up the drape.

"Look at me, baby. You just keep looking at me, don't stop. I'm right here, I'm right here—"

"It hurts!"

"I know, Mel. You just hang in there, I'm not going anywhere."

"Oh God, just make sure our baby's okay!"

"Chandler's gonna be fine, and you're gonna be fine, and we're all going to go home as a family. You'll see, baby." They put an oxygen mask over her face and I coached her, telling her to take deep breaths.

"That's it, deep breaths."

"Melody!" Doc called.

"Yeah?" she asked, voice muffled by the type of oxygen mask they'd put over her nose and mouth.

"Can you feel this, honey?"

"No!"

"Good! That's good, honey. We're almost there, just a little bit more okay?"

"I don't feel anything this time! Are you cutting? Doc, why aren't you cutting? Get him out! You have to get him out!"

I looked over the drape and oh, holy fucking shit! Mel's insides were on the outside, my baby still in his sack laying out, Doc ripping it open and getting the cord off from around my baby boy's neck. I felt tears sting my eyes for the first time in a long time. He was perfect, he was perfect in every way, except he wasn't making any sounds.

A nurse took him over to a lighted table and they frantically worked on our son, and I turned back to Melody, "He's perfect, baby! He's perfect!"

A high, thin wail went up from his tiny body and I swear on my colors, all my insides went liquid with relief. The nurse brought him over and laid him on my wife's chest and we marveled at our son, our beautiful baby boy with his mamma's hair, and eyes too dark to tell if they would be mine or hers yet.

"He's beautiful!" Mel said and she looked exhausted. She dragged her head woozily to look at Doc over the drape and asked, "Why don't I feel right? The room is spinning, and I—"

Her eyes rolled back in her head and her arms dropped. If I hadn't had a hold of Chandler she would have surely dropped him. A nurse reached around and straightened me up.

"Doc? What's happening?" I demanded but the old man ignored me, in favor of digging around in my wife's stomach.

"God damn it!" he cried. "I can't fucking find it. Where are you, you little bastard?"

Something was terribly wrong with everything that had just come out his mouth. I shifted from foot to foot and said, "Talk to me, man! What's wrong with my wife?"

"Get him out of here, take the baby, let me get this done – suction!"

I was ushered out into the hall and stood numbly outside the OR doors, watching Doc's back through the little pane of glass as nurses and more doctors rushed around my wife. Alarms were going off, saline and even bags of blood were hung as they worked frantically to save her.

I cradled Chandler to my chest, as he wailed and cried repeatedly for his mother and it was everything I could do to stay sane and not completely lose my shit. I watched, and watched, and the seconds dragged on into minutes and the minutes on into tens of minutes and Doc continued to work frantically, ceding to an actual surgeon who had come onto the floor, *running* down the hall, to push past me and my newborn son.

I watched monitors and numbers flash, lines bounce, readouts grow fainter, the alarms in the room screeching almost louder than my boy when a hand touched my shoulder. I jerked back and looked down at the nurse who was speaking, but I couldn't process what she was saying. She was trying to take Chandler away from me, and I let her – something in the back of my brain agreeing that *yes, this was best* for him. She said, "I'm going to take him to the nursery, he's just fine. You stay here with your wife."

The sympathetic look she gave me was enough to make me want to throttle her, and then I don't know how, but Rush and Nox were there, standing shoulder to shoulder with me, holding me up as the line on the screen went flat and I just couldn't watch anymore. I couldn't watch her die. I couldn't do this without her...

I turned around and collapsed back against the wall, sliding to the floor, the twins bracing me as the sobs came and wouldn't stop. She was everything to me, and I couldn't fathom it. I couldn't fathom doing *any of this* without her. That's just not the way it was supposed to *be*.

Mel had a fire inside, and it wasn't supposed to be snuffed out like this, there was nothing tiny nothing spark-like, she had *a fire* inside and this was not how it was supposed to go out!

I bowed my head and raised my knees, bracing my forearms on them and lost my fucking shit in the hallway. I sobbed like a little fucking girl and didn't give a shit who fucking saw me.

Melody, our family, our love and life together. We were just getting started and if there was a God, which I didn't personally believe there was, he was a cruel fucking bastard if he was going to rip it away like this. I closed my eyes, supported by my two brothers and pulled out all the stops, powerless in the face of all of this, I did something I had never done before, not once, not ever…

I fucking prayed, *If you're up there, you son of a bitch, prove it to me. You leave her alone. You don't take her from me, not now, not yet. Just leave her here. For our sons, for me, for everyone's life she just makes brighter just by breathing… you leave her down here for us.*

Frantic voices filtered through the doors to one side and at my back. Shouting messages back and forth, all indistinct enough I couldn't make out words, but distinct enough in the emotion that they held. They were losing this fight and I was losing my wife; my children were losing their mother.

"Please, God don't you take her from me," I uttered and Rush and Nox both did their best to shore me up but there wasn't anything they could do, just like there wasn't anything *I* could do. I was helpless, powerless to stop this from happening and it was probably the worst fucking feeling in the world.

The door swung open, and Doc came out into the hallway. He bowed and rested his hands on his knees for a minute before straightening up. He pulled at the surgical gown, saturated with Melody's blood and swept the surgical cap off his bald head. I looked up, and just stared, waiting, breath held…

Doc looked down at me, the tension draining from his shoulders, his face unreadable, and my whole fucking world crashed and burned, skidding along the asphalt of the road called life leaving me raw all the way to the fucking bone.

EPILOGUE

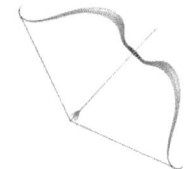

A rcher...
Four months later.

Shit, we were going to be late. Noah was standing next to me on the family courthouse steps while I held Chandler in my arms, and he was being a demanding little shit.

"Daddy up! I want up! Daddy!"

"Noah, you need to stop, Little Man, I got Littler Man here, I can't hold you both!"

"Daddy!" Noah held his chubby little arms up and opened and closed his hands and I swore to myself in my head.

"I'll take him, so you can get Noah," Nox said and I passed my baby boy to my brother so I could lift my big boy up. Of course the second I relinquished Chandler to Nox was the second he started to fuss and cry, kicking his little legs in their blue-footed onesie and declaring his unhappiness with a sharp, piercing cry.

I picked up Noah who was yelling louder and louder for me to do so and hitched him high on my hip. I guess I couldn't blame Noah for wanting to be the center of attention, it was, after all, his day.

Still, and not for the first time since Chandler was born, I thought to myself, *I just can't do this alone.*

"I've got it! Let's go!" Melody called and came running up the steps, her stylish flats slapping the cement.

I smiled at my beautiful wife and breathed easier. Thanks to Doc and the efforts of the hospital staff, I wouldn't ever *have* to do it alone… but it'd come at a price. Mel had been bleeding so bad, they'd had to do a partial hysterectomy. Noah and Chandler were it for us, but all four of us were alive, healthy, and happy which hadn't been the case the day Chandler had been born.

I'd lost my beautiful wife for four minutes. Her heart had stopped, and she'd been clinically dead for the most agonizing four minutes of my fucking life… but then she'd come back and it'd been a fuckin' miracle. *My* fuckin' miracle, and I'd thanked God just about every fuckin' day since.

"Are you ready?" Mel asked, smile sparkling, Noah's baby book with his birth certificate clutched against her chest.

"I am, you?"

"Ohh, as soon as I get Chandler to calm down!" She thrust the book at Rush and he took it. She took our squalling son from Nox and turned around discreetly, fishing in the top cup of her dress."

"Free the nipple!" Rush said grinning and Melody scowled at him.

"Oh, you hush! Just stop!" she told him and I called out to him.

"That's my ol' lady you're talking about there."

Nox helped to situate a baby blanket over my wife's chest so she could feed and calm our son, saying "Worse than that, that's your *sister* you're talking about there you sick—"

"Language!" Mel and I barked simultaneously.

Nox and Rush fell out laughing, slapping each other on their suited backs. It was just them with Mel and me for adoption day. The day I legally made Noah my son on paper. We didn't feel the need to make everyone dress for court, so the rest of the club was back at the club-house getting the party ready for when we got there.

Noah was playing with the gold disc at the end of my braid, and Melody smiled up at me. I bent down and kissed her and Noah cried "Eww!" Just another charming thing that his uncle Rush had taught him – that kissing was gross; like worms or dirt except worms were cool or some shit.

It'd been a long road full of red tape to get this far in the adoption proceedings. I'm pretty sure I'd filled out a couple of phone book sized stacks of paperwork over that time, and today was the day to get a new birth certificate and social security card issued for Noah with my name on it.

Noah Jerimiah Turner.

My first son.

We went in, and remained seated until we were called up. With a funny quiver of excitement in my chest, we filled out the last of the paper-work and a judge blessed it and the courtroom applauded and we had our first official picture taken with all the proper documents as a family. A legally recognized family, which I honestly couldn't have given a shit about that last part.

We'd been a family a long time without no stamp of approval from a citizen court of law. We were a family, in every way that counted.

I leaned down and kissed Melody, my heart made whole, mended just like magic, the moment she'd opened her eyes, touched the side of my face, and asked for our sons. I kissed my woman, my wife, my ol' lady, the mother to my children and for the first time in my life since my broken as fuck childhood, I not only felt whole but like a man should.

I was more than just Archer now. More than just an outlaw rider. I was a brother, a father, a husband and this woman's ol' man.

Family. I had a family, and it was the center of more than just my fuckin' world. It was the center of my universe.

"I love you," I whispered to Melody and she smiled up into my face and said, "I love you, too."

The End

ALSO BY A.J. DOWNEY

Indigo Knights

1. Her Thin Blue Lifeline

2. His Cold Blue Command

3. A Low Blue Flame

4. His Wild Blue Rose

5. Her Pained Blue Silence

6. A Cold Blue Call

7. Her Reluctant Blue Cavalier

8. Forged Under Fire

9. Under A Blue Moon

10. Sound of Blue Thunder

Sacred Hearts MC Pacific Northwest

1. Over the High Side

2. Wind Therapy

3. Apex of the Curve

4. Low Sided

5. Eating Asphalt

6. Hammer Down

7. Only Fool Riding

The Voodoo Bastards MC

1. Bourbon & Blood

2. Whiskey Shivers

3. Moonshine Lullabies

4. Cognac Secrets

5. Tequila Damnation

Iron Wraiths MC

1. Original Syn

2. Love & Fear

3. The Hangman's Rope

Royal Bastard MC: St. Augustine Chapter

1. Iron Hearts

Paranormal Romance (with Ryan Kells)

1. I Am The Alpha

2. Omega's Run

3. Hunter's End

Indigo City Darker (with Jared KingPacal Lain)

1. Triple Threat

2. Double Shot

Standalones

Synchronicity

ABOUT A.J. DOWNEY

A.J. Downey is a Pacific Northwest girl living in an East Tennessee world who finds inspiration from her surroundings, through the people she meets, and likely as a byproduct of way too much caffeine. She specializes in real and relatable romance stories featuring that real-life kind of love that everyone craves.

Stalker Information:

Website
www.ajdowney.com